SEALED WITH A KISS

"I accept your proposal." She watched as the smile he returned grew until it glowed with self-satisfaction before she added with wide-eyed innocence, "There is one small condition, however."

"Certainly," he murmured. "Anything you want."

"The marriage is to be in name only. There is to be no intimacy in our marriage, and the only exchange of affection will be for the benefit of an audience."

He continued to smile, but the warmth in his eyes cooled to a glacial glint. "It's to be a battle to the finish, is it, Miss Elliott? Well, never mind. If that's what you want, then I agree to your condition."

He rose slowly from the chair and pulled her up beside him. "I think it's time I left, but before I go, I think we should seal our disreputable bargain with a kiss. Just for practice, you understand."

JUDITH CONKLIN

MISTRESS OF THE MOORS

LEISURE BOOKS   NEW YORK CITY

A LEISURE BOOK ®

May 1991

Published by

Dorchester Publishing Co., Inc.
276 Fifth Avenue
New York, NY 10001

Printed in the United States of America.

Chapter 1

"But, Mr. Feeny, there must be some mistake," cried Raven, clutching the offensive letter. "Why, my father would never make such a demand of me. Oh, no, I'm sorry, but there has been a terrible misunderstanding here."

Lucius Feeny, a shriveled-up little man resembling a prune and with a disposition matching his looks, peered sourly at his client. His whole being was a reflection of his dingy and cramped little law office. Raven suspected he had deliberately chosen just such a place to conduct his profession because it suited his personality so well. It certainly wasn't because of an empty purse since his fees were healthy and his clientele numerous. His reputation was that of a shrewd and tenacious paladin to those who culled his services, and that determination reflected in the small rodent-like eyes challenging her now.

He adjusted the pince-nez attached to his nose before leaning over his desk with exaggerated gravity. "There is no mistake, Miss Elliott. As you can see, the letter is written in your father's own hand. When he delivered it into my keeping, he informed me of its contents and said that undoubtedly there would be vigorous objections from you. That is why he left instructions that I should not relinquish the letter to you until I notified Major Mallory of your father's demise and received instructions from him as to how to proceed in this matter."

Raven was finding it difficult to breathe. It was mid-July, and London sat wilting in the middle of its severest summer in 50 years. The temperature in the claustrophobic room discouraged even the slightest movement. Raven mentally thanked her father for stipulating no mourning upon his death, otherwise she would have succumbed to the heat long ago. Even now, the delicate gauze blouse she had carefully chosen for her excursion into the sweltering streets did nothing to relieve the unrelenting build-up of warmth between body and blouse.

She reached up and pulled the diaphanous material from her damp skin. "But, Mr. Feeny, my father would never oblige me to marry a complete stranger. You know that. I mean, I have never even met this . . . this Christopher Mallory. Why, I've never even heard of him.

Now, why would my father ask such a thing of me? I tell you, it's insane!"

The shrunken little solicitor, looking cool and comfortable in his stiffly starched collar and black cutaway, donned his most haughty look. "Miss Elliott, I cannot pretend to know what was behind your father's logic. After all, I was not his confidant; I was merely his solicitor. As such, it was and is my duty to see that his wishes are carried out."

Raven needed air. She snatched up a folder from a messy pile of papers on his desk and began fanning herself irritably. "I understand that, Mr. Feeny, but surely at the time he made this ridiculous provision, you must have questioned his sanity. You know how much my father loved me, and you know that under normal conditions he would never make such a request of me. Now, are you saying that you didn't find this request just a bit unbalanced?"

"Miss Elliott, it is not my place to question the lunacy of my clients. As I said before, I do not know what prompted him to make this stipulation, but, unbalanced or not, that is precisely what he has done." He leaned back, nearly disappearing within the folds of his overly large chair, and smiled blandly. "Of course, he did provide an alternative, if you found his first proposal distasteful, that is."

A puff of warm air, laced with the stench of street odors, drifted in from the two grimy windows propped open with law books. The

7

grudging breeze tickled the straying black locks pasted to Raven's neck, and she sighed in relief. "Well, of course, I find his first proposal distasteful. Now, for heaven's sake, Mr. Feeny, just tell me what the alternative is. Whatever the condition, I am certain it will be more appealing than marrying someone I don't even know."

He raised himself up out of the clutches of his chair, becoming all business again, and shuffled through the stack of papers before him until he found the one he sought. "Ah yes, here it is." He glanced at her over the top of his spectacles and grinned with satisfaction. "Well now, Miss Elliott, the alternative is this. If you should refuse to marry the gentleman aforementioned and still wish to receive your inheritance, then you may reside under the protection of your aunt, Mrs. Charlotte Grummon, until your twenty-fifth birthday. If you choose this course of action, upon that day you shall inherit your father's entire estate, amounting to . . . let's see, oh yes, approximately 52,462 pounds. I say approximately because, of course, that figure does not take into account the amount accrued upon the sale of the house." He grinned again, this time in greedy anticipation. "That, quite naturally, will be variable, depending upon the compensation we receive for the structure."

Raven wasn't listening and had turned pale. "Aunt Charlotte?" she gasped. "Oh no! Mr. Feeny, no one could live with my Aunt Charlotte. I don't know how Uncle George managed it all those years before his death. Believe me, no one could survive three years under her protection and nothing short of divine intervention could induce me to try."

"Yes," he mumbled sourly. "I am acquainted with Mrs. Grummon, and I must admit she is somewhat eccentric."

"Eccentric! Mr. Feeny, that is like saying the flood in the Bible was nothing more than a slight rain shower. My Aunt Charlotte is a tyrant with some rather queer ideas on how one should behave and how one should think, and she thrusts those ideas upon everyone around her by sheer force of will and contrivance."

The spectacles threatened to topple as he wrinkled his nose in feigned shock. His expression, vapid and patronizing, was a blatant insult, since it was designed to pacify an overemotional female with a childish intellect. "Come, come, Miss Elliott, I'm certain you must be exaggerating."

Raven's black eyes glittered ominously. She had been plagued with a lively temper since birth, a characteristic undoubtedly inherited from her mother's Irish ancestry. Most of the time, she managed to keep it in check, but occasionally it bubbled out of control, especially when provoked by high-hatted remarks, implying she was witless. She yearned to give him a good lashing with her tongue, but instead she choked back the fires of indignation and returned his smile.

"Am I?" she cooed with sarcasm. "Do you know she believes that sunlight causes tumors of the brain? She absolutely forbids so much as a ray of light from ever entering her house, and the place is boarded up like some forbidding fortress. She dictates to everyone around her how they are to dress, how to wear their hair, what to eat and when. She controls what they read, think and have opinions on, who their friends are, and when and where they go. Now, would you be willing to live under those conditions, Mr. Feeny?"

The pallid little solicitor snatched up a pen and began twisting it in his fingers. "My living arrangements are not in question here, Miss Elliott. Yours are." He threw down the pen and shifted in his chair. "Miss Elliott," he began in a softer vein, "can't you see what your father was trying to do? I can. Now, you are a very attractive young lady, and you have no other relative to look out for you other than your aunt." He looked uncomfortable and nervously tugged at his collar. "In these times, a young lady in your predicament is in a most vulnerable position. You see, there are many, well, unscrupulous people out in the world just waiting to prey upon innocent young women such as yourself."

"You mean men, don't you?" supplied Raven. "You may say the word, Mr. Feeny, without fear of me swooning."

"Please try to understand," he moaned. "You are not experienced enough to avoid the perils that await you. With this stipulation, your father is merely trying to save you from that peril. That's why he wants you safely married."

Married! There it was again. For the last three years that word had been flung at her from all directions. Her father had preached on the subject. Flora had praised its virtues. Her friends had highly recommended it. Well, she had no revulsion to matrimony. She wanted home and husband, but not just for the sake of convention—and it wasn't as if she hadn't had any offers. Actually, she had had quite a few. But she knew very well that most of the people indulging in that well-respected pastime plunged into it with not a whit of affection for the person to whom they were pledging themselves. As a result, their lives were cluttered up with mistresses and paramours behind every door. Well, that wasn't for her. When she entered into such a solemn alliance, it was going to be for love, and so far, she hadn't found it.

Mr. Feeny's wheezing voice broke into her thoughts. "Miss Elliott, I am certain your father had your best interests at heart when he made this provision in his will. That is why I strongly advise you to accept his wishes in this matter and marry this young man he has chosen for you."

Raven wanted to scream. The heat, the street noise and the smell of dust and moldy books were all contributing to the queasy feeling in the pit of her stomach. She closed her eyes, took a deep breath and prayed for patience. Somehow she had to get through to this man. "Mr. Feeny," she began calmly, "what if this Christopher person doesn't wish to marry me? Is he aware of this arrangement? Does he agree to it? And who is he, for heaven's sake? What information do you have about him?"

Mr. Feeny looked a bit perplexed, shifted in his chair and began to organize the papers on his desk. "As to that, Miss Elliott, I cannot say. I'm afraid I am unacquainted with Mr. Mallory, and I have no information on him or his family other than they are considered highly respectable and live in Devonshire."

"What?" she exclaimed.

He raised a hand to silence her. "Please, Miss Elliott, you really must control yourself. Now, I have told you all I know, and the choice is up to you. You may either reside with your aunt until you become eligible to receive your inheritance, or you may marry Mr. Mallory. In either case, the conditions in your father's will shall be met." He sighed wearily. "Now, I know all this is a shock to you, but perhaps this will help." He opened a desk drawer, pulled out a neatly wrapped parcel and handed it to her. "This is for you. Inside you will find a letter from a Major Roger Mallory. He is Mr. Christopher Mallory's father. It will explain everything, I am sure. Now, why don't you go home and read what Major Mallory has to say before you make your final decision. After that, if you have any questions, I shall be happy to talk with you again."

It was no use arguing further. Raven took the parcel and left.

She made her way along the grimy hallway and started down the narrow wooden stairs

which led to the ground floor, feeling helpless
and more than a little out of sorts.

She hated this part of London. Beecher Street
lay in the middle of the less prosperous part of
the business district where both wages and
rental property were below standard. As a result, impoverished families, often consisting of
eight or nine members, lived in single rooms
above the shops and offices lining the street.
Their laundry, hanging from sagging cords,
connected one building to another over the
alleyways like forlorn banners attesting to their
plight. Children, scores of them, dirty and
threadbare, ran rampant in the streets, darting
through traffic like little crazed animals. And the
odor was horrendous. Gutters reeked of sewage
being thrown out of windows as a matter of
course. All in all, it was a dismal and unsightly
place, and Raven was grateful Jeremy and his
carriage were waiting for her.

As she stepped out into the sunlight, the blast
of heat nearly caused her to faint, but then she
saw the gleaming black carriage waiting patiently at the curb. The carriage door swung open,
and she stepped inside. The door snapped shut,
and the well-sprung coach pulled into traffic,
sending up a gritty cloud of dust.

Jeremy Frasier sat across from her, grinning
like the overgrown schoolboy he was. "Well, my
lovely little waif, are you a grand heiress now?"

Raven looked at the handsome young man
facing her and felt a sudden pang of regret for
not loving him. Tall and blond, he sat there,

resplendent in his toffee-colored attire and matching boots, his brown eyes twinkling.

At 25 and quite unattached, Jeremy was the toast of every fair maiden of good breeding shopping for a husband. He was gay, charming and had a natural gift for flattery. It was no wonder every matron with an eligible daughter considered him a prime candidate for the role of son-in-law. Raven often marveled at how he continually managed to evade such a ruthless and predatory pack.

As usual, his blond locks needed attention, and she reached up and smoothed the unruly curls back into place. The gesture was an unconscious act, one she had performed many times, the habit second nature to her.

He laughed, revealing a dazzling set of white, even teeth. "Ah, love, you're always taking care of me. I often wonder what I would do without you."

She looked at him and frowned. "You would probably have to grow up," she replied with a slight hint of irritation.

"Ugh. Now, why would I want to do that? Being grown-up is dull and boring, and life is too short for that. No, I want to remain just as I am—happy and carefree."

Raven sighed in defeat. That was Jeremy. But she couldn't really fault him for his cavalier attitude toward life. She blamed his family. Since the day he was born, he had had too much, too soon. His family, although not titled, were wealthy beyond reason, due to his grandfather's shrewd investments and business sense. As a result, life to them meant nothing more than one frolic after another. There was never any serious thought for the future, let alone the present, in any of his relatives.

If only she could love him, she thought miserably. She had tried to, she wanted to, but that elusive emotion just wasn't there. Why, she didn't know. He had asked her to marry him, and all her troubles would be over if only she would say yes—but she couldn't. Something just wouldn't let her.

"Jeremy, would you be too disappointed if I asked to be excused from dinner with you tonight?"

She watched his face fall and felt a tinge of guilt.

"I suppose not," he said, clearly disappointed. "What's the matter, love, didn't it go well?"

Raven grimaced. "No, it didn't."

Jeremy, of course, bounced back immediately. He took everything, especially problems, as mere adventures in life and never spent more than 30 seconds worrying about any of them.

"What's the trouble?" he said with impish delight. "Did the old boy leave more credit than coins? Well, that's no reason to cancel an amusing evening of fun and frolic with a dashing chap like me. After all, you don't have to worry about money. Heavens, I've got enough to keep us well-padded for life."

Raven sat back in the luxuriously cushioned seat and tried to ignore the subtle throb in her temples. It was true. Jeremy had an allowance of 20,000 pounds a year and more if he needed it. It would be so easy for her to just marry him and go through life dabbling in whatever petty pleasures were in vogue at the moment.

She closed her eyes and blotted the perspiration forming on her brow with a delicate lace handkerchief. "Jeremy, please. If that is another proposal of marriage, it will do you no good. I've told you before that I love you dearly, but not in that way."

"Well, how do you know?" he exclaimed, theatrically. "You've never tried. We've always been just friends. But if you would give it a chance, you might find that you love me very much—and in *that way*, too. Besides," he suddenly whined, "I love you, Raven, and we could have a smashing time together."

Raven wasn't listening. Deep in her thoughts, she was trying to imagine what sort of man this Christopher Mallory must be to agree to marry a woman he had never seen. He would have to be an utter weakling in both body and spirit, she thought miserably. At least Jeremy was pleasant to be around. What if he did drink a little too much and gamble a little too heavily? He was handsome, charming and very wealthy. Maybe being married to him wouldn't be so bad after all.

Jeremy continued on with an accolade of

himself, and her headache increased in intensity as the carriage rumbled away from the sun-baked streets of lower east London.

When she returned home, Flora Higgins greeted her anxiously at the door.

Flora was a unique figure in the Elliott household and the only retainer left at 27 Darcy Square. She had started out as Raven's nanny and had progressed through the ranks of governess and housekeeper until now she was considered Raven's companion, although she wielded as much power as any family matriarch. Thin and wiry, she had a stringent disposition and a sharp tongue, but Raven adored her because her friend and companion had lovingly filled that terrible void in a young child's life when its mother is suddenly taken away.

Drying her hands on a stiff white apron, Flora followed Raven into the parlor like a dog seeking a treat. "Well, my dear, what did that old crook have to say? Are we going to be able to continue eating?"

Raven flopped down on the sofa dejectedly and unfastened the first three buttons of her soggy blouse. "That all depends, Flora."

"Don't talk in riddles, my girl. Your papa has been gone for a month now and not a farthing has come into this house since. Now, didn't that ol' fool give you anything to live on until your inheritance is settled?"

"No, Flora, he didn't—and that's not all. It seems Father put a condition in his will that I cannot inherit anything unless I do one of two things, both of which are completely insupportable."

Flora's most prominent feature was a rather substantial nose resembling the beak of a hawk, and she twitched it in disgust.

"I knew it! I knew the moment your dear mother died that that wooden-headed father of yours would make a mess of things, and in the twenty years since her death, he never proved me wrong. Well, out with it. What's he done now?"

Raven frowned in concentration. "Flora, did you ever hear Father speak of a family named Mallory?"

Flora settled on a footstool in front of Raven. "Mallory, Mallory. No, I don't think . . . wait a minute! Wasn't there a good friend of his by that name in his regiment many years ago?" She shook her finger at Raven. "Yes, there was . . . and I remember now. He used to get mail from someone named Mallory. Why?"

"Because Father has stated in his will that I may not inherit tuppence unless I marry someone named Christopher Mallory. Apparently, this Christopher is the son of his friend, a Major Roger Mallory. The other choice I have is to go live with Aunt Charlotte for the next three years. I would then receive my inheritance upon my twenty-fifth birthday."

"What? Why, that old fool!" she thundered. "He must've been as crazy as that sister o' his when he made that will." Sparkling blue eyes squinted out from under gray bushy brows. "I hope you're not contemplatin' moving in with that unhinged aunt o' yours."

"Flora," Raven scolded, "you know very well Aunt Charlotte is not crazy. She's just notional, that's all."

"Humph," snorted Flora. "You may call it what you want, but anyone who shoots at a person just because they approach your door is crazy in my estimation, even if it is your lawyer. And remember, I don't like lawyers."

"Yes, well, you know how Aunt Charlotte is. Besides, you know very well the incident was investigated and declared an accident. Otherwise, they would have prosecuted."

"Accident? In a pig's eye! The whole town is afraid of her, the old harridan. It's because she's got all that money. Why, she could probably break half the people in London if she had a mind to." She made a face, as if tasting a foul medicine. "Oh, blast the old biddy. Why doesn't she just help you? Lord, she's got so much money, she'd never miss it."

"You know why," Raven sighed. "She's wanted me ever since Mama died. She somehow thought that I would only survive the rigors of growing-up under her expert tutelage. And now that I'm grown? Heavens, at twenty-two and unmarried, she wishes more than anything to take charge of me and begin to groom me for what she perceives to be a proper marriage." She sprang from the sofa. "Flora, what am I going to do? We have to have money to live on."

"Am I to assume, then, that you have dismissed the idea of us becoming inmates in that lunatic asylum your aunt runs?"

Raven waved a hand at Flora in disgust. "Oh, Flora, for heaven's sake, will you be serious for a moment?"

Flora shrugged. "Well, tell me about this young man you are supposed to marry. What's he like? Do you like him?"

"Flora," Raven muttered in exasperation, "haven't you been paying attention? I don't know the man. I've never even heard of him until today. For all I know he could be an axe murderer with a penchant for chopping up unsuspecting brides."

"Good heavens," choked Flora, "didn't that goose of a lawyer give you any information about him? I mean, how on earth are the two of you supposed to get married if neither of you know each other?"

Raven remembered the parcel Mr. Feeny had given her. "The package, Flora. I came in with a package. Where is it?"

They looked around and found the bundle in a chair by the door. Raven snatched it up and went to plop down on the sofa once again. "Mr. Feeny said this was from Major Mallory and that it would explain everything."

"Well, don't just sit there," Flora grumbled. "Open it up and let's see what the good major has to say."

Raven tore the parcel apart and found two envelopes, both addressed to her. She chose the lighter of the two and opened it up. Inside was a letter which she began to read aloud.

"My Dear Miss Elliott,

Please accept my condolences for your father's death. It saddened me to hear of his passing since we shared a close kinship for one another, and I shall miss him greatly.

As you probably know by now, your father and I discussed your future before his death, and we concluded that a marriage between you and my son would be the wisest course of action.

Since you are alone now, it is imperative that you come at once and reside here until your marriage. I know this must seem strange to you, but I assure you, everything will be explained to you once you are here.

Best Regards,
Maj. Roger Mallory"

"Well, that wasn't a lot of help, was it?" Flora said sarcastically.

Raven tore into the other envelope and spilled its contents out on the sofa. "Look, Flora—money!"

There was, indeed, money along with several papers which Raven picked up and began to study.

"According to this, Major Mallory has an estate in Devonshire called Heathglade, near a town named Dunsford."

Flora wasn't interested in geography. She had grabbed the various notes sprawled on the sofa while Raven was speaking and had feverishly ascertained the amount lying in her lap.

"Well, there's enough here to pay the butcher off and get us to that Mallory fellow, but that's all."

"Are you saying we should go?"

Flora frowned impatiently. "Well, we can hardly take the man's money and not pay him a visit."

"Why take the money at all?" Raven asked. "There is another solution, you know. I could just marry Jeremy and be done with it."

Flora looked at her as if she had lost her mind. "Marry that mutton-headed dandy? Not if I can help it! No, I think we should pay a visit to this Major Mallory and see what he has to say. Who knows? You may find that you like this future husband of yours."

"Never," Raven cried vehemently, springing from the sofa once more. "Oh, honestly, can't you just imagine what sort of a man this Christopher Mallory is to allow himself to be cajoled into a blind marriage? Why, I can just see him—a malnourished, little, pasty-faced excuse of a man, trembling in his boots as his father informs him of his arranged marriage. Ugh, what a repugnant idea!" She began to pace about the room. "Of course, the rest of what you propose may have merit. After all, I'm sure this Major Mallory is a sensible man. If I put in a personal appearance, maybe I can convince him of the ridiculousness of this compulsory marriage and actually enlist his aid in collecting my inheritance without it." She suddenly whirled around and squealed happily. "Oh, Flora, it should be easy!"

Flora sighed and rose from the footstool. "Well, while you're celebrating your victory, I'll go start dinner. After we fight over the few crumbs we've got left, I'll drag out the trunks, and tomorrow we can start packing."

Once in the kitchen, Flora smiled to herself as she reached into her apron pocket and felt the letter she had put there for safekeeping. So far, everything was going according to plan, and she gave herself a mental pat on the back for her, up until now, untested acting ability. Now, all she had to do was get her charge to the malnourished, pasty-faced excuse of a man William Elliott, the Major and herself had conspired to match her with.

She chuckled. She had never met the Mallorys, but Flora had a feeling this Christopher was more of a man than even she expected. William Elliott may have been a passive parent, but he had loved his daughter dearly, and in this instance, Flora trusted his judgment implicitly.

She picked up the big kitchen knife and began to slice the last of the mutton off the bone. As she worked, she remembered him saying something about leaving his daughter something more important than money. He was leaving her a legacy beyond price. It was a legacy of love.

Chapter 2

F ive days later, the hired chaise Raven and
Flora had procured in Dunsford moved
up the entrance drive to the Mallory estate. They had watched the imposing edifice of
Heathglade grow in size for several miles, catching glimpses of the house through the treetops
as they cleared each rise in the road. Every time
they assumed the expanding girth of its walls
was merely an optical illusion. They had been
mistaken. When, at last, the driver halted the
carriage at the front door, both women were
struck dumb.

The home, three-stories high, stood gleaming
like a giant beacon in the afternoon sun. It was
built of stone, but the surface had been diligent-
ly scrubbed and maintained to keep a fresh and
clean appearance. Softening the stark white
exterior, every so often, lacy patterns of sturdy

ivy curled gracefully skyward, while surrounding the structure, a beautifully manicured lawn spread out from its base, bearing the likeness to a green velvet sea. Decorative shrubs of rhododendron and peony sat scattered among giant oak and spruce trees, resembling flower boats floating on an emerald ocean. Raven could only blink in wide-eyed wonder at the sheer beauty surrounding her, for she had never witnessed anything comparable.

The driver, a slight little man made swarthy by a lifetime of toiling in the sun, abandoned his place in the driver's seat with a fluid leap to the ground but aided his passengers to alight in a more sedate manner.

Their journey had been tiresome with three days of steady traveling, stuffed in overcrowded coaches filled with unwashed bodies, and both Raven and Flora were stiff and sore from their ordeal. But now that it was over, they each breathed a sigh of relief as their feet touched solid ground.

"Ohhh," Flora moaned, trying to stand straight. "If I ever again see that last ruffian masquerading as a coach driver, I'll have him drawn and quartered. I swear the hateful beast deliberately aimed at every bump and hole between Exeter and Dunsford."

"Never mind that now," Raven replied. "Just concentrate on what is ahead of us."

"And just what would that be, besides permanent disablement?"

Raven smiled. "A cool bath, a palatable cup of tea and a soft bed."

As they waited for the driver to tote their valises up the impressive fantail steps, Flora surveyed the house and grounds with her usual blunt appraisal. "Quite a little hovel your major lives in, isn't it?"

"He's not my major, Flora," Raven grumbled, taking off her bonnet, "and neither is his son. And will you please stop trying to assess his value? I know what you're up to."

Flora looked at her innocently. "Why I don't know what you mean. All I did was offer a comment regarding the Mallorys' accommodations and you get—"

"Flora, I am not marrying Christopher Mallory—and that is final. Now get that covetous look off your face and let's get on with what we came here to do."

They followed the driver to the door and watched as he flung their baggage down with the same care he would give sacks of grain. Flora flinched but remained silent as she dug deep into her reticule and doled out the driver's fee. He took the money and counted it carefully before doffing his hat. He then turned and left without saying a word.

"Uncivilized brute," she snorted, watching the carriage rumble down the long drive. "You'd think he would at least have had the courtesy to wait and see if we might need additional assistance. And did you see the way he treated our luggage? After all, that was good money we just paid him and—"

"Flora, please," Raven sighed, shaking the dust from the skirts of her rumpled traveling suit. "At least we're here. Honestly, I am so tired . . ." She took hold of the elegant brass door knocker and rapped firmly.

As they waited, Raven reveled in the steady balm of a cool breeze and watched it tease the delicate leaves of the ivy just beginning to peep over the doorsill.

The temperature was much cooler here, perhaps ten or so degrees less than in London, and it was evident in the lush vegetation covering the landscape. In London, what little foliage there was had long since wilted and faded into varying shades of brown, but here the rich color of emerald green announced the robust health of abundant plant life.

After several moments of waiting, Raven reached up to knock again when the door opened a few inches.

"Yes?"

Peering through the opening, a pair of frightened blue eyes, surrounded by a halo of stringy blond hair, scrutinized them warily.

"Good afternoon," Raven began. "My name is Miss Elliott, and this is my companion, Mrs. Higgins. We are here to see Major Mallory. I believe he is expecting us."

After a slight hesitation, the door swung open. Before them stood a young girl of about 15 or

16 years of age. The traditional servant's garb, a starched white apron over the inevitable gray dress of austere cut and quality, hung about her sparse frame, and only her overlarge ears prevented the smudged dust cap from completely swallowing her head. In her hand she held a polishing cloth, and the aroma of lemon oil and beeswax emanated from her. She stood there, frozen with what suspiciously resembled fear, and Raven was at a loss to understand why. What could be so terrible about answering the door?

The young girl gawked at them for a moment and then, as if remembering her manners, bobbed an awkward curtsy. "Oh, yes, Miss. We was expectin' ya, a'right. Uh, won't ya come in, Miss?"

She moved aside and allowed Raven and Flora to enter a massive foyer with white marble flooring, white walls inlaid with peach-colored paneling and an impressive sweeping staircase leading to the upper floors.

As Raven stepped through the threshold, she caught her breath. The foyer, spacious and airy, contained only one piece of furniture, a massive round table, polished to a mirror finish and placed directly in the center of the room. A large bowl of roses, varying in shades from rich cream to bright coral, was its only decoration. Overhead a chandelier dripping with hundreds of crystal prisms hung in opulent splendor. At the moment, the sunlight streaming through the transom above the door caught in the glass droplets, causing a shower of diamond-like reflections to fill the room.

The sound of an angry male voice broke the spell of enchantment, and the little maid flinched and hurled a hasty glance toward a row of rooms opposite the staircase. "If you'll jus' wait 'ere, Miss," she requested anxiously, "I'll be gettin' Mr. Purdy." And then she darted off like a frightened bird.

The sound of another angry voice broke into the first, and now Raven understood the girl's odd behavior. They had arrived at a very awkward moment. Apparently there was some dispute going on between members of the household, and all the servants, including the butler, had judiciously scattered into the deeper recesses of the house. Only the little scarecrow, probably because of her inexperience, had been left to face the unpleasantries.

"My word," Flora mumbled in awe, "it's a bonny palace."

Raven stood, transfixed, watching the room sparkle. "Money isn't everything, Flora," she commented softly.

Flora snorted. "Yes, well, I'll be sure and tell the butcher that the next time I see him."

"Shhh," Raven hushed. The argument was heightening, and Raven strained her ears, hoping to overhear its subject matter. "Listen. Where is it coming from?"

Flora shrugged. "I don't know, but it's none of our business anyway."

Raven started toward the series of rooms.

"Raven Elliott," Flora hissed, "get back here and remember your manners. Young ladies don't eavesdrop on private conversations, you know."

Raven stopped and spun around. "Flora, how can anyone eavesdrop on a shouting match that is easily audible throughout the house? Now come along. Aren't you in the least bit curious as to what the quarrel is about?"

"Certainly not," Flora replied, indignantly. "And neither should you be. Raven Elliott, come . . ."

Raven was already halfway across the foyer, and there was nothing else for Flora to do but follow.

In a matter of moments they located the disturbance. The heated discussion emanated from the third room down, and the door stood slightly ajar.

"You may argue all you like," blustered a gravelly voice, "but you know I'm right. Ever since Robert's death, you've known that the responsibility of inheritance has fallen to you. And it's not as if I haven't given you ample time to find a suitable wife and settle down. Good God, Christopher, it's been three years."

Flora realized who the participants were and the topic of dissension at the same moment Raven did. She grabbed Raven's arm and frantically tried to pull her back into the foyer, but Raven twisted free and crept closer to the door.

"And just what does time have to do with it?"

shouted a deep resonant voice. "My Lord, this is 1817, not the dark ages. Why do I have to marry in order to inherit? Bachelors can manage business affairs just as well as married men, you know."

"That's not the point, and you know it. I'm not saying you can't handle things. Lord knows, you've been a marvel at handling our operation in the Indies. It's your choice of women that concerns me." The gruff voice softened. "Listen to me, Christopher, I want you settled and happy before I die, and that harem of sordid women you keep collecting is not my idea of suitable candidates for the mother of my grandchildren. Besides, you're thirty-three years old. It's time you settled down."

"And so you've decided to saddle me with a shriveled-up, pinch-faced prude that will be ever so proper and socially acceptable but, undoubtedly, dull as a toad. Dear God," the deep voice finished.

"You don't know that. Why, from everything William has written about her, she sounds like a lovely young woman."

"Oh? Then why hasn't she found her own husband? No, thank you. Do what you will, disinherit me if you like, but I'm not about to marry some homely spinster just to keep a promise you made to an old army chum."

Christopher Mallory calling her a homely spinster was the last straw. Raven felt a surge of heat color her cheeks as the combination of humiliation and blazing fury consumed her.

"Did you hear what that pompous oaf called me?" she hissed. "Why, I'll . . ." And before Flora could stop her, Raven grabbed the door, yanked it open and marched into an imposing study.

Like the foyer, the study was an impressive room. At one end, a massive fireplace dominated almost half the wall with a sofa and several chairs surrounding it, forming a cozy area for conversation or reading. At the other end a large desk with two chairs positioned in front sat before a row of large windows. The rest of the room sported bookshelves from ceiling to floor, each shelf filled to capacity.

There were two men in the room. One, an elderly gentleman seated behind the desk, appeared to be in his sixties. The top of his head reflected the filtered light pouring in from the windows, but the rest was covered by a thick layer of gray hair. He had a very round face, mottled from long years of being in the sun, and an impressive silver mustache decorated his upper lip. Even without the red and gold military uniform, Raven knew at once he was the Major Mallory she had come to see.

The other was much younger, very tall and broad shouldered. He stood in front of the desk, leaning slightly forward with his hands resting on the edge. Both men started as she made her abrupt entrance.

Christopher Mallory straightened up, irritation plainly written on his face. "And just who might you be?"

Raven stared into a pair of dark chocolate eyes. Even in anger, he was the most handsome man she had ever seen. Standing straight, he stood well over six feet tall and had a healthy crop of lustrous hair the shade of rich coffee. White even teeth contrasted sharply with the coppery tan of his smooth skin, and occasionally a set of deep dimples broke the sculptured line of his upper jaw whenever he moved his mouth a certain way.

Unlike his father, Christopher Mallory was dressed casually. A spotless white shirt, loose fitting and of superb quality, covered his well-defined upper torso. Below, a pair of fawn pants hugged a slim waist and lean hips and continued down a set of muscular thighs only to be lost in a pair of dark brown riding boots, polished to a gleaming finish. Unfortunately, Raven was too angry at the moment to be swayed by the appearance of her adversary.

Instead, her black eyes glittered with rage. "I, sir, am the shriveled-up, pinch-faced prude who is unable to find her own husband."

His deep brown eyes registered astonishment before a myriad of expressions, from disbelief to comprehension to embarrassment, flashed across his face.

"Oh Lord," he muttered, sagging against the desk. "Please, Miss . . . Miss Elliott, is it? Please, let me apologize if I have offended you. It's just—"

"You are too boorish to be offensive, Mr. Mallory," Raven interrupted between clenched teeth. "And after you hear what I have to say, you may very well decide that an apology is unnecessary."

She watched in helpless frustration as an amused expression settled on his face. He folded his arms across his chest and propped one splendid boot over the other. "Pray continue, Miss Elliott. I am certain we are all most interested to hear what you have to say. But please, before you begin, try to remember that you are a lady. Judging from your mood at the moment, I think it best that you be reminded of it."

Her eyes smoldered with the flames of righteous anger as she retaliated. "The only thing I have to say to you, sir, is that you needn't fret any longer about having to marry this homely spinster since nothing—do you hear me?—nothing could induce me to marry you. You may take your happy bachelor existence and wallow in it for all I care. Believe me, I would rather starve to death than be wedded to anyone as crass as you."

The brown eyes were dancing now, and he pushed away from the desk to walk over and make a slow circular inspection of her. "You know, sir," he commented sedately, "she really isn't too bad looking, is she?"

The major nearly choked on his cigar. "What? Oh, no, no, she isn't." And then he grinned. "As a matter of fact, my boy, I think she's quite lovely."

Raven cringed inwardly. She knew how she must look. Her thick mass of black curls had always been a problem to control, even when she wore it up. No matter how many pins were used, a generous supply of stubborn ringlets always managed to escape their captivity. They teased her neck, tickled her cheeks and harassed her brow. And that was during the best of times. But now? If only she hadn't removed her bonnet, she thought miserably. She already knew her amethyst traveling suit was rumpled and stained from the rigors of the trip. And her face? She reached up and brushed her cheek. She could feel the dirt and grime on it.

He finished his inspection by stopping directly in front of her and smiling. "Yes, well, once she bridles that temper, has a good scrubbing and someone to curry those wild tresses, she might turn out to be tolerable."

Flora turned the color of parchment. She knew very well the limit of Raven's self-control, and Christopher had just passed it. She opened her mouth to try and ward off the inevitable explosion, when Major Mallory caught her eye. Still grinning pleasantly, he put a finger to his lips, indicating that she should remain silent.

Raven, on the other hand, had turned a bright scarlet. "Tolerable!" she shrieked. "Why you, you . . ." She frantically searched about for something to throw at him.

Christopher threw back his head and laughed uproariously. "Please, Miss Elliott," he sputtered between snorts of laughter, "I apologize again. It's just that you were so angry, and I suddenly visualized myself playing the part of

Petruchio to your portrayal of Katharina. You must admit our situation bears a slight resemblance to Mr. Shakespeare's comedy."

Unable to find anything suitably heavy enough to kill him with, Raven turned and stared at him, with an expression that nevertheless declared her intent. "The only resemblance I see, sir, is your likeness to Petruchio, but somehow I cannot perceive you agreeing to the paltry price he did. After all, Baptista only offered him a mere 20,000 crowns." She walked over to stand very close to him, her face only inches away from his. "But you, sir, are so much more the catch. Dare any of us hope that there is enough money in your father's coffer, indeed in the whole world, that would persuade you to give up your precious freedom?"

Christopher's smile vanished, and his brown eyes glittered dangerously. "The face of an angel with the tongue of a viper," he murmured. "Katharina has, indeed, come to life."

They stood there for a moment, their eyes locked in a sort of perverse duel. An eternity passed until, at last, Raven tore her eyes away from his and adjusted her gaze to the middle of his broad chest. "Good day to you, Mr. Mallory," she managed to say, "and good-bye."

She didn't remember leaving the room or even traversing the foyer, but all at once, she was fumbling with the latch of the front door when the major caught up with her.

"Miss Elliott, please," he pleaded breathlessly. "This is most embarrassing. Oh, my dear, surely you are not considering leaving us? Oh no, no! Now, please come back and let us apologize properly."

"Major Mallory," Raven muttered angrily, tugging on the doorknob, "I'm certain you are a very nice man. But your son is insufferable!"

The major began to perspire. "We meant no disrespect, my dear. It's just that, well, sometimes our sense of humor oversteps the bounds of good manners. But we meant no harm, honestly."

"I think you should listen to the major, child," Flora recommended, catching up to them. "After all, I seem to remember you having some rather peculiar opinions of Mr. Mallory yourself. Now, be sensible and think. Just where were you planning on going, and on what?"

Raven gritted her teeth. She hated it when Flora expressed good sense, and she was always doing it. It was maddening to always be wrong and, worse yet, having it pointed out to you constantly. Still, Flora was right. She had been just as opinionated toward Christopher Mallory as he had been toward her. And just where was she going? She couldn't go back home. Mr. Feeny had hired an agent to close the house and put it up for sale. And even if she could, she had no money to get there. Why, she couldn't even go to Aunt Charlotte without money.

She had no choice, and she knew it. Besides, the wretched door refused to open. She turned around and faced the major. "Very well," she said calmly. "It seems we must stay, at least for the moment."

"Excellent," he responded enthusiastically. "Now, where is that Lizzy? Oh, there she is."

The scrawny young girl who had met them at the door melted out of the shadows from beneath the staircase.

"Lizzy, please show Miss Elliott and her companion here, Mrs. Higgins, to the rooms we have prepared for them. And then find Purdy and see that their luggage is attended to." He turned to Raven. "And now, my dear, I want you to go upstairs and have a nice rest. If there is anything you want, anything at all, just tell Lizzy and she'll see to it. Then, as soon as you feel like it, I should be pleased to receive you in my study where we can begin anew with a proper introduction and a pleasant chat."

"Thank you, Major Mallory," Raven replied stiffly, "but I must warn you, the only chat we will have will be regarding my immediate departure."

As Lizzy led them upstairs, Raven suddenly realized that Christopher Mallory had conveniently disappeared into thin air. Strangely, she felt a pang of disappointment, and the sensation only tweaked her already wounded pride. It's just like him, she thought grudgingly. He's as spineless as he is arrogant.

Forty-five minutes later, Raven stepped into a cool bath, bubbly and scented with the delightful aroma of jasmine soap shavings. The frothy liquid felt wonderful, and she sank down until only her shoulders were above water.

Flora busied herself by draping Raven's petticoats about the room in an effort to give them a quick airing before being put into use again. She appeared to be completely occupied with her task, but she wasn't. Her mind labored over trying to decide what to do next.

One thing was certain. She couldn't let Raven leave. If she did, then the whole scheme would be foiled, and that would never do. After spending many hours with William Elliott, worrying over Raven's future, they had both decided this would be the best solution. Raven, for all her London airs, was just too naive and too impetuous to be left alone in the world. She needed someone strong enough to capture and control that impulsive nature of hers. She needed protecting, and now that Flora had met Christopher Mallory, Flora knew he was the perfect choice to do just that. The only problem was that both principals were blatantly resisting.

There was one hope, though. During that horrendous scene in the study, Flora had watched Christopher's and Raven's reactions to one another, and she had noticed a certain response between the two that, mad or not, held promise. There was something there, all right. All it needed was a bit of cultivating. Now, if only she and the major could keep them together long enough for nature to take its course, then happiness would reign supreme.

She deserted the petticoats and went to pick

up a soft washcloth draped over the back of the bath. She doused it in the cool, soapy water and began a slow circular motion across Raven's back. "Well, he certainly isn't the malnourished, pasty-faced excuse of a man you thought he was, is he?" she commented casually.

Raven whirled around, sending a soapy wave spilling to the floor. "He's worse!" she flared. "He's a . . . a swine!"

Flora thought Raven's reaction was a little too vehement to be natural, and she smiled to herself. Things may work out after all. "Well, swine or not, he's the most desirable man I've ever seen, and if I were forty years younger, I'd find out if the product performs as well as the package promises," she replied calmly.

"Flora Higgins," Raven gasped, "will you listen to yourself?"

Flora snorted. "No, you listen, my girl. If you would stop fighting and fuming long enough, you'd see that man's got something."

"Oh, Flora, he's an impossible man. Did you hear what he had the gall to call me? How dare he!"

Flora snickered. "Well, I seem to remember you had a rather jaundiced opinion of him, too. Surely, you can't fault the man for exercising the same doubts you had. Now, if I were you, I'd . . ."

Raven stood up and grabbed a towel. "Go away, Flora. If you're going to defend him, then I'd just as soon be alone."

Flora abandoned the washcloth and rose to

her feet. "All right, but, as I was saying, if I were you, I'd take a second look at that young man. He's a man, my girl, a real man from head to toe, and there's not many of them left." She paused at the door and watched Raven envelop herself in the soft towel. "No indeed, there's too many Jeremys in this old world and not enough Christophers, if you ask me." And then, she disappeared through the door.

Raven dried herself off and slipped into a clean shift, muttering the whole time. What did Flora know, anyway? She wasn't the one being forced into an unwanted marriage. She wasn't the one who would have to live with a condescending womanizer suffering from an inflated opinion of himself.

She stretched out on the bed and closed her eyes, intending to take a short nap, but Christopher Mallory's face kept intruding. Still shaken from that intense moment when they had looked into each other's eyes, she felt her face flush as she remembered the expression in his eyes when he made that frank appraisal of her. It was as if he could see . . . everything! The impudence of the man, she thought angrily, and turned over to beat a fist into the innocent feather pillow. If only he wasn't so handsome. That's what his trouble was, of course. He had a lofty opinion of himself since probably every woman he came in contact with threw herself at him. Well, not her—not for any inheritance, not for any price.

After several minutes of trying unsuccessfully

to wipe him from her mind, she sprang from the bed. "Well, handsome or not," she hissed defiantly, "I'll show him just how resistible he really is."

She wanted to look her best for her meeting with Major Mallory, because if she intended to charm him into helping her, then she needed every feminine wile at her disposal. The dress she had in mind to accomplish her aim was a dusty pink muslin, trimmed with an exorbitant amount of white lace. The gown looked lovely on her; everyone said so.

She began to rummage through her valise, and then she remembered. She had packed the garment in one of her trunks. Overwhelmed with frustration, she tore into her bag, scattering nightgowns, undergarments and hairbrushes about the bed until she found a lilac skirt and white gauze blouse with long puffy sleeves and a lace collar. It was all she had packed in her valise.

When she finished dressing, she looked in the floor mirror and frowned. She resembled an old maid school teacher. Why, she thought miserably, did everything seem to be against her?

She slipped downstairs and knocked on the study door. A voice she recognized as Major Mallory's answered, and she entered.

He was, as before, sitting behind his desk. She had assumed he would be alone, but as she walked into the room, Raven noticed his detestable son lounging in one of the chairs facing her host.

The major smiled happily. "Oh, there you are, my dear. I hope you had a pleasant rest?"

Both men rose and remained standing as she approached the desk.

"Yes, thank you," she lied.

"Excellent," he exclaimed. "Now, please have a seat, my dear, and let us begin anew."

She took the spare chair in front of the desk.

"Major Mallory, I do not wish to appear rude, but I would rather our little chat be private."

She didn't look at him, but she felt Christopher stiffen beside her. Apparently he wasn't used to having women snub him, and she felt a perverse pleasure in being, perhaps, the first to do so.

"Are you hinting that I should leave, Miss Elliott?"

This time she did look at him. "I am not hinting, Mr. Mallory. I am stating, quite plainly, that my conversation with your father is personal and should be confidential. If that is not explicit enough, then let me be more specific. It is none of your business."

"So was mine," he murmured icily, "but that didn't stop you. At least, here I am visible. I do not huddle behind closed doors eavesdropping as seems to be your practice."

"I was not huddling, and the door was not closed," she cried with indignation.

Christopher smiled at her, but there was no mirth in the expression. "A minor point, Miss Elliott, and completely irrelevant since you knew perfectly well the conversation you were listening to was meant to be private."

Raven opened her mouth to issue an angry retort, but the major intervened. "Please, children, we must stop this sniping at one another. Now, let us forget the past and concern ourselves with the future."

"That is exactly what I'm concerned about," Christopher commented drily. "Oh, the face and figure are appealing enough, but I have, as yet, to see the young lady when she wasn't in a high rage. Now, I don't mind a woman with spirit. Sometimes it can be quite delightful. But a steady diet of it can be wearing, especially if there are no assuasive moments from time to time to offset the fire and fury."

Raven's black eyes sparkled with defiance. "I hope you are not hinting that the future you are so concerned about will be in any way connected with me or my temperament. If you are, then let me rectify that misconception immediately."

Christopher grinned at his father and rose from his chair before facing her. "I'm afraid, Miss Elliott, that it is you suffering from the misconception, not I. You see, my father and I have already worked out the details for our wedding. It's to be in one month's time. So, rage or not, it seems I am stuck with you. I only hope I have the stamina Petruchio had."

Her mouth flew open, and she looked up at him in astonishment.

Christopher chuckled. The mellow rumble reminded Raven of distant thunder, full of energy. The analogy sent a pleasant tingle through her.

"Well, don't look so shocked, Miss Elliott. After all, things could be worse. You could be marrying Jeremy Frasier." He reached down and, with the tip of his finger, gently pressed the bottom of her chin up until her mouth shut. "In any case, Miss Elliott, I shall bow to your wish and remove my detestable presence from this happy gathering."

He picked up her hand and bent over it. "Your servant, ma'am." And then he strode from the room, whistling.

Chapter 3

I t took a little over an hour for Raven to agree to the marriage.

After her second encounter with Christopher Mallory, Raven was even more determined than ever to free herself from any entanglement with him. What she hadn't reckoned on was his father's persuasive skills. Major Mallory turned out to be a master of entreaty, and Raven soon realized she was no match for him. She did, however, manage to gain two important pieces of information. She learned the circumstances linking the Elliotts and the Mallorys together, and as a result, the reason behind her father's provision.

According to the major, he and William Elliott had become friends when their regiment, the Seventh Royal Fusiliers, had been sent to quell a

47

disturbance in the West Indies some 40 years before.

"Oh, my dear, it was a devilish position we found ourselves in, I can tell you that," he stated between puffs on a newly lit cigar. "Quite explosive. You see, the native population there had begun to organize against the slavery being forced upon them by the white settlers spilling into their land, and by the time we arrived, a number of small plantations had already been raided and serious trouble was brewing." He shook his head. "It was a nasty business. The natives were completely primitive, you see, and their methods particularly savage and brutal. When they raided, those they didn't kill outright were taken prisoner and tortured in ways that were unspeakable." He sniffed in disapproval. "Unwholesome piece of business, I must say."

Raven's interest was aroused. She knew her father had served in the West Indies, but he had never elaborated on the circumstances surrounding his assignment there. Now was her chance to find out. "Please, go on, Major," she encouraged.

He flicked the ashes of his cigar into a lovely crystal receptacle. "One night, shortly after our arrival, a tribe of jungle-dwelling Indians attacked our outpost. Many in our troop were killed, and William was wounded. I was a lieutenant then and consumed with proving my courage in battle. I stood up in the middle of the attack, shouting orders and waving my sword like a bloody fool." He sighed. "Silly bit of nonsense, it was. Anyway, instead of being killed as I well-deserved, I was captured and dragged off into the jungle. William jolly well knew what would happen to me, and so, after being patched up, he organized a small band of surviving troops and came after me.

"It took a day and a half for them to track my unfriendly hosts to their refuge deep in the jungle, and it was none too soon. By the time William and his merry band arrived, the natives were in the midst of some gruesome ceremony, and I had been stripped naked and trussed up to dangle from all fours on a crossbeam." He chuckled as if remembering some pleasant experience. "I remember at the time I felt like a pig ready for the spit, but it wasn't so amusing then. Believe me, if William had not come when he did, in another few minutes I would have no doubt been the evening's entertainment."

The major told his story, leaning back comfortably in his chair behind the desk. When he finished, he sat up and looked at Raven with earnest blue eyes. "Now do you see, my dear, why I have respected and admired your father all these years? If he had not come after me, I would have suffered a terrible death."

Raven sat before him, shocked and confused, silently trying to sort out her feelings. On one hand, she felt a great sense of pride in her father for courageously putting his life in jeopardy to save a friend. On the other, anger and resentment stirred within her for never being told of his heroism. In all the years she and her father had lived together, he'd never spoken of his military exploits. Oh, she knew he had been to many exciting places and had served his country honorably. He'd even had a box of medals and ribbons to prove it, but she had never paid any attention to them. She didn't think there was any reason to. Now, she felt cheated for being denied that sense of pride a child feels when her parent proves superior or exceptional at some feat.

"I'm sorry, Major Mallory," she said at last, "but all of this is a revelation to me. You see, I never knew anything of my father's life before, well, what I could remember observing for myself. He never talked to me about anything other than the most trivial matters, and he never once spoke the name Mallory, even in passing."

The major looked sad. "That sounds like William. He always did keep his own counsel, even among his friends, so it doesn't surprise me that he should do the same with his family."

"But why?" Raven asked. "What was so secretive about it?"

The major rose and turned toward the row of airy windows behind him to gaze out at the late afternoon sunshine. "Oh, it wasn't that," he confided. "Your father, my dear, was a very modest and benevolent man. To receive praise of any sort was an embarrassment to him." He chuckled. "I remember at the time I felt such a sense of indebtedness to him that I nearly drove him crazy trying all sorts of ways to repay him. When our friendship became strained because of it, we finally settled the issue by making him promise to let me repay him someday if he ever needed anything."

He turned back to her. "Years passed. We kept up with each other through letters, and we visited together whenever I got to London. As time went on, it looked as if I would never be able to repay my debt to him, but I never forgot it." He returned to his chair and snuffed out what remained of his cigar. "Then, one day I received a letter from him, telling me he was ill and was worried about you. He asked if I would look after you if he should die. Well, of course I agreed immediately. You see, that was the first time he had ever asked anything of me, and it was my chance to clear the slate, so to speak."

Raven's head swam. Having her whole perception of someone, especially her own father, suddenly exposed as inaccurate was devastating. Still, she knew the major's assessment of her father's character was true. Looking back, she now realized how she had misread his shyness and modesty as signs of weakness and lack of ambition. If only they had been closer, talked more, been more open with each other, then maybe Raven would have seen the true man he had been.

Raven frowned. "But, Major Mallory, why this stipulation that I marry your son? Why didn't he just request that you become my guardian? I mean, to ask someone to forfeit their child into a blind marriage just to repay a debt seems to me a bit excessive, don't you think?"

The major leaned back in his chair and smiled. "That was my idea."

"What?" Raven exclaimed, unable to credit his response.

His smile faded, and he leaned forward once more. "Listen to me, my dear. The reasons are not important, but just know that at the time your father made that request, I was desperately struggling with a crisis here. When I got your father's letter, it was as if God had sent the answer to both our dilemmas."

Raven looked at him in bewilderment. "I . . . I'm afraid I don't understand. How could marrying me off to your son help with any dilemma you may have?"

The major evaded her eyes and shifted in his chair. "My son is in trouble, Miss Elliott, serious trouble. The specifics I cannot and will not divulge, but your marriage to my son can save him from a terrible tragedy."

"But how on earth could a contrived union between the two of us help him? I mean, if he is already in some sort of difficulty, wouldn't such an irksome liability as an unwanted marriage only complicate matters further?"

The major shook his head adamantly. "No, no. Please, Miss Elliott, just trust me. I love my son, and I would never do anything to hurt him. And please understand, I would never do anything to hurt you, either. I loved your father too much for that. It's just that the reason Christopher is in this predicament is because of me. I brought him back, you see, and by doing so opened Pandora's box. Now, it is up to me to close it."

"Back?" Raven asked in surprise. "Was he away somewhere?"

He shook his head wearily. "All of that is superfluous. What is important now is that you marry my son." He smiled at her.

The kind and gentle expression was genuine enough, but there was something else marring its effect. In his eyes, Raven recognized desperation.

"You know," he continued, his voice growing solemn, "there is a strange parallel to all of this that perhaps you will find strikingly poignant. I know I do."

"What is that?" she asked, with suspicion.

He leaned back, threaded his fingers together across his stomach and at last met her gaze. "Once, long ago, I prayed for help. God heard me and sent William to my rescue. Not too long ago, I prayed once again for the same thing— only this time the plea was for my son. I believe He heard me, just as He did before. This time, He sent you. Strange, is it not, that once again an Elliott is placed in a position to save a Mallory? I think, my dear," he finished quietly, "that God in His infinite wisdom has ordained the Elliotts to forever be the Mallorys cherished preservers. What do you think?"

Raven sat motionless, staring at him. He was a devil. He knew precisely the effect those last few words would have on her, and he used them with skill and expertise. She knew now that she would never be able to talk him out of her marrying his son, let alone helping her gain her inheritance. That parental instinct to help and protect one's own offspring was simply too great a force to defeat.

"If you will marry my son, Miss Elliott, I promise you will not regret it. Christopher is a fine young man. He is intelligent, responsible, and has a great sense of honor. He will be an excellent husband to you, and I believe the two of you will find great happiness together."

What could she say now? She was beaten, and she knew it. Still, something pricked at her. Was his argument just melodrama? Coincidence? Or was it something far greater? Deep inside, a little voice kept telling her to stop resisting and accept the marriage. But was that soft whisper merely the echo of his overpowering influence or the gentle urging of an authority beyond refusing? Whatever the source, Raven accepted defeat.

Shortly after the major's unfair but decisive victory, they moved into the main salon for tea, and Flora joined them there. Almost immediately, Flora and the major settled into a comfortable fellowship, chatting pleasantly between themselves. They tried to draw Raven into their conversation, but Raven only managed an occasional comment here and there. She tried to pay attention to their dialogue but couldn't. She was too wrapped up in her own jumbled thoughts.

What sort of trouble could Christopher possibly be in? It couldn't be anything criminal, otherwise a marriage wouldn't help. Money, perhaps? No. The Mallorys had more wealth than she could ever imagine. Health? Marriage certainly wouldn't help there either. So what was left? She had tried, of course, to get the major to tell her what the trouble was, but he had flatly refused to elaborate on the matter. Apparently, he expected her to blindly sacrifice her life in marriage to a man she knew nothing about and be quite happy to do so without any explanations.

Here it was again, she grumbled to herself, that subtle conspiracy men used to keep women blithely ignorant. No wonder women were considered feather-headed and unable to have any serious opinion when they were constantly kept unaware of anything that might stimulate an intelligent thought or a decision, especially when it might clash with the male's point of view. The longer she thought about it, the angrier she became, and her mood only darkened when Christopher put in an unexpected appearance.

He entered the salon, wearing evening clothes and looking even more handsome than before. Raven studied her future husband and bristled. She realized he was going out for the evening, but that wasn't the reason for her ill-humor. It was his attitude. If he was in some sort of trouble, either he was unaware of it or he was treating his predicament in a very cavalier manner. He appeared to have not a care in the world.

"Well, it looks as though I missed a very

pleasant tea," he remarked, smiling, as he walked into the room.

Raven couldn't help noticing the dimples cutting deep slashes in his smooth, tanned skin, and her defenses went up. Angry or not, she felt a certain response to him that made her wary. She may have to marry him, but she had better not ever fall in love with him. There was something unnatural about this whole situation, and she was astute enough to know she could be badly hurt if she didn't keep her guard up. Whatever troubles plagued the Mallorys, she knew she would be the last one considered in any situation.

"Christopher," his father said, beaming, "do come in and join us."

"Thank you, sir, but I can't. If I don't leave now, we shall be late. The Carltons are having a dinner party, and I am escorting Serena Faraday."

The major smiled. "Ah yes, Miss Faraday is a lovely young lady and quite charming, too."

Christopher glanced at the mantle clock. "Yes," he replied absently, "she is, but I'm afraid patience is not considered one of her better attributes. She is most probably wondering where I am now. As it is, I only popped in to pay my respects to the ladies and let you know I was leaving."

"Well then, you must go, of course."

Christopher walked over to his father and bowed respectfully. "I hope you have a pleasant evening, sir. I will, of course, give your respects to the Carltons." He turned to Flora and repeated the bow. "Mrs. Higgins, I hope you will excuse my absence this evening. If so, then I promise to redeem myself tomorrow evening."

Raven's temper flared. Flora sat grinning up at him like a besotted goat. He's got her completely charmed, she thought cynically, just like his father. Well, they weren't fooling her for a moment. Something was wrong here. The whole scene smacked of a stage play with all the characters acting out their parts. Only she was unfamiliar with the script.

At last, he turned to Raven.

Flora and the major were seated on the sofa, and Raven occupied a chair diagonal to them. Christopher took a couple of steps until he stood directly in front of her. He reached down and captured her free hand.

He raised her hand to his lips, but instead of touching her warm flesh, he whispered, "We need to have a private talk. Tomorrow?"

She snatched her hand away and glared at him. How dare he glide into the room and announce his plans to be with another woman after becoming engaged to her. To go out for the evening was one thing, but to do so in the company of another female was quite another. The unmitigated gall of the man was appalling. Was he completely insane or just conceited beyond reason? At that moment, she wanted to scratch his eyes out.

"Tch, tch," he uttered with a grin. "You really should do something about that temper of yours." And then he was gone.

By supper, she was beside herself. What was the matter with her? she kept asking herself— but of course she knew. She was angry because he was handsome to the point of distraction. She was angry because he was with someone else tonight even though they were betrothed. She was angry because she was not finding him as resistible as she'd thought. But most of all, she told herself, she was angry because she was compelled to marry him in order to save him from some vague disaster, and he didn't appear in the least appreciative.

Supper was a miserable affair. Flora and the major didn't seem to notice her subdued mood, or if they did, they chose to ignore it.

The meal, hastily designed to welcome and honor her, went almost untasted by Raven. She felt guilty for not adequately appreciating the cook's efforts on her behalf, but she couldn't help it. The longer she sat, picking at each course, the more furious she became. How dare he flaunt his dalliances in front of her? Was this an example of what she could look forward to? Undoubtedly it was. Of course he was only doing it to humiliate her further. But why? After all, she had agreed to marry him, hadn't she? What more could he want?

After an hour or so at the dinner table, the threesome retired to the salon, and the major and Flora took up a rousing game of cribbage while Raven tried to concentrate on a book from one of the shelves. She sat staring at the pages until the mantle clock mercifully read 10:30. That was late enough. She had done her duty.

In her room, she found the mess she had left on her bed cleared away and her prettiest nightgown spread across the folded down covers. Apparently, she had unconsciously packed the pink, silk garment in her valise. She smiled to herself as she scooped it up. This was just what she needed to soothe her jangled nerves.

She actually began to hum happily as the cool, delicate fabric slid down her slim figure, and then she turned her attention to the wash basin where soap, toothbrush and tooth powder waited.

Next, she took a seat at the dressing table and attacked the thick cloud of black curls with a stiff hairbrush before adding a soft pink ribbon, tied in a bow. She looked in the mirror and studied her appearance. She wasn't too unbecoming, she thought. She had good coloring, and the soft pink color of her nightgown complimented her complexion and offset the dark color of her hair, eyes and brows. Her eyes were too large, of course, but she had an attractive nose and her mouth was quite appealing. She screwed up her features and made a face in the mirror.

"Shriveled-up, pinch-faced prude, huh? Well, Mr. Christopher Mallory, you agreed to this marriage, but it won't be on your terms. You may think you're just adding another diversion to your harem, but you're sadly mistaken. Go ahead and have all the women you please, but you won't have me." She got up and went to bed.

Sometime late in the night, Raven was awakened by a soft rapping on her door. She struggled to a sitting position and fumbled with the candle on her bedside table until it reluctantly took hold. "Who is it?" she called softly.

"It's Christopher."

She threw the covers off and yanked on the filmy peignoir matching her gown before creeping over to the door.

"What do you want?"

"I want you to open the door," he replied with a note of impatience in his voice.

"It's late."

"That is precisely why I do not wish to stand out here banging on the door. Of course, if you don't care whether the whole house is awakened, then . . ."

She unlocked the door and yanked it open.

Her heart skipped a beat. He stood leaning against the threshold, his jacket and cravat thrown over his shoulder, looking oh so elegant and oh so attractive.

The tanned face smiled appreciatively. "Well now, if this is a sample of what I should look forward to, then I can scarcely wait for the wedding." He glided past her into the room.

"You can't come in here!" she screeched. "This is my bedroom."

He stopped and gazed about the room. "Yes,

60

undoubtedly it is since there is a bed and you're standing there in your nightdress." He flashed her a lecherous glance. "And a very fetching nightdress it is, too."

She hastily wrapped the peignoir around her. "Will you please stop annoying me and leave before someone discovers you are here?"

"Tell me, does your hair always do that?"

Her hands automatically flew up to her hair. "Why?" she asked defensively. "Is there something wrong with it?"

He pulled a chair over next to the bed and grinned at her. "Oh, nothing is wrong with it. That's the problem."

"Please," she moaned, "you have to go. This . . . well, this isn't proper."

"Oh, poppycock," he grumbled and settled into the chair. "We are engaged and will be married within a month. Besides, everyone is sound asleep. Now, come here and sit down. I told you I wanted to talk to you tomorrow. Well, this is tomorrow."

She went to sit on the edge of the bed and noticed he had tossed his jacket and cravat across the foot of it. Why did the sight of his clothes on her bed look so pleasant and yet fill her with such panic?

"Now, Miss Elliott," he began and then paused. "Well, I suppose I should call you Raven by now. Anyhow, I wanted to talk to you about a proposal I have for you."

She blinked at him. "Proposal?"

"Yes. You see, I realize that you are steadfastly

against this marriage." The dimples danced mischievously. "You have made that quite clear. Well, so was I until my father explained the predicament you were in. What you may not know is that I find myself in a somewhat similar predicament. So I started thinking, and finally I came up with a feasible plan that would be beneficial to us both."

"You have?"

"Yes. Here is my proposition. If you will marry me and stay with me for six months, then, at the end of six months, you may take your inheritance and we shall part company. By then, you will have received your father's legacy, and I will have fulfilled my father's wish to marry."

She looked at him with suspicion. "Why the six months' wait?"

"My dear Miss El . . . I mean Raven. We must make the marriage look sincere. It would be embarrassing for us and my father, otherwise. Oh—and one more thing."

"Yes?"

"We must make everyone believe that we are in love." His eyes raked over her seductively. "We must be convincing."

"And just what does that mean?" she challenged.

"That means," he murmured, still surveying her frame, "that there should be an open display of affection between us. I mean, how would it look if we behaved like two surly cats fighting it out in a burlap sack?"

Raven gritted her teeth. She knew it! She

knew he would expect to enjoy the intimacies of marriage with her and at the same time continue his libertine lifestyle with other women.

"Won't that be a little difficult with you cavorting about the countryside with your endless list of ladyloves?" she asked sweetly.

He winced. "Ouch. I see my reputation has preceded me." His dark brown eyes twinkled with amusement. "I assure you, ma'am, a man's reputation with the ladies always exceeds the reality. But, if it will make you feel better, I promise to behave like a model husband for as long as we are together. How's that?"

Raven looked into his handsome face. So, he only wanted a marriage for six months. How like a man to want nothing permanent, just a pleasant diversion until the newness wears off.

"And just how, if I may ask, are we to dissolve the legal bonds of marriage once we have entered into them? I mean, I know it won't matter to you since you intend to enjoy the pleasures of bachelorhood for all eternity, but I, sir, may one day wish to marry again and that may be a little difficult with a husband still in tow."

He waved a hand in airy nonchalance. "My dear Miss Elliott, there is nothing that cannot be accomplished with the right legal advisor and enough money. Believe me, a dissolution of marriage is quite possible. It happens more often than you realize."

So, he had it all planned out. How very convenient for him. Very well, she thought smugly, if he wanted only a temporary mar-

riage, then she was only too happy to comply—
except she had a few plans of her own concerning their arrangement.

She smiled at him. "That's very clever of you, Mr. Mallory. I accept your proposal."

She watched as the smile he returned grew until it glowed with self-satisfaction before she added with wide-eyed innocence, "There is one small condition, however."

"Certainly," he murmured. "Anything you want."

"The marriage is to be in name only. There is to be no intimacy in our marriage, and the only exchange of affection will be for the benefit of an audience."

He continued to smile, but the warmth in his eyes cooled to a glacial glint. "So, Katharina still lives. It's to be a battle to the finish, is it, Miss Elliott? Well, never mind. If that's what you want, then I agree to your condition."

He rose slowly from the chair and pulled her up beside him. "I think it's time I left, but before I go, I think we should seal our disreputable bargain with a kiss. Just for practice, you understand."

His suggestion sent a tingle through her, and she recoiled, trying to ward off her reaction to him.

"Ah, ah," he warned huskily. "You're supposed to love me, remember?"

Raven's worst fears were realized. The moment his lips touched hers, she was lost. The aroma of him, the very feel of him, drugged her senses, and she promptly complied to a call as fundamental and ancient as life itself. As his lips caressed hers with a sweet tenderness, her arms slid up his back and explored the firm, warm frame hidden beneath his silk evening shirt. His arms tightened, molding her body to his, and she heard a soft moan escape his throat.

Finally, he nestled his lips in the crook of her neck. "You missed your calling, Miss Elliott," he whispered. "You should have gone on the stage."

The sound of a soft bump and then a scratching noise within the wall brought him to attention, and his head snapped up. "Damn," he muttered.

"What is it?" Raven asked breathlessly.

"It's probably Aunt Jessica."

"Who's Aunt Jessica?"

"She's my father's sister. Aunt Jessica lives with us. She has a suite of rooms on the top floor, but she sometimes prowls around in the passages at night. You see, she's a bit batty. She apparently has learned about you and is about to pop in to pay you a visit."

"Passages? Do you mean to tell me there are hidden passages behind the walls?" Raven found the whole idea of hidden passages incredible, but Christopher responded as if the subject bored him.

"Oh yes, the bloody house is riddled with them."

"But that's terrible," she cried. "Why, that means that anyone could just walk into my bedroom any time they wished."

The dimples appeared. "It's a tantalizing thought, isn't it?" And then he put his finger to his lips. "Shhh."

He crept over to the wall and waited. Sure enough, there was a click and one of the wall panels swung open.

Jessica Mallory staggered out of the woodwork and glanced about the room, blinking as if the light from the one bedside candle illuminating the room hurt her eyes.

She was dressed in a hopelessly outdated garment of yellow and green brocade, topped off by a ruby-red ornamental shawl. The fringe dragged along the ground and impeded her movements since her feet kept becoming entangled in the trimming. Several strands of beads, pins, a mixture of bracelets and a gaudy pair of earrings contributed to a feeling of her being weighted down by their sheer numbers. In her arms she clutched a fat yellow cat, and Raven was unsure whether the animal was unconscious or just completely contented.

Raven, trying not to giggle, slowly backed up and sat down on the edge of the bed. Aunt Jessica tottering forward, swaying to and fro, reminded Raven of a little old lady who had fallen into a ragman's cart and had crawled out with an assortment of his wares clinging to her.

The apparition shuffled toward her until she was close enough to peer into Raven's face.

"So you're the young lady that's going to marry my Christopher. Tell me, young woman, am I going to like you?"

Raven studied the elderly face before her. She would have been quite lovely in her youth, Raven decided, but now the ravages of time had done their damage. An abundance of silver mingled with the reddish-gold strands straying from a week-old hair style. Bright red circles decorated overly powdered cheeks, and a heavy layer of black pencil almost obliterated the pair of watery-blue eyes. Batty or not, Raven liked her.

"I hope so, ma'am. My name is Raven, and you must be Aunt Jessica."

Jessica Mallory studied Raven intently. "Well," she said at last, "you're a pretty little thing, but I don't know. You look like her, you know."

"Who?"

"Ivy, of course," she snapped. "She took Albert away from me, and that was a bad thing to do. Are you going to be bad?"

"That's enough, Aunt Jessica," Christopher said, stepping out from behind the panel.

The sound of his voice startled his aunt, and she whirled around. "Christopher," she cried, "what are you doing in Ivy's room?"

He walked over to her and took her arm. "That's not Ivy, Aunt Jessica. That's Raven, my fiancée. Now, come along. It's late, and you shouldn't be prowling around this time of night."

Christopher's aunt resisted his gentle nudge toward the door. "Your fiancée, you say? Oh dear, Camilla is not going to like that. It's just like before, Chris. Camilla said one day Ivy would come back—and now she's come for you."

Raven watched as Christopher put his arm around his aunt's shoulder and patted her affectionately. "No, no, Aunt Jessica, I told you. That's not Ivy. All that happened a very long time ago. That's Raven, Raven Elliott, and she's my fiancée. Ivy is probably dead by now so you don't have to worry about her any more."

They had started for the door when Jessica Mallory suddenly stopped. "Your fiancée, you say?"

"Yes. Raven and I are to be married in a month's time."

Christopher's words seemed to frighten his aunt, and she dropped the cat. "Oh dear, Christopher, does she know? Does Camilla know about her?"

"No, Aunt Jessica. She and Julia are not back yet. But you are not to worry about that. Now, come on. It's late, and we must let Raven get some rest."

She thought for a moment and then nodded her head. "Oh yes," she agreed, "she must get some rest before Camilla arrives. Oh dear, Camilla is not going to like Ivy being here. It's just like before. There's going to be trouble, I know."

Christopher and his aunt were at the door

when Raven caught his arm. "Christopher, who is Ivy and who are Camilla and Julia?"

He leaned down and kissed her cheek. "Don't worry about that now. I've got to get Aunt Jessica back upstairs. I'll explain everything tomorrow."

After they had gone, Raven stood staring at the closed door for a few minutes, feeling strangely abandoned and uninformed. Just who were Ivy, Camilla and Julia? Were they relatives? Did they live here? And if so, why did Aunt Jessica seem so concerned about them?

She walked over and closed the wall panel before turning back toward the bed. Apprehension now mingled with confusion, and a frown formed on her smooth brow. Aunt Jessica had predicted some kind of trouble connected with someone named Camilla. Was she, perhaps, the crux of Christopher's problems? Could Christopher and this Camilla person be involved in some sort of love entanglement the major wished discouraged? If so, then that would explain why the major appeared so anxious for her to marry his son. But if indeed Christopher was romantically involved with this mysterious woman, then why would he agree to marry someone else? Raven shook her head. She was too tired at the moment to unravel the tangle.

She went to climb back under the covers and noticed Christopher's jacket and cravat still lying at the foot of her bed.

As she picked them up, that delirious scent of

his drifted up to her nostrils. She began to tremble. What had she gotten herself into? What a fool she had been to think she could come out of this arrangement with her emotions intact. Christopher Mallory was a dangerous man. Already he had broken her condition of no physical involvement between them, and she had quite willingly responded. And that was only the beginning. If her perception of the situation was correct, she was being drawn into an emotional triangle not of her choosing, and of the three principals involved, she would be the most likely to be hurt.

As she slipped between the cool sheets, Raven knew she had been wise to insist that there be no intimacy in their marriage. Whatever the reasons were for her being here, she knew that love and commitment were not among them. She must remember that because already her feelings for Christopher Mallory were becoming uncomfortably pleasant.

When she finally did get to sleep, Raven's dreams were disjointed and tumultuous with harrowing escapes through dark passages filled with cobwebs and vermin, of wild natives creeping silently through thick jungle foliage and of handsome heroes with dimples.

Chapter 4

When bright sunshine assaulted Raven's sleepy eyelids, she rolled over in languid rebellion. The brilliant light had disrupted some pleasant dream, and she wanted desperately to learn its outcome. Then the sound of quarreling sparrows nesting just below her window sent the last threads of the dream into oblivion, and she raised up angrily only to see the sun high in the open window. She jumped up, embarrassed at the thought of sleeping so late.

She stumbled over to the wash basin and poured a generous amount of fresh water into the delicate porcelain bowl. Scooping up a handful, Raven doused her face, just as a knock sounded on her door. Thinking it was Flora with her breakfast, she called, "Come in," and gave herself another sobering splash.

"The more I see that nightdress, the more I like it."

Recognizing Christopher's voice, Raven gasped and began to grope around on the stand, frantically fumbling for a towel. Feeling embarrassed at being caught at a disadvantage, her quick temper blazed to life. Did the wretched man have no sense of propriety at all?

Christopher walked over, picked up the towel and handed it to her. "I've been waiting for you for hours, so I thought I would come up and see if you had expired in the night. Tell me, do you always sleep this late?"

Raven clutched the damp towel to her, trying to hide her state of undress. "Will you please leave?" she grumbled angrily. "You know you are not supposed to be in here."

He grinned mischievously. "You invited me in."

"Don't be obtuse," she snapped. "You know very well I didn't know it was you."

Christopher rested against the washstand with maddening familiarity and folded his arms across his chest. "And if I had identified myself, would you have let me in?"

"Certainly not!"

He smiled. "In that case, I would have missed the pleasant opportunity once again of seeing you in that fetching nightdress."

"Mr. Mallory," Raven muttered, "I realize this is your home and you very probably are used to running rampant throughout its length and breadth, but these are my private quarters. As such, you have no right to come barging into them to view me in any state of dress and you never shall."

Christopher chuckled softly. "That, Miss Elliott, remains to be seen." He left the washstand and walked over to the window. "Actually, there was a reason for my barging in, as you put it. You see, I've made plans for us today, and your lazy habits are spoiling my schedule." He turned back to her and shrugged. "Well, somebody had to come and rouse you, and I was the only one left."

Raven's eyes narrowed in suspicion. "What do you mean, you're the only one left? Where's Flora?"

"My father has taken your delightful Mrs. Higgins on a sightseeing tour. I expect they will be gone most of the day, so I've made a few plans of my own."

By now Raven had decently covered herself. "Mr. Mallory," she snapped, "your plans, whatever they are, are of no interest to me. Now, why don't you just leave and get on with them?"

He grinned at her. "I see that temper of yours hasn't diminished any. Very well," he sighed, as if placating a small child, "I'll leave. But do hurry, will you? Just dress in something comfortable because I've got cook busy packing us a picnic basket and we will be out-of-doors most of the day."

"Perhaps *you* will be," she stated, "but I intend to stay right where I am."

Christopher, heading for the door, stopped

and slowly turned back to her. "That is where you are mistaken, Miss Elliott," he commented with deadly resolve. "I am taking you on a picnic, not to your execution. Now, you may go willingly or not, but go you shall."

Raven stiffened. She wasn't used to being ordered about, and she certainly didn't like being told where to go and when. On the other hand, he seemed to show a distinct penchant for giving orders and expecting them to be obeyed without question. Well, she was about to break him of that nasty little presumption, at least where she was concerned.

She looked at him mutinously. "Mr. Mallory, I have no intention of going anywhere with you, especially unchaperoned. Now, I realize this isn't exactly London, but surely, even in these outer provinces, the rules of civilized behavior are still practiced, and I intend to abide by them."

Christopher looked amused. "Are you afraid of my intentions, Miss Elliott?" he challenged. "How very quaint!"

His patronizing tone stoked Raven to fume in earnest. The fact that he always managed to have the upper hand whenever they met infuriated her almost beyond endurance.

"Quaint or not," she hurled back, "the truth is I know nothing about you, but from what I've witnessed so far, you are completely without scruples and shouldn't be trusted without an armed guard present."

Christopher's face darkened, and he started toward her. "Now you have offended me, Miss Elliott," he replied silkily. "I'll have you know, I am a gentleman of the first water. It's one of my more sterling qualities, and I admit to a certain pride for possessing such a lofty attribute. Your implication that such a trait is either lacking or insupportable in my character wounds me to the core."

All the while he was speaking, he had kept advancing on her until Raven was forced to retreat backward in order to keep any distance between them. The window sill abruptly halted her strategic evasion.

He pinned her against the opening by placing a hand on either side of her, and Raven had to lean slightly out the window in order to avoid him. "But I'll tell you one thing, Miss Elliott," he murmured softly, his face only inches from hers. "If I ever do decide to have my way with you, I will not take the time to drag you out into the countryside. I will take you here—in the hall, on the dining room table, wherever it suits me. Is that clear?"

Raven stared into his face, alive with promise, and struggled for breath. She hung there, trembling and pale, her eyes brilliant with fear. She nodded hastily and extravagantly.

Christopher backed away abruptly. "Excellent," he continued, suddenly changing the mood. "Now that that is cleared up, I shall expect you downstairs in ten minutes. But I warn you, I'm not a patient man, and if you're not there by then, I'm coming up to get you, dressed or not."

He was almost to the door when he noticed his jacket still lying at the foot of Raven's bed and walked over to retrieve it. As he scooped the coat up, he spied his cravat tangled among the bed pillows. It was obvious she had slept with it. He pulled the scarf free and turned to her, smiling. "I hope this didn't cause you any loss of sleep last night." Then, he was gone.

Convinced he would be true to his word, ten minutes later Raven stepped off the last step of the staircase just as Christopher strode into the hall carrying a large picnic basket. There hadn't been time to do anything except slip into the same gauze blouse and lilac skirt she had worn the day before and tie a ribbon around her hair. Without breaking his stride, Christopher took her arm, and she barely managed to snatch her bonnet and shawl from the nearby hook as he propelled her through the door.

Outside, she and the picnic basket were loaded into an awaiting curricle and they were off.

As they headed out into the wilderness, Raven became enthralled with the beauty of the Devon countryside. She and Flora hadn't had a chance to see much of it on their trek out, crammed as they were into an enclosed coach, but now all its beauty and splendor was laid out before her.

The Mallory estate sat nestled in a small valley

surrounded by an endless succession of softly rolling hills called moors. Raven had always heard of the windswept moors and imagined them to be great expanses of drab wasteland, but that certainly wasn't the case here. In Devon, the moors were a vital and colorful place, teeming with life. Wildflowers bloomed riotously among the stout and sturdy heather, displaying a breathless variety of hues and textures pleasing to the eye. Birds, darting and swooping, feasted upon the insects thriving within the vegetation, and occasionally some furry little beast would pop its head up out of the undergrowth, startled at their unexpected intrusion.

The day itself was lovely. The sun shone brightly, tempered by a soft breeze, and large puffy clouds paraded across the sky like huge piles of raw wool. Even the air was delightful. It was crystal clear and smelled of a sweet freshness that had long disappeared in the London atmosphere of soot and teeming humanity.

Raven must have uttered an exclamation of delight because Christopher turned and smiled at her. "I see you're impressed with our little corner of England."

She removed her bonnet and shook her head to allow the warm breeze to slip through her hair. "Ohhh," she breathed. "It's all so lovely. I could stay out here forever."

They were on the crest of a small hill, and Christopher stopped the carriage. "Yes, it is beautiful, isn't it? But don't let its beauty fool you. The moors can be a very dangerous place, especially for newcomers."

"But why?" she asked in surprise.

"Because. Look." He pointed toward a succession of identical-looking hills. "Can you tell one slope from another?"

Raven studied them. Each looked exactly alike. Each had the colorful shades of summer interlaced with an intricate network of trails cut into the foliage by thousands of sheep over eons of time. It looked like a beautiful patchwork quilt draped over a bumpy bed.

"No," she admitted, at last. "But what does that matter?"

"It could matter immensely if you had to find your way home by yourself. Believe me, it's not uncommon for strangers to become lost out here. It happens all the time and sometimes with fatal results. That's why I want you to promise me that you won't wander out here by yourself. Will you promise me that?"

She assured him she wouldn't.

By early afternoon, they had traveled far enough onto the moors to be completely isolated from the outside world. Christopher pulled the carriage into a small grove of trees, oddly out of place on the open landscape.

"We're here," he announced pleasantly and jumped down to help Raven out.

"Here?"

He snatched the picnic basket and a blanket from behind the seat of the carriage and started toward a flat shady area among the trees. "Yes. Here. I don't know about you, but I'm famished and I intend to devour whatever delicacies cook has managed to stuff in this basket. If you want your share, you'd better hurry."

Raven was every bit as hungry as he since she had missed breakfast, but this unusual haven, appearing in the middle of nowhere, fascinated her. She ignored him and began to investigate the area.

"I wouldn't go traipsing about in the under-brush if I were you," he warned, spreading the blanket out. "In case you are unaware of it, this is a bog and very dangerous."

"A bog?"

"Yes. It's another danger the moors have to offer that I failed to mention earlier. A bog is an area of soft, marshy ground. If you should stumble into one, you can't get out and will be sucked under. It's very unpleasant which is why you had better know what you're doing before you come out here."

She immediately took his advice and went to huddle nervously on the edge of the blanket.

Christopher chuckled pleasantly, and the deep, rich rumble sent a wave of exhilaration through Raven.

"Well, it's not that bad. I just meant that you shouldn't go wandering off into the foliage."

He sat down, stretched out on his back, his hands behind his head, and watched as Raven began to unload the contents in the picnic basket. "You know, it occurs to me that I know absolutely nothing about the woman I am about to marry. Tell me about yourself."

Raven stopped her unpacking and glanced at him. "I'm certain there is very little I could say that you wouldn't already know."

He looked surprised. "Oh? And what makes you think that?"

"Well, for instance, you seem to know all about Jeremy Frasier. That means you probably know everything else about me."

Christopher chuckled. "Oh, that! Well, I got that piece of prattle from my father. Apparently your father was concerned about your involvement with good old Jeremy, and he expressed his misgivings in his correspondence to my father. But that's the extent of my information about you, and I'd like to know more."

She went back to unloading the food. "Why?"

He batted at an aggressive insect buzzing dangerously close to his face. "What do you mean, 'why'? Isn't it perfectly natural for a man to want to know something about his future wife?"

"Ordinarily, yes. But there is nothing ordinary about our arrangement, is there?"

He looked at her and frowned. "What difference does that make?"

"I just wonder how wise it would be for us to delve into each other's private lives when our relationship is to be only transitory."

Christopher raised up on one elbow. "Is there something in your past, or perhaps in the present, you wish concealed, Miss Elliott? Because if there is, then I think I have a right to know. I mean, if there is a possibility that I may be shot dead by a jealous lover or an irate husband then I think it would be only common courtesy for you to advise me of the probability."

Raven glared at him. "I assure you, Mr. Mallory, there is nothing in the least sordid about my past or present. Actually, I was attempting to save you from any embarrassing confessions, since last evening your aunt specifically implied that my presence was about to create some sort of difficulty with someone named Camilla."

Christopher thought about her explanation for a moment and then settled back down. "That's very considerate of you, Miss Elliott, but I'm afraid I have no secrets. You see, every sordid detail of my private life has been open to glaring scrutiny almost from the moment anything happens. Sorry to disappoint you."

What was she supposed to do now? She had given him a perfect opportunity to explain who Camilla was and why Aunt Jessica predicted trouble. Was it possible she had reached the wrong conclusion? Could Aunt Jessica just be creating fantasies concerning the people around her? It was possible, of course, very possible. Still, he had neatly avoided answering the question of just who Camilla was, and that troubled her. Why? What was he hiding?

His voice broke into her thoughts. "Well? Out with it, Miss Elliott. I have to know something about you so when my friends ask about you, as they undoubtedly will, I will be able to speak about you with some intelligence."

Raven realized the sense of what he said. "Well, there isn't much to tell. I am twenty-two years of age, I am an only child, and my mother died when I was two. Flora raised me."

His eyebrows registered surprise. "Is that all?"

She shrugged. "What else is there?"

"Well, what was it like? Were you a happy child? And I'm sorry, I don't mean to be unchivalrous, but why haven't you married by now?"

The dappled shading on his handsome face caused a warm wave to wash over Raven. She began to fix their plates. "I suppose I did have a happy childhood. At least, I don't have any bad memories of deprivation although we were not wealthy by any means. But we had a comfortable life, and I had everything I needed. You see, I am a very complacent person in that I don't require a lot of material fripperies to assure my happiness."

Christopher snickered. "I'm sorry, but with that temper of yours, complacent is the last word I would use to describe your nature."

Her face became stormy. "If I do have a temper, it's because I don't like being pushed or forced into doing something I have no say in. And anyone with an ounce of backbone wouldn't like it either. Somehow, I don't think it's strange to want to have some measure of control over your own life."

He sat up, reached over for a bottle of wine Raven had retrieved from the basket and began the task of uncorking it. "Is that why you never married, then? You didn't want to relinquish any of that control?"

With one hard yank, the cork burst from the bottle, and he poured the pale gold liquid into two waiting goblets before setting the bottle down.

Raven thrust a plate full of edible delights at him. "The reason I haven't married, Mr. Mallory, is because as yet I have not found a man worth marrying."

He took her offering, propped himself up on one elbow and plucked the cold chicken leg off his platter. "Perhaps your qualifications for a husband are a bit extravagant. Just what are they, by the way?"

Raven knew very well he was mocking her. "Extravagant or not," she replied, "you fall far short of them. However, as you said earlier, we are stuck with each other. So if you have a right to know my past, I have a right to know yours."

He washed down a mouthful of chicken with a healthy gulp of wine. "Very well, Miss Elliott. Fair is fair, although you will no doubt be disappointed." He looked skyward as if seeking divine assistance. "Well, let's see. First of all, I'm thirty-three years old, and I have a sister, Julia, seventeen. I had an older brother, Robert, but he died three years ago. He was thrown from a horse. Anyway, at the tender age of twenty-two, I was sent abroad. We have a sugar plantation in the West Indies, and we needed someone to run it. That was me. I came home three years ago when Robert was killed and have been here ever since. End of story."

Well, at least now she knew who Julia was, but he still hadn't mentioned Camilla or what her association was to the family. Raven realized that the omission earlier and now was deliberate.

Raven swallowed a mouthful of hard cheese. "Weren't you a little young at twenty-two to be sent overseas to manage a plantation by yourself? Seems to me your older brother should have been the one to go."

Christopher tossed the skeletal remains of the chicken leg into the nearby shrubbery. "Who, Robert?" he exclaimed. "Oh heavens, no. Robert was much too sober and scholarly for that. Besides, he was busy being groomed to become my father's heir."

Raven glanced at him hesitantly. "Sounds like you didn't like your brother very much."

For a moment, she regretted her comment because he frowned suddenly and became very serious.

"On the contrary," he answered quietly. "I loved my brother very much. He was kind and gentle to a fault and, looking back on it, perhaps that was the trouble. You see, he lacked a certain amount of grit. He was easily manipulated, and people ended up managing him instead of the reverse."

Raven could see he was speaking in broader terms than merely his brother's ability to manage a plantation and she hoped he would elaborate, but he didn't. "What about your mother?" she asked, offering him a variety of fresh fruit nestled in a basket.

He accepted the basket and began rummaging through the contents. "My mother died when Julia was born. I would have had several brothers and sisters between Julia and me except that something always went wrong. By the time Julia came along, my mother didn't have the strength to survive."

"I'm sorry," Raven murmured.

"Oh, don't be. My mother had a very full life and died doing what pleased her most, bringing new life into the world." He chose a plump apple and began polishing it on the front of his shirt. "What of your mother? You only mentioned her in passing, you know."

Raven smiled. "My mother also died doing what pleased her most. She was trained as a nurse, and when an outbreak of cholera hit a less fortunate section of London, she was called in to help. Within a week, she had become a patient herself and died soon after. I was just a child at the time, but I remember her very well."

The core of the apple joined the chicken breast. "Well, Miss Elliott, it seems we both come from noble stock. Even our fathers distinguished themselves in the service of their country. You know what that means, of course."

"No, what?"

"It means that we have an obligation to our families to follow in their exalted footsteps. Tell me, do you have any grand schemes in that direction?"

They finished their lunch, chatting amiably about their hopes and desires for the future until Christopher became drowsy. He stretched out once again and closed his eyes, leaving Raven to clear away the luncheon remnants in silence. As she worked, she kept glancing at him.

What was he really like? She knew he was handsome and could be quite charming when he wanted to be. He had proved that today. But what was underneath the facade? Was he temperamental? Did he drink heavily or gamble too much as Jeremy did? Was he an honorable man? There were a hundred questions she wanted to ask, but she had noticed a reluctance in him to discuss anything truly personal. Was that the reason he refused to mention the mysterious Camilla? Did she fall into that hidden realm he considered his personal privacy?

Raven finished her chore and then turned to watch him in repose. His face, completely relaxed now, was even more appealing than in animation. His dark hair, tousled by the wind, reminded her of Jeremy's unruly mop, but she longed to touch Christopher's in a way she had never felt when straightening Jeremy's. She forced her eyes away from the silky temptation and allowed them to travel down his face, past the dark lashes and the straight nose, finally to settle on his lips. She recalled the soft, warm sensation of them when he had kissed her the night before, and a very pleasant ache spread through her. Raven couldn't stand it any longer. She had to know the answer to at least one question.

"Christopher," she murmured quietly.

"Hmmm?"

"Why did you agree to this marriage?"

He opened his eyes and looked at her. "Does it matter?"

She regretted asking the question. "No, I suppose not."

He sat up and frowned at her. "Why did you ask?"

"I don't know." She shrugged. "I suppose I'm just a bit curious about your motives, that's all. What with Aunt Jessica mentioning someone named Camilla not liking you having a fiancée and all, I can't help wondering . . ."

His face hardened. "Camilla and my motives are none of your business, Raven."

"I'm sorry," she almost whispered. "It's just that I feel as if I've stepped into something rather awkward. If I have, then, perhaps—"

"The only thing awkward is your inquisitiveness," he replied curtly. "Now, I have agreed to this marriage. That should be enough. Just don't start prying into things that don't concern you." He got up briskly. "It's getting late. We'd better start for home."

He grabbed the picnic basket, pulled her up and escorted her to the carriage where he threw the basket in and turned her around.

"Look," he muttered, "I'm sorry I pounced on you just now. It's just that my reasons are very private and perhaps a little too complex for you to understand." He reached up to caress a lock of her hair. Their eyes met. "Damn," he sighed.

"What's the matter?"

"You are. You're very much the matter." Slowly his head bent toward hers until their lips were almost touching. "You're fast becoming a complication I hadn't counted on, Raven," he confessed huskily, "and it's deuced inconvenient. Unfortunately, it's a complication I'm finding myself quite willing to take on, and that could be my undoing. That's why I'm asking you not to ask any questions."

Her eyes, fixed on his moving lips, became sleepy with desire. "I'm . . . I'm sorry," she whispered before his lips stilled the trembling of her own.

Christopher's arms, as they encircled her, hinted at a surprising strength, carefully checked. It was as if she had been snared in some velvet trap from which she had no desire to escape. She simply relaxed and allowed herself to be captured. As his kiss deepened, she slipped her arms around his neck and returned the kiss as passionately as he gave it. Suddenly, she didn't care if it was ladylike or not. All she could think of was sating the delirious hunger she felt for him. But when he lifted her off her feet and started back to the blanket, propriety returned.

"Christopher, no," she begged.

He stopped, hesitated and then set her down. As soon as his breathing quieted, he gave her a peck on the forehead. "Get in the carriage. I'll get the blanket."

Raven had been holding her bonnet in her hand, but during their ardent embrace, she had dropped it. She watched him walk back to the blanket before reaching down to retrieve her bonnet.

It was then she heard a loud noise and felt something slam into her cheek. Knocked off-balance, she fell to the ground.

The sound caused Christopher to look up and see her fall. "Raven," he shouted, as he scrambled toward her frantically.

When he reached her, Raven was lying on the ground, holding her cheek, her hand and bodice already covered with blood.

"Dear God," he muttered, pulling out his handkerchief. "Here, let me see." He pulled her hand away and began blotting the wound.

Raven looked up at him, dazed, and then she winced. "What . . . what happened?"

"You've been shot. That's what happened," he growled furiously.

"Am I hurt bad? Ouch!"

He had been dabbing at the wound, and now it was beginning to sting like fire.

"Sorry, love. No, I don't think so, but you're

going to need a doctor. Here, put your arms around my neck. I've got to get you home before you bleed to death."

Raven did as she was told, and he scooped her up and gently deposited her inside the carriage.

As he climbed in beside her, Raven clutched his arm tightly and looked at him, her eyes frightened. "Christopher, did you see who did it? Was it a hunter? What if he's still there?"

Christopher slipped his arm around her so she could lean against him. "No, he's gone," he replied tightly. "I heard him ride off on the other side of the bog. But it was a hunter all right. It's what he was hunting that bothers me."

Their arrival home was anything but sedate.

Crashing through the front door with Raven in his arms, Christopher shouted, "Purdy. Come quick. There's been an accident." He slammed the door shut with his foot.

"Christopher, what on earth is going on?"

The young girl speaking stood midway up the staircase. As Christopher rushed up the stairs toward her, she caught sight of the blood covering both of them and shrieked.

"Not now, Julia," Christopher grumbled, reaching her. "You can faint later. Right now, get to Bridges and tell him to go for the doctor. Now!" he thundered, and then he continued up the stairs, two at a time.

Within a few minutes, a crowd of servants had gathered outside Raven's bedroom door, murmuring speculations. Christopher was administering his rudimentary nursing skills when the young girl reappeared.

She pushed her way into the room and hovered over Christopher's shoulder. "Christopher, is this the young lady Aunt Jessica was telling us about? What happened to her? Is she hurt badly?"

Christopher sat back and glared at her. "Not now, Julia, and would you please stop that infernal chattering?"

"Well, for heaven's sake," she whined, "I was only trying to find out who she is. Aunt Jessica kept telling us that Ivy had returned. Of course, Camilla and I knew better, but Aunt Jessica was in such a state of excitement that we couldn't get anything else out. of her. Just that Ivy had returned and that there was going to be trouble. Christopher, are you really going to marry her?"

Exasperated, Christopher threw a bloody towel into the basin and turned to face her.

"Yes, Julia," he said calmly, "I am going to marry her—that is, unless she bleeds to death before that blasted doctor gets here. Now, will you please be quiet and go see what's happened to that indolent Lizzy? Oh, never mind," he grumbled. "Just get me some clean towels, fresh water and some smelling salts. And, oh yes, bring a bottle of brandy back with you. Now hurry!"

Raven was beginning to feel light-headed. "Christopher," she sighed drunkenly, "who was that?"

"It's just my sister, Raven. You remember. I told you about her."

"Oh yes," she mumbled vaguely. "But I don't remember her. Why don't I remember her?"

"That's because you haven't met her yet. She and Camilla have been on a shopping spree in London."

Christopher's concerned face swam crazily in front of Raven. "Who is Camilla?" she finally asked.

"Never mind that now," he said patiently. "Just relax and rest, if you can. I'm sure the doctor will be here any minute."

Sight and sound faded in and out as Raven fought to stay conscious. Once she heard a strange man's voice say something and Christopher's voice responding.

"I don't care what you have to do. Get out there and see if you can find out who fired that shot. I want that blackguard found. Now!"

The strong odor of smelling salts immediately cleared the cobwebs. Then Christopher forced a glass to her lips.

"Here, drink this," he ordered. "It'll help."

Just then, there was a commotion in the doorway and a very beautiful young woman pushed her way into the room.

"What on earth has happened here?" her lovely voice cried. "The boy at the stable said someone had been shot."

Christopher rose from the side of the bed and faced the attractive newcomer. "It's all right,

Camilla. Everything is under control, and a doctor has been sent for."

From the bed, Raven saw the woman's enchanting face turn to chalk as she noticed Christopher's shirt. The left sleeve, as well as most of the front, was pasted to his body by a generous supply of wet, sticky blood.

The young woman Christopher had identified as Camilla gasped in horror. "Oh no," she whispered hoarsely. "It was you. You were the one shot." And then she sank gracefully to the floor.

Chapter 5

Raven didn't remember much after that. She was aware of people stirring about from time to time and of the doctor attending to her. There was pain, a foul-tasting liquid and then blissful oblivion.

It was morning before her senses completely returned and with them came the memory of being shot. Instinctively, she reached up and gingerly touched her cheek. A thick bandage, covering half her head, prevented any further exploration of the severity of the wound, but considering the size of the wrapping, and the sharp pain experienced when she flexed her facial muscles, Raven judged it to be extensive.

"How do you feel, child?"

Sweet, wonderful, reliable Flora sat in a chair beside the bed. She had apparently been there all night because she looked a bit disheveled and her eyes bore the marks of fatigue.

"How bad is it, Flora?"

Flora leaned forward and patted her hand. "Well, you're a very fortunate young lady, that's for sure. The doctor said it's nothing that won't heal. There is some damage, though. The bullet nicked your cheekbone and a bit of flesh is gone. I'm sorry, but I'm afraid you'll have a respectable scar there to mark the event. Do you mind?"

Raven tried to smile, but the intense discomfort prevented her from completing the expression. "I suppose not," she sighed. "At least I am alive."

Flora grinned. "That's my girl. I told Mr. Chris there was more to you than a pretty face."

Raven raised an eyebrow. "Mr. Chris? Are the two of you on a first name basis now?"

Flora blushed. "Well, you know how an emergency can break down the barriers of formality. Anyway, when we were talking about you, he gave me permission."

Raven's pulse quickened. "Talking about me?"

"Yes. When the doctor told us about the damage and the scar and all, well, he threw a royal fit. But I told him you were above all that."

"Was that all?"

"Well, yes, I think so. You see, he was out most of the night along with some of the hired help. They've been combing the area, trying to find out who shot you." She leaned even closer. "Can you tell me anything about it, child? Do you remember how it happened?"

Raven thought for a moment. "I don't know, Flora. It just happened so quickly and without warning. One minute I was fine, and the next I was on the ground."

"You do know that Mr. Chris thinks it wasn't an accident, don't you? He thinks someone deliberately tried to kill you—and so do I."

"Oh phooey," Raven chided. "Flora, it was an accident, pure and simple. It was just some careless hunter out searching for rabbits or something, and his shot went astray. That's all. Besides, who would want to kill me? Nobody here even knows me yet."

"In a pig's eye!" Flora scooted the chair closer and lowered her voice. "I've heard talk. The servants are saying it was probably some silly aunt living here. They say she's absolutely balmy. She's supposed to be living on the top floor, but the family lets her run loose, for heaven's sake. They say she thinks you are some woman that took an old beau away from her years ago and now you've come back, although for what reason I'm not sure."

"Flora," Raven replied, "that would be Aunt Jessica, and believe me, she wouldn't hurt a fly. Oh, I admit she's a bit peculiar, but she's perfectly harmless."

"My word," Flora grumbled, "you haven't noticed the similarity between this aunt and another aunt we know that is also known for her peculiarities? And she shot a man on her doorstep, for pity's sake. Harmless, my Aunt Fanny!"

"Flora, I assure you there is no comparison between Aunt Charlotte and Jessica Mallory. Aunt Charlotte is opinionated and set in her ways to the point of trying to force her will on others. Aunt Jessica simply lives in a dream world and sometimes has trouble distinguishing reality from fantasy. That's all. She isn't mean or malicious. Believe me, she is quite harmless. And besides, how in the world could she have gotten way out on the moors? My word, we must have been ten or fifteen miles out in the wilderness. Now, even if she could get there, how would she know where to look?"

A gentle rap sounded on the door before it swung open and the beautiful young woman Raven now knew was the mysterious Camilla glided into the room.

"May I come in?" she asked.

Flora rose. "Certainly, Mrs. Mallory. I was just about to check on our patient's breakfast anyway. Perhaps you could stay with her until I get back?"

Camilla smiled. It was a lovely smile that enhanced her beauty. "But of course. I just came by this morning to see how Miss Elliott was doing and to introduce myself. Now apparently I will be of some use as well." She glanced over at Raven. "How do you do, Miss Elliott. My name is Camilla Mallory, and I am very pleased to meet you at last."

Camilla Mallory was even more beautiful than Raven had remembered. Very much like a china doll, she possessed a creamy complexion, sapphire eyes and hair the color of burnished flaxen. That alone was enough to shake Raven's confidence, but add a figure that was something beyond belief and Raven felt absolutely eclipsed.

Nevertheless, Raven responded politely. "How do you do, Miss . . . Did Flora say Mrs. Mallory?"

Raven must have looked puzzled, for an effervescent bubble of amusement escaped Camilla's dainty throat. "I see no one has as yet bothered to explain my place in the family. I was married to Christopher's brother, Robert. I am his widow."

Raven thought she looked anything but a widow. Standing there in a pale yellow gown made from the finest silk available, she radiated an air of youthful beauty combined with a provocative innocence any man would find devilishly appetizing. Raven immediately thought of Christopher and the first pangs of jealousy flickered within her.

"May I sit down?"

The question jarred Raven out of her unhappy thoughts. "Oh yes, please do."

Camilla sank gracefully into the chair Flora had vacated. "I must say, Julia and I were astonished when we arrived home yesterday and learned of your and Christopher's impending marriage. I mean, it seems so sudden. We had absolutely no idea Christopher had developed such a close relationship with anyone."

An alarm went off. So much for the inquiry into her health. But that wasn't what really bothered Raven. It was the fact that Camilla didn't know. Was no one in the family aware of the particulars concerning her and Christopher's marriage except those directly involved? Aunt Jessica didn't know, she was certain of that. Now she knew Camilla was ignorant of the facts and most probably Julia, as well. Raven remembered Christopher emphasizing the importance of everyone believing in the sincerity of their marriage, but she had thought he was speaking of outsiders. If, indeed, he had meant to fool the whole family, then she and Christopher were in for a stressful six months because they would be living a lie day after day under close scrutiny.

Raven propped herself up on the pillows. "Yes, I suppose it is rather sudden."

"It's quite unlike Christopher, too," Camilla continued. "He usually isn't so secretive. If anything, he's a veritable chatterbox. But then, that's a man for you. They are annoyingly unpredictable."

Raven couldn't help smiling—or at least trying to. "I don't believe Christopher could have predicted anything like this, and I know I certainly couldn't have."

Camilla's expression remained pleasant and friendly except for the lovely blue eyes. "How cryptic you are, Miss Elliott. Now, of course, you must tell me all about it. It sounds terribly romantic and I must know everything, beginning with how the two of you met and all the events leading up to this monumental turn of events."

What was she supposed to do now? "I'm afraid I don't know where to begin," Raven answered evasively.

"Well, however did the two of you meet? Oh, I know you must have met in London, but how? Were you introduced to each other? And how long have you known Chris?"

The time had come to make a decision. Should she try to invent some story that was sure to be exposed as a lie at the first slip of an unwary tongue, or should she tell the truth? The answer was simple. It was always better to tell the truth.

"I'm afraid Christopher and I only met each other two days ago."

Raven watched Camilla's lovely face turn pale.

"I see," she mumbled.

For a moment, Raven thought she glimpsed a crack in that placid expression, or was it perhaps only confusion?

Raven felt suddenly relieved. Well, now that the deed was done, she might as well explain. If there was to be any reparation to be made, then let the Mallorys pay it. After all, they were responsible for this ludicrous situation, not her.

"If you're thinking our affection for one another is a bit too rapid to be believable, it is. You see, there was an agreement between our fathers, a legal agreement, that up until a few days ago neither Christopher nor I was aware of. Our marriage is simply a fulfillment of that agreement."

Raven wasn't mistaken now. Camilla's eyes glittered with what Raven recognized immediately as anger and possibly hate. But to whom was it directed? Her? Major Mallory? Christopher?

"You say there was an agreement between your father and Roger. May I ask the reason for that agreement?"

Although Camilla's hands were resting in her lap, Raven could see them trembling. She suddenly knew that Camilla's feelings for Christopher were much more than a mere sister-in-law should have, and Raven almost felt sorry for her. "It's a financial agreement," she replied, kindly, "involving inheritance rights."

When Camilla spoke again, Raven barely recognized her voice. "And you say Roger had a part in this agreement?"

Raven didn't have the heart to tell her it was actually his idea. Instead, she simply nodded.

Camilla stood up abruptly. "If you will excuse me, Miss Elliott, I just remembered something very important that I must attend to. I'm sure you will be all right until Mrs. Higgins returns."

Raven watched her hurry from the room and knew exactly where she was going. She also knew something else. Camilla was in love with

Christopher. All at once, there was a sick feeling in the pit of her stomach. Did Christopher love her as well? Was that what he meant by her being an unexpected complication? But if he did love Camilla, why hadn't they married? Of course, it was possible he didn't return her love. No, Camilla was too lovely. Any man who could resist the willing affections of a woman as beautiful as Camilla was no man at all, and that certainly didn't apply to Christopher. At the very least, he was having an affair with her.

As she watched the door close behind Camilla, Raven remembered Aunt Jessica's prophecy that there would be trouble. Now she understood the full impact of her words.

Raven's mind whirled. Maybe Christopher doesn't know Camilla is in love with him—but of course he must! If she could see it, so could he. So, what follows? Either he does not return her affections, or he does and something is preventing them from consecrating their love. If the first assumption was true, then things may be a bit uncomfortable for awhile, but eventually everything should settle down. If the second was true, then Aunt Jessica's prediction of trouble was a gross understatement, and Raven suspected that was the case. Otherwise, Christopher wouldn't have been so unwilling to speak of Camilla.

Of course, the immediate question now was, where did she fit into this tragic set of circumstances? Being a woman, Raven knew very well

Camilla's ultimate goal was marriage. Women in love invariably wanted a permanent and binding commitment with the men they loved. But were Christopher's ambitions as honorable? Not necessarily. Raven was certainly no expert on men. Still, she knew enough to know that a man could love a woman and yet not wish to marry her, but somehow she couldn't picture Christopher as that type of man. There was something about him that attested to his sense of integrity. But then again she couldn't credit a man like Christopher agreeing to marry a woman he didn't even know, let alone love, just to please his father, either. After all, where did his sense of integrity fit in that situation? No, something was wrong. Everything had a false ring to it. Nothing was what it seemed, and she had felt it from the beginning.

"Why are you looking so serious, and where is Mrs. Mallory?"

Startled, Raven looked up and found Flora standing by the bed with her breakfast tray. Raven had been so caught up in her thoughts that she hadn't heard her come in.

"She's gone, Flora. I'm afraid she left rather hurriedly."

Flora placed the tray in Raven's lap. "Well, what do you think of our young and lovely little widow?"

Raven frowned. "She's in love with him, Flora," she answered absently.

"Who? Who are you talking about?"

"Camilla. She's in love with Christopher."

Flora snorted. "Bah. Women like that don't love. They don't know how. But that isn't what I asked you. I asked what you thought of her."

Raven took a generous sip of tea and felt the warm liquid slide down her throat. "I think she is very beautiful and probably very intelligent and, from a man's point of view, very desirable," she answered grudgingly.

Flora, as usual, had no patience for diplomacy. "Pshaw. She's a predator, pure and simple. She's as slippery as an eel, wily as a cat and as dangerous as a stag in rutting season."

Raven put her cup down. "Flora, has anyone ever told you your choice of words can sometimes be a bit indelicate?"

Flora refused to be swayed. "Go ahead and criticize me all you like," she responded, as she settled back into the chair beside the bed, "but I've been watching that pretty piece of petticoat, and she's not the poor little bereaved widow she would like everyone to believe her to be."

Raven became disinterested in the scone she was buttering and glanced at Flora. Whatever faults Flora had, Raven knew her to be an expert judge of character. "What do you mean, Flora?"

"Well, I don't know how to say it. She just isn't right, that's all. Now take last night. She wasn't at all interested in finding out the identity of the culprit responsible for shooting you. She seemed to dismiss it as unimportant. All she wanted to do was talk about her trip to London and to discuss the people she had met there and the clothes she had bought. She seemed uncommonly interested in having Mr. Chris see some ball gown she had purchased for an upcoming festivity. She wanted his opinion on it, and when he told her he didn't have time to discuss fashions with her, she went into a sulk. Now, I know she is young and young people sometimes don't have the right perspective, but even that untried sister of his showed more interest in the proceedings than our pampered little powder puff."

"Well, of course she wasn't interested," Raven argued. "Don't you see, Flora? She has just come home to discover the man she loves is engaged to another woman. Of course she tried to divert his attention. My heavens, she must be beside herself."

Flora shook her head adamantly. "No, no! There's more to it than that. Oh, I'm not saying she isn't interested in Mr. Chris. My word," she muttered, "any woman between the ages of three and ninety-three would be. But if it is jealousy, she has the strangest way of expressing it I've ever witnessed."

Flora rambled on, but Raven's mind stubbornly refused to change direction. Whatever way Camilla chose to express her jealousy was immaterial. The simple fact was that Camilla was in love with Christopher, and Raven couldn't help feeling a sort of sisterhood with Camilla because of her own growing attraction to Christopher. She could well sympathize with

Camilla's jealous feelings, if that is what they were. After all, what else could they be?

By luncheon, Raven's head reeled with unanswered questions and outrageous theories.

Her noon meal turned out to be the predictable and dreaded marrowbone broth that was always administered to patients suffering from substantial blood loss. All was not lost, however. Served with it were several slices of cold lamb, a serving of mixed vegetables and vanilla custard with rum sauce. It was, of course, too much, but Raven did her best.

After lunch, she spent the afternoon receiving a parade of visitors. Her trunks had arrived only shortly before the flow of well-wishers began, and Flora busied herself with the unpacking, seemingly oblivious to the continually changing audience.

Major Mallory was the first to arrive. He theatrically voiced his outrage over her accident and assured her the culprit would be found and properly punished. Christopher stuck his head in but stayed only a moment, saying he had something to attend to. He seemed distracted and paid little or no attention to her attempted responses to his disjointed questions. Various servants, including little Lizzy, paid their respects as well, but it was not until late afternoon that Christopher's sister, Julia, arrived.

She was a pretty young girl but still awkward in her deportment. She breezed into the room like a young colt out for a romp.

Unlike Christopher, Julia had a very fair complexion, and scattered across her dainty nose were several freckles, giving her a healthy and well-scrubbed appearance. Raven could see the family resemblance between brother and sister although Julia's hair was light chestnut and her eyes were green rather than the deep brown her brother possessed.

"Well, you don't look a bit sick," Julia commented bluntly. "Honestly, everyone has been telling me not to bother you because you needed your rest." She walked over and inspected Raven carefully. "Well, I suppose you do look a bit pale, unless of course that's your natural complexion."

Raven smiled. "Sit down, Julia. Actually, I'm very glad you came because I wanted to thank you for your help yesterday."

Julia ignored her invitation to be seated. Instead, she went to finger the rumpled dresses Flora was unpacking. "My help?"

"Yes. I remember Christopher asking you to fetch some water and towels and whatnot, and you did."

"Oh, that." She waved a hand in dismissal. "Ohhh, this is pretty. Is it new?"

Julia had picked up a dress of pale green muslin, and Raven glanced at it. "Fairly new. Of course, what you have on is very pretty, too."

Julia glanced down at her own gown. She wore a pale yellow muslin trimmed with coral ribbons at the neck and around each puff sleeve. "I suppose," she replied with boredom. She dragged Raven's gown over to the floor mirror and held it up to her. "Yes, this is nice, but Camilla's clothes are much prettier."

She turned around and threw the dress back into the pile. "You shouldn't have come, you know."

Raven became wary. "Why not?"

"Because you're spoiling everything. It is Camilla that Christopher should be marrying, not you. You don't belong here. Camilla does."

"Don't you think your brother should be the judge of that?"

Julia began to roam about the room, picking up hairbrushes, smelling a bottle of cologne. "Oh, he would love to send you packing if he could. You see, everything was going along nicely until you arrived. Now, of course, he has nothing to say in the matter. Papa has seen to that, and I think it is very unfair of him, too."

Raven was becoming depressed. "I see," she murmured.

"No, I don't think you do." Julia glided over to the window and glanced out briefly before turning around to face Raven belligerently. "Actually, it isn't your fault, I suppose, since it is apparent you are completely ignorant of certain facts, but after I explain them to you, perhaps you will understand and leave quietly."

"Please do, Julia," Raven replied with a steadiness she hardly felt. "It is always best to know as many facts as possible before making any decision."

Julia smiled and went back to the pile of clothes thrown across the bed. "You see,

Camilla and Christopher were lovers before she met Robert." She glanced up at Raven, grinning with mischief. "You didn't know that, did you?"

Raven felt her heart begin to pound. "No, I didn't."

Julia's eyes glittered. "I didn't think so."

Raven met Julia's intimidating stare with one equally formidable. "Go on, Julia," Raven replied boldly. "You mustn't become fainthearted now."

Julia obviously hadn't expected Raven to be as indomitable an opponent as she appeared to be. Finding her offense suddenly met and challenged, she tore her eyes from Raven's intense gaze and concentrated on a stack of nightdresses on the bed. "Well, that's all, really. As soon as she married Robert she realized she had made a silly mistake and married the wrong brother, but by then it was too late. But now, they have another chance to put things right, and I think they should have it."

Raven knew idolatry when she saw it. "I would hardly call marrying the wrong man just a silly mistake, Julia, but never mind that. I can tell that you like Camilla very much, don't you?"

Julia's defensive instincts took over. "Everyone makes mistakes—even you. You did when you came here. Anyway," she spat out defiantly, "I think Camilla is the most beautiful and charming person I have ever known. She knows everything. She knows about fashions and entertaining and music and . . . and just everything.

She is more than my sister-in-law; she is my friend."

"I've no doubt of that," Raven replied calmly. "And you're right about Camilla being beautiful and charming. But perhaps you are wrong about Camilla and your brother being in love. Otherwise, why haven't they married by now?"

Trembling in apparent frustration, Julia whirled around and stomped back to the window. "It's Papa," she cried vehemently. "He's never liked Camilla and for no reason, too. Now he's talked Christopher into marrying you." She began to cry. "Why, I . . . I think it's just awful what he's done." She sniffed dramatically and then picked up her skirts and fled the room before Raven could respond.

"Such a sweet child," Flora sneered after Julia had slammed the door. "It's just a shame that all-knowing sister-in-law of hers didn't teach her any manners along the way."

Raven moaned. It was becoming all too clear. Camilla and Christopher were in love, very much in love, but for some reason Major Mallory disliked his daughter-in-law and was opposed to Christopher marrying her. So much so that he contrived to bring her here to put a wedge between the two lovers, and somehow he had managed to bribe Christopher into marrying her.

She sighed in misery. "Oh, Flora, what am I going to do?"

"Bah. You don't mean to tell me you're going

to pay any attention to that hateful little snip, are you? Can't you see what she's doing? Why, she's so crazy about that painted-up doily of a sister-in-law that she'll do anything to please her. And it's plain to see that the merry widow of Heathglade wants you gone."

"Oh, Flora, this whole situation is impossible. Julia is right, and we both know it. I don't belong here. Whatever the difficulty is between the major, Christopher and Camilla, my being drawn into it isn't going to change the fact that Christopher and Camilla are in love with each other."

"And just how do you know that?"

"Flora, please," Raven muttered. "You heard Julia. Why would she lie about something like that?"

Flora snorted. "On my word! You know, you really are the most vexing person I know. You have the most annoying habit of letting minor trivialities get in the way of major issues." Flora left her chores and plopped down in the chair beside the bed. "Now, listen to me. I've no doubt that that silly child believes every word she told you. And I've no doubt that Mrs. Mallory wants Mr. Chris. But remember, I've seen them together. You haven't. And I'm telling you, it just ain't so."

Raven sat up on the side of the bed. "Then perhaps you can tell me what *is* so. There's something going on, Flora. If it isn't a love affair, then what is it?"

Flora frowned. "I can't tell yet. Last night was

such a hectic night that it was impossible to know. But Mr. Chris didn't show the slightest sign of affection for her, I can tell you that. If he cared about her at all, wouldn't he appear to be glad to see her, I mean, especially since she's been away?" She shook her head. "No. She may have an itch for him, but he isn't scratchin'."

Raven stood up and swayed unsteadily.

"And just where do you think you're going?"

"I need to get up, Flora. I'm going balmy lying in this bed."

"Well, the doctor said you would be weak as a kitten for awhile and that you should stay in bed until you are feeling stronger."

"All I want to do is sit in a chair by the window. I need some fresh air."

Flora continued to grumble but nevertheless helped her patient get settled at the window and then got back to the unpacking.

Several minutes of silence passed between them before Raven finally spoke. "Flora, it's no use. We have to leave here."

Flora, putting away a stack of Raven's shifts in the chiffonier, slammed the drawer impatiently. "If you run away now, it'll be the biggest mistake you ever made. Mr. Chris is a fine man, and he's worth fighting for. If you walk away and leave him to that predatory female, I'll be ashamed I raised you."

"Flora, I can't marry a man who loves some-one else—and he does, regardless of what you say. I mean, it's bad enough that we are not in love. But for him to be in love with another woman—and remember, we would be living in the same house with her—well, I don't even want to think about it. No, we will just have to go to Aunt Charlotte. That's all there is to it."

"Well, it certainly is nice to know that you can read minds," Flora retorted.

"Please don't badger me, Flora."

"Well, how else could you know that Mr. Chris is in love with her? Has he told you he is? Have you seen any evidence of it? And what if what that snippy little sister of his said was true about them being lovers before she married Mr. Chris's brother. It doesn't mean it's still true."

Raven's interest caught on something outside. "Oh, Flora, please—"

"No, I won't, please! Now, just think for a minute. If you were a man and in love with a woman, and she left you to marry your brother, would you go back for a second helping? Not likely. Not unless you were thickheaded, that is, and Mr. Chris is not thickheaded."

"Apparently he is," Raven murmured. "Come here, Flora."

Flora obeyed and followed Raven's gaze out the window. Down below, Christopher had dismounted and was helping Camilla off her horse. He reached up, took hold of her tiny waist and lifted her out of the saddle. He set her down, but before he released her, Camilla stretched up on tiptoe and lightly kissed his lips. Then she turned, looked up at their window and waved to them gaily.

"Lord help us," Flora groaned.

Raven didn't hear Flora's plea to the Almighty. She heard, instead, that same small voice from somewhere inside her, telling her not to believe what she saw but to listen to her heart instead. The only trouble was that her heart had broken.

Chapter 6

That night, Raven received her second nocturnal visit from Jessica Mallory.

Sleep had been hard to come by after witnessing Camilla's affectionate display toward Christopher—not so much because she offered it, as Christopher's ease in accepting it like an everyday habit.

Nevertheless, sleep did come late in the night, but the respite was short-lived. The familiar bumping and scratching within the wall awakened Raven, and by the time her bedside candle was lit, the panel swung open and Aunt Jessica teetered into the room.

Aunt Jessica wavered in the candlelight adorned in a hideous, magenta, taffeta gown. Large red roses had been randomly attached to the dress but in no discernible pattern that Raven could define. The ever-unconscious cat

was draped about her shoulders, its head bobbing limply as she stumbled along. This time,
Raven thought Jessica Mallory resembled a
great lady who had been attacked in a rose
garden by a group of marauding felines and had
barely survived.

"Ohhh, how pleasant," Aunt Jessica crooned.
"I see you were expecting me. It's so nice to
arrive for a visit and discover that you were
anticipated."

Raven smiled. "Good evening, Aunt Jessica.
It's nice of you to pay me a visit although it's a bit
late, don't you think?"

Christopher's aunt's eyes, half-hooded under
heavily painted lids, looked wary. "You're angry
with me. Everyone is always angry with me."

"Heavens no! Please come and sit down. Ah, is
your friend there all right?"

Reassured now, Aunt Jessica trotted forward,
reached up, grabbed the cat and flung it down
on the bed. "Oh, that's Marigold," she
announced absently. "He's always like that, the
lazy sot. Likes his brandy, you know."

The cat raised its head sluggishly and eyed
Raven with apathy before giving one side of its
whiskers a lavish sweep with a pink, serrated
tongue. Then its head fell down abruptly as if it
had been shot.

Aunt Jessica stood there for a moment, rummaging through the various layers of clothing,
until she drew out a fresh bottle of dark amber
liquid, two small glasses and a saucer. "I've
brought you a present." She beamed happily.

"After your frightful ordeal, I thought you might need a little something to help you brace up." She set the bottle and glasses on Raven's bedside table and then patiently waited for Raven to offer back a portion of her gift.

"That's very thoughtful of you, Aunt Jessica. Please. I don't think I'll have any just now, but you must have some, of course."

Aunt Jessica poured herself a full glass, took a healthy gulp and settled in the chair beside the bed.

"Hmmm," she murmured, studying Raven from under her dark blue eyelids. "Are you sure you're not Ivy? If you are, then I'm not going to like you."

"No, Aunt Jessica, I'm Raven Elliott. Don't you remember? You came to see me night before last and Christopher introduced us."

"I know what Chris said," she grumbled. "I'm not dim-witted, you know. But what does he know? You could be Ivy. You look like her, and Camilla said that Ivy would be coming again."

Raven was confused. She had assumed that Ivy was the woman responsible for taking Aunt Jessica's beloved beau, Albert, away from her. Now she wasn't so sure. If that were so, then how could Camilla possibly know her or anything about her comings and goings? That had happened many years ago, before her time.

"Aunt Jessica, just who is Ivy? Does Camilla know her, and is she supposed to be coming here?"

"Ivy is Ivy," she growled, exasperated. "Oh,

she's a clever one, all right. I thought she was my friend, but she wasn't. She pretended to like me but she was jealous, jealous of all my beaus but especially jealous of Albert. He was so handsome and charming. All the girls wanted his attention, but he chose me for his sweetheart—that is, until Ivy lured him away. Now she wants to take everyone I love away from me. Camilla says so. She took Albert away, and now Camilla says that Ivy is going to come back one day and take Marigold away. But this time we're ready for her. We're watching."

"We?"

"Yes. Me and Marigold. We watch for her."

The cat recognized its name and raised up long enough to wink at them sleepily, then drifted off once more.

"You see? He's always watching."

Raven glanced at the cat. It lay there like a fat fur rug, snoring contentedly. The cat wasn't watching anything. It was dead drunk, and Raven suspected that Marigold wasn't the only one with a penchant for brandy.

"Aunt Jessica, when did all this happen? I mean, when did Ivy take Albert away from you? Was it, say, within the last ten years?"

Aunt Jessica concentrated. "It was the fourth of April, 1779. I ought to know because it was three days before Albert and I were to be married."

"But Aunt Jessica, that was almost forty years ago. How on earth could Camilla know her? And if she doesn't know Ivy, then how could she know that Ivy was coming back?"

Aunt Jessica frowned. "I know. Marigold and I have puzzled over that before. We asked her once, but she got so angry we never asked again. You see, Camilla never liked us. She used to kick Marigold whenever she thought no one was around, but then she changed one day and said she wanted to help me and Marigold. Said she heard Ivy was coming back to have me locked up and was going to steal Marigold. She said we should hide in our rooms, so when Ivy came she couldn't find us."

Raven was beginning to dislike Camilla more and more. "When was this, Aunt Jessica? Do you remember?"

"Well, of course I do," she replied huffily. "It was just after she and Robert were married. That was, let's see, five years ago. I was happy until then. . . ." And then she trailed off into a world of her own.

Raven sat there for a moment watching her, wondering where she was and what she was thinking. Finally, Raven called out to her. "Aunt Jessica?"

Startled, Aunt Jessica darted a glance at Raven, and Raven noticed tears in her eyes.

"I miss Robert. He was such a gentle boy, and he liked me. He used to spend time with me and talk to me before he married Camilla, but now I spend all my time hiding from Ivy."

Suddenly Raven nearly choked on the bile

that welled up inside her. Camilla! It always came back to Camilla. Camilla seemed to have some strange power over Heathglade and everyone in it. Christopher, Robert, Julia and even poor Aunt Jessica hadn't been able to escape from her influence. And the major? Did he know of Camilla's hateful ways? Was that the reason he disliked her? If so, then why hadn't he just taken her to task? After all, he was master of this house and his word should be law, unless, of course, he was afraid of her. As a matter of fact, everyone seemed intimidated by her in one way or the other, so why should the major be any different?

But Aunt Jessica was the one Raven was most concerned about at the moment. It sounded very much as if Camilla had used Aunt Jessica's unhappy past to gain control over her. She had fed on her fears and, ultimately, caused a great deal of unnecessary misery to a helpless and gentle human being.

In that instant, Raven made up her mind. Just a few scant hours ago, Raven had been ready to leave the Mallorys to their own devices, but now her stubborn streak refused to let Camilla win by default. She would stay. If the fates had declared her destined to save one Mallory from a life of misery, why not all of them? And Camilla was the key. Raven was determined to break Camilla's hold on the Mallorys, and she would start now with this innocent and tortured soul.

"Aunt Jessica, you don't have to worry any more about Ivy. She isn't coming. I guarantee it. You and Marigold are safe. I will see to it."

Marigold, as if relieved of a great burden, chose at that moment to sober up enough to stand. He dragged himself up, stretched luxuriously and began to groom himself with deliberation.

Aunt Jessica beamed happily. "Did you hear that, Marigold? We're safe. Ivy isn't coming after all."

Raven's mind began to work at a fever pitch. It suddenly hit her that Aunt Jessica was very probably a veritable fountain of information regarding Camilla and the complex relationships within Heathglade. All she had to do was tap its source and then attempt to distinguish fact from fantasy.

She was about to open her mouth to begin the first delicate attempt at probing for information when Aunt Jessica, as if somehow warned about what was coming, got up, draped the cat over her shoulders once again and started toward the open panel in the wall.

"Oh, Marigold, I am so happy. I think we should go and have a little nip to celebrate, don't you? I just knew something good was about to happen. I told you, didn't I? You remember? I just knew it."

"Aunt Jessica, please don't leave yet. I mean, well, we haven't finished our visit yet."

"Oh, I must go, dear," Aunt Jessica mumbled.

"You see, Marigold is anxious to get back upstairs, and when he wants something, then there's no help for it, I'm afraid."

She stepped through the open panel and then turned to face Raven. "I am so glad that shot wasn't fatal, my dear. They meant it to be, you know, but then I'm sure they thought you were Ivy."

Aunt Jessica's cryptic words sent a shock of uneasiness through Raven, and she threw the covers off and swung her feet over the side of the bed. "Who, Aunt Jessica? Who are you talking about?"

Aunt Jessica seemed not to hear Raven but continued on with maddening vagueness. "But just to be on the safe side, I'd be very careful if I were you. They don't want you here, you know."

"Who doesn't want me here?" Raven asked with impatience. "Aunt Jessica, who are you talking about?"

"I knew there would be trouble. I told them, but no one listens to me. Oh well, no harm done."

Raven sprang from the bed and started across the room to stop her from leaving, but before she could reach the wall, the panel had snapped shut and Raven was left facing an empty wall.

Raven felt cold. What was she saying? Did she know something, or was it just the ramblings of a fertile and slightly muddled mind?

Raven crept back to bed and sank into deep deliberation. Well, here was the first test of her ability to decipher Aunt Jessica's babblings. Was it possible that someone actually did try to kill her? That certainly was what Aunt Jessica was saying. Flora thought so and said that Christopher believed it, too. And who were 'they'? 'They' implied more than one person. Or did it?

Raven began to shake, and she huddled further down in the covers but made no attempt to put her candle out. No, this was fantasy, she decided. Jessica Mallory was undoubtedly out of touch with reality, and it would be less than sensible to put any credence into anything so outlandish. And Flora? Well, she could have just been overreacting to the accident.

After several minutes of sound reasoning, Raven dismissed her doubts as being the results of an overactive imagination fed on by a series of upsets and bizarre incidents. After all, what Aunt Jessica was proposing only happened in cheap mystery novels, not in real life. In the mundane world of reality, people just didn't go around trying to commit murder at the drop of a hat. It just wasn't done. Nevertheless, Raven felt more secure with some light in the room, and the candle was left burning all night.

The next morning Raven went downstairs. She still felt weak, but she had to get out of her room. Now that the decision to stay had been made, she was anxious to get on with it, and the first order of business was to discover the extent of Christopher's and Camilla's relationship. The only way she could do that was by observation, and the sooner the better.

She walked into the dining room and found

everyone seated over breakfast. The major, seated at the head of the table, spied her first as she paused in the doorway.

"My dear!" he exclaimed jubilantly. "What a pleasant surprise. Do come in and join us."

Christopher, sitting at the opposite end of the table with his back to the door, turned, saw her and immediately rose from his chair.

When he reached her, Christopher took both of her hands in his and glared down at her angrily. "What the devil are you doing out of bed?" he whispered.

Raven smiled, raised up on tiptoe and kissed him on the cheek. "Tch, tch. Why, Mr. Mallory, you really should do something about that temper of yours." She skirted past him and went to the sideboard to dish up her breakfast.

She filled her plate and then turned toward the table. The only space available was beside Christopher, to his left. Camilla, firmly entrenched to his right, looked quite comfortable and natural there. That meant, of course, that Raven and Camilla sat across from each other, face to face, with Christopher in-between. The irony of the situation was almost comical, and as she sat down, Raven wondered how many others at the table were aware of it.

The major's face was flushed with excitement, and he rubbed his hands together gleefully. "Well now, this is most pleasant. But you must be careful, my dear, and not tax your strength. Dr. Lamb said you had lost a lot of blood."

The sharp crack of a metal fork against fine

china caused everyone to start. "Oh pooh," barked Julia, "she looks perfectly fine to me— fine enough to travel, I'd say."

Raven smiled at her. "Why, thank you, Julia. And you're quite right about me being fit enough to travel. As a matter of fact, I was thinking about asking Christopher if we could resume our tour of the countryside today, since the previous attempt was cut short because of my accident."

Julia glared at Raven. "I would think," she sputtered, "a coach trip back to where you came from would be more sensible."

Raven laughed innocently. "Heavens, Julia, now why would I want to do that? After all, I am already very well acquainted with the sights of London but not nearly as familiar with my new home and surroundings. Now, since I shall be living here permanently, I think I should remedy that appalling lack in my education immediately."

Julia first turned pale, then a bright scarlet. She sprang from her chair and flounced out of the room, leaving her breakfast unfinished.

The major sighed and shook his head wearily. "Mercy, I wish I knew what has come over that girl. She has become quite choleric lately."

"Roger, please," Camilla said pleasantly. "Everyone knows that young ladies go through a number of difficult stages in their development, and Julia is no different. She's just going through an awkward time at the moment, what with the house steadily filling up with females and all. I'm sure she is just feeling a bit threatened at the moment and perhaps wonders where her place is within the family." She focused her gaze on Raven. "Don't you agree, Miss Elliott?"

Raven met Camilla's icy expression with equal intensity. She hadn't missed the double meaning in the beautiful widow's words, nor had Camilla meant her to. Raven knew that Camilla expected her to cower under her intense gaze, but Raven had a surprise for her. The first shot was about to be fired in an ugly battle for supremacy, and Raven felt the exhilaration one feels when one is about to strike a well-deserved blow.

"If you mean that any change in a person's status, whether real or imagined, gives that person the right to exercise bad manners, then no, I do not. Julia may be young and lacking in sophistication, but she is not mentally impaired. She knows exactly what she is doing and, personally, I think she needs a good paddling."

Almost as soon as the words were out of her mouth, an unnatural cough exploded from Christopher along with much clanging of teacups and water glasses. By the time he had run out of things to drink, the tension had eased and breakfast was continued, although on a more somber note than before.

Immediately after breakfast everyone departed for their various planned activities. The major excused himself, explaining that he had some paperwork to look at concerning the West

Indies operation. Julia sent word that she had plans to spend the day with a young friend at a neighboring estate, and Raven discovered that Camilla and Christopher apparently had a standing appointment to go riding every morning after breakfast. To give credit where credit was due, Christopher did try to get out of it, but Raven insisted that their routine should not be changed because of her. Actually, Raven was not that charitable; she just needed some time alone with Flora to make plans.

As soon as everyone was off, Raven called Flora into her room and locked the door.

"Flora, I'm staying," she began.

Flora grinned. "Now, that's the Raven Elliott I raised. I knew it was only a matter of time before you fell in love with him. I told myself, I said—"

"Flora, I hardly know the man. Now, will you get hold of yourself? Honestly, can't you think of anything else besides love and romance?"

Flora shrugged nonchalantly. "In a word, no. It's what makes life worth living, although you don't know it yet. Now, if you would just give Mr. Chris a chance, you'd know what I mean."

Raven grabbed Flora's hand and dragged her over to the chair beside the bed. After stuffing Flora into the chair, Raven climbed up on the bed beside it. "Listen, Flora, I am marrying Christopher Mallory for two reasons. One, to get my inheritance and two, to break Camilla's hold on this family. Nothing more."

Flora snickered. "Whatever you say. But I

don't understand what you mean about Mrs. Mallory's hold on this family. Does she have one?"

Raven sighed in irritation. "Of course, she has one, Flora. What else do you think we were discussing yesterday?"

Flora waved her hand in dismissal. "Oh, that. I was only trying to warn you of her designs on Mr. Chris, but heavens, child, you're making it sound as if she has the whole flock of them under an evil spell."

Raven wiggled. "She has, in a way. Now think, Flora. First there is Christopher. He was in love with her once, and she jilted him for his brother. Now even you said he would have to be crazy to get involved with her again, but, crazy or not, he is."

Flora squirmed with impatience. "Bah," she grumbled. "Why, that little peck we witnessed doesn't mean a thing. Now, if that's all you have to base your suspicions on, then—"

Raven raised a hand, commanding silence. "Hear me out, Flora. Next, there was Robert. Now, don't tell me he didn't know that Camilla and Christopher were lovers before he became involved with her. Any brother with an ounce of sensitivity wouldn't take his brother's love away from him, and Christopher told me himself that Robert was a very kind and gentle man. Yet that's exactly what he did."

Flora sighed. "I can see you don't know much about men, do you?"

Raven ignored her. "Now we come to Julia.

Need I say more? Why, she's so mesmerized by Camilla that she is no longer able to think for herself. Didn't you notice that little tantrum she pulled at breakfast? I swear, it was like Camilla talking through a puppet. And then there is the major."

Flora sat up abruptly. "What about the major?"

"Flora, I am convinced that something quite dangerous is going on between the major and Camilla. You heard Julia say that the major disliked her. Well, I believe he knows something about her that is unsavory, yet he's afraid of her. It's the only explanation for him arranging this marriage. It's Christopher, you see. He knows about their affair, and he's trying to prevent Christopher from marrying her. It's the why of it that I don't understand yet."

By now, Flora was caught up in Raven's speculations. "You know," she said, frowning, "now that you mention it, I have noticed a bit of stiffness between those two every time they are in the same room together. It's as if each is expecting the other to say or do something, but nothing ever happens. Yes," she mumbled, almost to herself, "they're waiting for something to happen."

Raven felt a sense of relief sweep over her. She wasn't crazy after all. Something was wrong, and there was comfort in knowing that someone else felt it also. Feeling confident now, she plunged on. "But the worst of all, Flora, is poor Aunt Jessica. Do you know that Camilla is telling

Aunt Jessica that the woman her old beau ran off with is coming back to have her locked up in an asylum and is going to steal Marigold, the one thing she loves most in this world?"

Flora looked at Raven in confusion. "Who's Marigold?"

"Marigold is Aunt Jessica's cat. It stays in a perpetual alcoholic daze because of, I suspect, a steady diet of brandy. Anyway, she loves that cat more than her own life, and she is terrified it's going to be spirited away, thanks to Camilla. That's why you never see her. She creeps around in those hidden passages because she is afraid Ivy will see her and take Marigold."

Flora blanched. "Hidden passages?" she squeaked, her voice an octave higher than usual.

"Flora, buck up," chided Raven. "Yes, the house is full of them. That's why I waited until everyone was occupied before I talked to you. But from now on, we have to be careful what we say because everyone here knows about them and any one of them could eavesdrop on us through the wall when we least expect it."

Raven waited for a response, but Flora just sat there like a life-size doll.

Finally, Raven became impatient. "Well, what do you think about what I've said? Am I crazy or is there something wrong here?"

"Quiet," Flora barked. "I'm thinking."

"What is there to think about? Either I'm right, or I'm not. Now which is it?"

Flora got up and began to pace about the room. "The question isn't whether you're right or not—and incidentally, you are right, now that I think about it. There is a lot wrong in this house. The question is, is it any of our business? Now, you say the only reason you're marrying Mr. Chris is to get your inheritance. Is that right?"

"Yes. That and to stop Camilla. If she marries Christopher, then this family will never be free of her."

"Well, let's say you marry and get your inheritance. What happens next?"

Raven got up and joined her pacing. "Well, Christopher and I made a bargain. We will stay together six months and then part company. I go my way, and he goes his."

"Hmmm." Flora deliberated and then stopped. "Why the six months?"

"Christopher says we must make the marriage look genuine and show affection so everyone will believe that we are in love. Otherwise, it would be an embarrassment to all of us."

Flora shook her head in annoyance. "You know, for a smart young lady you show a shocking amount of ignorance. Can't you see what he's doing?"

Raven looked at her stupidly and shrugged. "No," she answered in innocence. "What is he doing?"

"My dear child, a lot can happen in six months of marriage with an open display of affection. He doesn't want a marriage for only six months. He's going to use that time to win your love, although it will be a wasted effort, since you are already in that happy state. Besides, within six months you won't be able to leave, and he knows it. He'll see to that."

"Oh? And just how will he do that?"

Flora rolled her eyes heavenward. "Because, my little simpleton, unless I've misread that look in his eye, you will be well on your way to producing an heir by then."

Raven couldn't look at Flora any longer. She turned her back and began pacing about the room aimlessly. "Oh, that," she said, nonchalantly. "That's all been taken care of. You see, our marriage is to be in name only."

Flora snorted. "And whose brilliant idea was that, as if I didn't already know?"

"Oh, Flora, what else was I supposed to do? The man is in love with Camilla. I'm nothing but a complication to him. He said so."

Flora chuckled pleasantly. "Oh, I've no doubt of that. Until you came along, he was in control of his feelings. Now you've knocked some pegs out from under him, and he's a bit off-balance."

"He's nothing of the sort, Flora. My word," she grumbled, "we've only known each other a few days. You're just dramatizing the situation because you want it to be that way. I tell you our marriage is nothing more than a sort of business arrangement. He wants it that way, and so do I."

"If you say so," Flora mumbled, and Raven noticed she was frowning.

"Flora, what's worrying you? What's so complicated about it?"

Flora had been pacing again, but now she

stopped. "I'll tell you what's worring me, and if you weren't so dense, you'd be worried about it, too. The simple fact is that someone tried to kill you, and you better recognize that before you go sticking your nose where it's not wanted. Besides, if you're not going to be a permanent member of the family, then why care? And, by the way, how is being married to Mr. Chris for only six months going to prevent Camilla from getting him in the end? You know good and well that an annulment of marriage will follow after you leave, and then she will descend on him like a hawk on a sick hare."

Raven squirmed uncomfortably. "I don't know," she grumbled. "I don't know anything Flora, except that I have to stay and fight."

Flora looked at her with that challenging expression that always made Raven feel like she had been caught with her hand in the cookie jar. "Well, it seems to me, before you do anything you ought to sit down and examine your true motives for wanting to stay."

Raven walked over to the window. "I've already told you, Flora. I'm staying to get my inheritance and to help the Mallorys."

Flora joined her at the window. "You know," she said calmly, "a certain amount of pride is a good thing, but too much of it can destroy you. There's a fine line between the two. Be careful, child. Make sure you know what you're fighting for. If all you want is your inheritance, then that's one thing, but if you want Mr. Chris the way I think you do—and I don't mean for only six months—then that puts a whole new complexion on things."

Flora was right, of course. She did want him but not for only six months. Within a matter of four days, she had gone from loathing him to loving him. How it happened and why, she couldn't understand, much less explain. Love was new to her, and the swiftness and depth of it frightened her. If Flora imagined Christopher being off-balance, it was nothing compared to what she was feeling.

Chapter 7

The next few days passed with almost unbearable normalcy. A week had passed since Flora and Raven had had their private talk and everything had been settled. Since then, Raven had taken each day as it came and told herself that when the six months were up she would be able to leave without any regrets.

During that time, Raven had closely examined her feelings for Christopher and had reached a startling conclusion. What she felt was not genuine love. Common sense told her that true love didn't happen that quickly or that fiercely. Love took time. It didn't sprout up overnight like a weed in a garden. The sincere and valid feelings of affection had to be nurtured and given time to grow. No, that sweet misery she felt every time he came near was nothing more than physical

attraction, something perfect strangers sometimes felt for each other. The phenomenon,
although common, defied explanation but certainly was not a permanent affliction. One got
over the disease, and now that she recognized
the symptoms, so would she.

Late one morning, she and Flora were sitting
on the terrace, having a glass of lemonade, when
Christopher and Camilla returned from their
morning ride. Aside from this single breach of
conduct, Christopher had been an ardent and
attentive fiancé. Why so, Raven couldn't fathom,
since everyone in the family now knew that love
had nothing to do with their marriage—well,
perhaps not everyone. Flora still clung to the
belief that love was in the air, and no amount of
convincing to the contrary was going to change
her mind.

As Camilla and Christopher broke through the
foliage separating the stable from the house and
started up the stone path, Flora snorted. The
unconscious gesture was always a preamble to
voicing some displeasure, and Raven smiled to
herself. If nothing else, Flora and her colorful
opinions kept life stimulating.

"Well, here comes Lucrezia Borgia and your
intended. I still think it's crazy for you to let him
go off with her every morning."

"Hush, Flora, I know what I'm doing."

"Well, it looks to me as if you don't care. And I
know that's not true. Oh, go ahead and deny it
all you want, but remember, this is Flora you're

talking to. I've seen you look at him. I wasn't raised in a hole, you know. I know that look."

Raven sighed. "Flora, will you please get your head out of the clouds and pay attention to what we're really about? Now, for heaven's sake, buck up and be pleasant."

Flora rose abruptly. "You can be pleasant for both of us. I'm going to my room."

She turned and marched into the cool dimness of the house.

"Ahhh, I see we're just in time," Christopher said, smiling as he and Camilla climbed up the steps to the terrace. He walked over to Raven and tilted her chin up. "Did you miss me?" He bent down and kissed her.

Camilla stopped at the table, looking beautiful in a blue riding habit. "Well, of course she did," she bubbled. "When a woman is in love, she wants to do everything with the man she loves. It's just a shame she doesn't ride. Of course, being a city girl, that is to be expected, I suppose."

Raven shifted uncomfortably on the lounge. Why did Camilla refer to her as a woman in love? Were her feelings that transparent?

Christopher seemed not to notice either the implication or the subtle criticism. Instead, he concentrated on pulling up a chair beside Raven and settling into it. "How is your cheek this morning? Is it still painful?"

Raven's heart jerked. That dreaded disease was showing itself again. He sat lounging lazily in the chair, his loose-fitting white shirt partially exposing a bronze chest topped with an equally tanned neck and handsome face. She gave herself a mental shake. Where was that common sense she possessed only moments ago?

"I'm fine," she replied. "It's a bit stiff and hurts when I smile, but otherwise I think it's doing very well."

An uncomfortable silence followed while Christopher poured himself a generous glass of lemonade. Raven glanced up at Camilla, intending to ask how the ride went, and found her watching them coldly. When Camilla realized Raven was observing her, she smiled brilliantly. "Well, if you will excuse me, I need to go and change." She whirled around and disappeared into the house.

After she had gone, Raven turned her attention to Christopher. He was looking after Camilla, a strange expression on his face.

"Christopher," Raven said quietly, "tell me about Camilla. I don't want to appear nosy, but Julia told me that you and Camilla were once . . . well, you know."

Christopher's face became stormy. "My sister needs a sound paddling and a lesson or two in diplomacy."

"Well, the lessons in diplomacy, perhaps, but not the paddling," Raven suggested. "You see, I believe her motives were honorable."

He looked at her in surprise. "You're very charitable. So tell me, just what do you suppose these honorable motives were?"

"She was trying to warn me that your affections lay elsewhere. At the same time, I imagine she was defending Camilla's interests. She is very devoted to her, you know."

"How very considerate of her, on both counts," he crooned sarcastically. "And it's comforting to know my sister has such an intimate awareness of my affections as to be assured in what direction they lie." He took a long, slow sip of lemonade and propped his feet up on the edge of her chair. "Very well, since my little sister has chosen to air the stuffy sanctum of my privacy, we might as well get on with it. What would you like to know?"

Raven was miserable now. She wanted to know—she was desperate to know—how he really felt about Camilla, and yet she feared the answer. "I . . . I'm sorry," she stammered. "It's really none of my business. After all, our relationship is only a business arrangement, and I have no right to pry into your personal affairs."

Christopher glared at her for a moment and then stood up and walked into the house.

Raven sat there, mentally berating herself, when he suddenly reappeared, puffing on a newly lit cheroot. He reseated himself as before, took a long draw on the cigar and began.

"Camilla's family owns a sugar plantation close to ours in the Indies. Unlike us, however, they live there. I didn't know it at the time, but they had left their daughter in England to attend school and learn to be a proper young lady. When she finished her schooling, Camilla went home to her parents. That's when I met her and we began seeing each other. Everything appeared to be fine, except for one thing. She hated Barbados. She hated the heat, the natives, the long hours I worked, the living conditions, the lack of social graces. Well, you get the idea. Anyway, we began to have arguments about my coming back to England. She wanted me to come back here to live. I wanted to stay. I kept telling her that there was nothing for me to do here, since Robert was the family heir and handled everything here. At least back there, I was of value, and besides, I loved my work. In any case, there came a time when I needed to come home to follow up on some shipping problems we were having, but at the same time I was needed there because of some production problems. By then, Camilla had had enough of Barbados, and she had decided to come back to England and live with some relative. She volunteered to deliver my suggestions to solve the scheduling of shipments to my brother. Well, she did. She met Robert and end of story."

"And now?"

"And now, what?"

"Well, things are different now. You are here. So is she. I'm sorry, but I can't help wondering why the two of you haven't married. I mean, it's plain to see that you still have feelings for each other."

His expression grew hard. "My feelings for Camilla, whatever they are, are none of your business, Raven. The reasons I choose not to marry Camilla are private and have nothing to do with our arrangement."

"I'm not concerned about our arrangement," she said irritably, "but whatever is between you and Camilla is my business if I am to be placed in the middle."

He threw the cigar butt down and crushed it out with the heel of his boot. "I don't know what you're talking about. There is nothing for you to be placed in the middle of. Whatever was between Camilla and me ended long ago. Now, she is simply my sister-in-law. That's all."

A feigned cough from the doorway interrupted their discussion, and Major Mallory stepped out onto the terrace. "I hope you will excuse this interruption, but I wish to speak with the two of you on a matter that has just been brought to my attention. Do you mind my intruding?"

Christopher stood up. "Not at all, sir. Please come and join us, if you like. Would you care for a glass of lemonade?"

The major waved a hand in refusal and settled into a chair. Christopher followed suit.

"As I said, something has just been brought to my attention that, I must confess, I had not thought about until now. It concerns your accident, my dear, and its close proximity to the wedding."

Raven and Christopher glanced at each other in mutual bewilderment.

"What does one have to do with the other?" Christopher asked.

The major cleared his throat. "Well, Camilla thought that perhaps Raven would like to postpone the wedding until her wound heals." He glanced at Raven, embarrassed. "She thinks you might be a little uncomfortable about appearing as a bride with your face in bandages. I'm sorry, my dear," he muttered apologetically, "but the possibility never occurred to me until Camilla mentioned it just now. Of course we will postpone the ceremony, if you would prefer."

For a moment Raven didn't know what to say. To be perfectly honest, the thought had never occurred to her either though perhaps it should have. Maybe a bride in bandages would be an embarrassment to Christopher. She was about to acquiesce when Christopher quickly dispelled that notion.

"Not likely," he interjected, before she could respond.

"But, my dear boy, I think we should leave the decision up to—"

"The decision has already been made, and we might as well get on with it. This was your brilliant scheme, remember? Well, so be it. In any case, the wedding is to be a small affair in the family chapel with only close neighbors attending. If the prospect of a bride in bandages offends them, then let them stay home!"

Raven sat there, stunned. Get on with it, he said. If Raven had had any illusions before, she didn't have them now. He couldn't wait to get the dastardly deed over with. The sooner they married, the sooner the six months would be over, and then he and Camilla could continue on with the love affair they were not involved in.

Christopher glared at her. "Well?" he challenged.

"I agree," Raven replied calmly, although she was anything but calm. "I see no reason to rearrange our plans."

Christopher stood up. "Good. Well, now that that's settled, I've got work to do. If you'll excuse me?" He didn't wait for a response but strode into the house, leaving Raven and the major staring after him.

After lunch, Raven went for a walk. It had become a fairly routine pattern for her each day, usually in the company of Flora, but this time Raven felt the need to be alone. She needed some time to think, and so she slipped away before Flora came looking for her.

The day was pleasant again, just like all the others, as she climbed the first slope past the stable and started toward the open moors.

She ambled along for awhile, not paying much attention to where she was going. She tried to concentrate on the scenery but could not. Instead, Christopher's angry face kept cropping up in her thoughts. Why was he so defensive of his relationship with Camilla? What difference would it make if she knew the truth? To them, surely she was only a minor inconvenience. Soon she would be gone from their lives—and then what?

She must have frowned because her cheek began to ache. Raven reached up and rubbed it gently. The action channeled her thoughts in another troubled direction. It had been in the back of her mind ever since Aunt Jessica's veiled indictment of her accident, and no amount of common reasoning could dismiss it. Now fear and suspicion had reared their ugly heads, and they were there to stay. Was it possible that someone had actually tried to kill her? Flora had never dismissed the idea and constantly brought the topic up in conversation. She speculated about the motives, the suspects and the benefits of each if the deed had been accomplished. So much so that now even Raven was beginning to believe in the possibility. She certainly wasn't wanted here, not by anyone. She was a complication to Christopher, a threat to Camilla and a troublemaker to Julia. Aunt Jessica, more often than not, mistook her for Ivy and therefore a threat. And the major? By now, he probably regretted ever bringing her here. But murder? No, the whole idea was absurd!

She stopped long enough to pick a wildflower and startled a bird out of its nesting place. She watched it fly away and then threw the flower down. She didn't belong here, she thought gloomily. Everywhere she turned she was upsetting the natural order of things. She had certainly upset the Mallory household. She had completely unnerved Aunt Jessica. Why, the poor thing had thought Ivy had returned to put her away and take Marigold. Christopher was being forced to marry a woman he didn't love. Camilla was having to watch the man she did love marry someone else, and Julia in her immature way was resentful because her fairytale dreams were not coming true. As for the major, he was having to take the brunt of everyone's discontent. Yes, she was a thorn in everyone's side, but was she enough of an irritant for murder?

Raven considered her suspects, and that's exactly what they were—suspects.

First was Camilla. She had the best motive, of course, but she had not known about Raven until she and Julia arrived home on the day of the shooting. And that was after she and Christopher had already left on their picnic. That automatically eliminated Julia for the same reason.

Aunt Jessica? Raven couldn't believe it. Oh, Aunt Jessica was unbalanced at times, but she couldn't believe that Jessica Mallory was capable of murder. Of course, at the time she did think Raven was Ivy, but Raven didn't believe Aunt Jessica would even know which end of a gun the bullet came out of. So who was left?

The major? No. He was the one responsible for her being here, and he wanted her to marry Christopher. As a matter of fact, he was insisting upon it.

That left only Christopher, but he was eliminated because he was with her when she was shot. Besides, why would he want to kill her? If he didn't want to marry her, all he had to do was refuse—unless, of course, he couldn't refuse.

Raven stopped suddenly. What if, knowing he had to go through with a hateful marriage, he decided to eliminate his unwanted bride? He could have hired someone to do it. It would have been easy. He had had the time. Maybe that's why he changed his mind so readily about marrying her. She remembered now. In the short time it took her to take that hateful rest, he had changed from risking disinheritance to eager fiancé. Why? Surely he must have known that Camilla would be incensed at the prospect unless, of course, he had plans to remove the irritant before Camilla learned of it. Had he already thought of the idea and merely agreed to the marriage to placate his father?

She started to walk again, but her pace quickened and became erratic as if fleeing from some stalking menace.

And then there was the hurried picnic, she thought frantically. The outing had been his idea. He hadn't asked if she would like to go; he had simply forced her to go. And what better place to arrange for an execution than on the isolated moors during a private picnic? Her head began to pound, and she gasped for breath. Execution! Christopher had actually mentioned something about her execution. Had it been some ghoulish hint on his part, a mere slip of the tongue or just coincidence? Of course, he did treat her with concern when she was wounded, and he did get her prompt medical attention. But then, what else could he do when the shot had not been fatal? Raven felt suddenly cold, and she pulled her shawl closer around her.

She felt sick to her stomach. No, Christopher couldn't do that! He couldn't plan to kill someone! Not Christopher. Not the man she had come to have such intense feelings for. Oh, why couldn't she figure it all out? The answer was there before her and yet, and yet . . .

The sound of thunder off in the distance broke into her concentration, and she looked up. Ugly black clouds were building up directly in front of her and were beginning to rumble warnings that a sudden and violent summer storm was approaching. She turned around to start back and then froze. The landscape behind her looked the same as in front. She scanned the horizon in all directions, but it all looked the same. Where was home? In what direction was home?

She began to panic. This is what Christopher had warned her about. Before, she had only gone a short distance from the house, but today she hadn't been paying attention and had gone too far. Now she was hopelessly lost.

The wind suddenly began to pick up, and she whirled around and watched, terror-stricken, as a brilliant slash of lightning lashed out of the angry thunderclouds and struck the ground. The storm was coming directly at her.

The wind, gusting to an alarming velocity, sucked up twigs and pieces of debris and began hurling them about, savagely pelting her. Raven picked up her skirts and bolted.

She ran as fast as she could for as long as she could, but she was losing the battle. Each time she glanced over her shoulder, the storm had gained ground and was growing in strength.

The afternoon had turned ominously dark, and the wind, by now, had become her worst enemy. It clawed at her, dragging her down and then nearly lifting her off her feet at times. It grabbed her shawl and sent the wrap flying away like some grotesque bird making its escape. Just as she was about to give up and let the storm take her, Raven spotted refuge. A small clump of shrubbery, nestled at the base of the rise she stood on, issued a silent invitation. She scrambled down the incline toward it.

She plunged headlong into the scraggly brush, thinking it would give at least some protection from the storm. It took her a moment to realize that something was wrong. When she tried to take a step, she couldn't. Her foot wouldn't budge. She looked down and found herself ankle-deep in a thick black ooze and sinking. A bog, she thought hysterically, and then she lost control and screamed.

The next thing Raven knew, she lay on top of another rise and her shoes were missing. How she had gotten there and how much time had passed, she had no idea. But one thing she did know. There was no escape for her. Either from the storm or from the fate that awaited her back at Heathglade. She took a deep breath, closed her eyes and waited for the storm.

Faces and words floated about in her subconsciousness. Christopher's angry expression. The hurried picnic. "Execution." "Inconvenient." "Complication." "Let's get on with it." Camilla's cold smile. Lovers. Julia's hateful sneer. A gunshot. Pain.

The faint whisper of her name echoing in and out of the howling wind roused her. Raven listened intently. There it was again. She hadn't been mistaken.

She was saved! She staggered up and watched as a horseman appeared on the neighboring hill. He stopped, shouted her name again and then spied her as his horse reared back on its hind legs.

Christopher! No, her mind screamed. He's coming to rid himself of his unwanted bride. She turned and shot back down the slope.

The storm was almost on her now, but she ran headlong into it. She had to get away. It was all so clear now. He was coming to kill her, and what better time and place than in the wilderness in the middle of a terrible storm? He could rid himself of her by throwing her into a bog, and who would be the wiser? Everyone would just assume she stumbled into one and was sucked under.

The wind was so strong, it impeded her flight.

Airy fingers caught at her clothing and tossed her hair into her eyes so she couldn't see where she was going. Still, she fought on.

"Raven. Stop. It's Christopher."

Large drops of rain began to strike her, but she wouldn't stop. He kept getting closer. She had to get away. She imagined herself sinking into a dark world of soft mud and suffocating as her lungs filled with water.

"Stop, damn it! It's Christopher."

She could hear the hoofbeats now, and they sounded like the crack of doom.

Suddenly the horse was beside her and then a strong arm encircled her and dragged her up off the ground.

Raven began beating and clawing at the arm. "No," she screamed. "Let me go. Let me go!"

Before she could catch her breath, she was tossed over the neck of the horse, face down, and the stallion took off into the storm.

He's taking me to a bog, she thought frantically. He's going to kill me. She began kicking and screaming. "No, no. Let me down."

A vise-like grip held her on the horse. "Stop it, damn it. Stop it," he growled viciously.

Time seemed to stand still. Then, without warning, the rain no longer flooded down on them and the horse stopped. Christopher slid out of the saddle, dragged Raven off the horse and whirled her around. He shook her roughly.

"What in blazes is the matter with you?" he shouted. "Have you gone crazy? Didn't you hear me calling you?"

They were in some kind of ruin. Outside the storm raged, but inside this part of the decaying structure it was still dry.

She looked up into his angry face. Christopher's wet hair looked coal black now and supplied the tiny rivulets of water streaming down his handsome face and dripping off his chin. His eyes, dark orbs of blazing fury, stared down at her hatefully.

"Please," she whimpered. "Don't hurt me. I'll do anything you want, just don't . . ." She couldn't finish.

He held her upper arms in a tight grip. He began to shake her again. "Hurt you? Hurt you? Dear God, I ought to beat you till you bleed. What in the bloody hell were you doing out here by yourself? Didn't I tell you how dangerous it was? Didn't I? And why in the hell did you run away from me like that? Have you lost your mind?"

"Please," she begged, and then her knees buckled under her.

He caught her up in his arms and carried her into a dark corner where he dumped her on a large pile of hay. "Don't move. Just stay there," he ordered, and then he went back to his horse.

Raven watched as he stripped the mount of its saddle and then rubbed the heaving animal down with the blanket before tying the reins to a secure post. Then he disappeared around a corner. She heard some shuffling and scraping noises before he came into view again, carrying a pitchfork. He came toward her.

Raven gasped and shrank back.

He stopped. "What is the matter with you?"

"What . . . what is that for?" she asked breathlessly.

Christopher grinned. "Well, I knew you were a city girl, but surely you know what a pitchfork is. It's for picking up hay." He stabbed the gruesome instrument into her rustic cushion, lifted up a shocking supply of straw and disappeared around the corner again. He made three trips.

At last he returned, empty-handed. "Your quarters await, my lady." He made an elaborate bow, then reached for her hand.

Raven allowed herself to be led around the corner, limping all the way, and discovered a vigorous fire crackling within a crumbling fireplace. In front of the hearth, a comfortable bed of straw had been fashioned.

He noticed her gingerly walk. "What's the matter with . . . Good Lord, you're barefoot! What happened to your shoes?"

She couldn't bring herself to mention the bog, thinking it might give him ideas. "I . . . I lost them," she muttered and sank down into the straw without elaborating.

Christopher sat down beside her, pulled off his boots and set them in front of the fire. "I'm dying to know how you lost them, but I won't press the point." Then he reached over his back and peeled off his saturated shirt, revealing a firm muscular chest and broad shoulders, both colored a rich golden brown. He draped the bedraggled garment over his boots.

When he had satisfied himself with the drying arrangements, Christopher turned and grinned at her. "Well, now it's your turn."

She blinked at him. "My turn?"

"Yes. If you don't get out of those wet clothes, you'll come down with pneumonia."

"Ohhh, no," she protested. "I'm fine, just the way I am."

He shrugged. "If you say so. But remember, I warned you, and don't expect a bit of sympathy from me when you come down all croupy. Now, let me look at those feet."

"Why?" she challenged and tucked them even more securely under her drenched skirts.

"Give me your feet," he grumbled and then began groping under her skirts until he located her ankles. With one hard tug, he unceremoniously yanked them out from under her. "Unless I've misjudged you, you're not used to running barefoot in the heath. I just want to see . . . Yes, it's just as I thought." He examined both feet and then released them. "Well, you're wounded, but not mortally so. And it's no more than you deserve, running off like that."

They sat there for awhile, warming themselves and listening to the storm unleash its fury. Raven was freezing, even though it was high summer, because of a strong draft blowing through the structure. She kept shivering in spite of herself.

Christopher, noticing her discomfort, reached over and threw an additional log on the fire before stretching out and propping himself up on one elbow beside her. "Now that you've calmed down, do you suppose you could tell me, between those chattering teeth, just why you ran away from me like that?"

When she looked down at him, her heart skipped a beat. It had become dark and murky except for the firelight illuminating the room with flickering shades of amber. Christopher's face, bathed in the coral glow, gazed back at her. In his eyes smoldered the unmistakable expression of desire.

"I . . . I didn't know it was you," she stammered and shivered again. Only this time, it wasn't because of the cold.

"That isn't why you ran, Raven," Christopher murmured gently. "You were afraid of something. Was it me, perhaps? Or was it something within yourself?"

"No! Honestly, it's just that I . . ."

He reached up and pulled her down on top of himself. "Come here," he whispered.

As she drifted down toward him, he wrapped her in his arms before rolling over and trapping her beneath him. "This is what you have been afraid of," he commented softly. "We both were. But it's too late, Raven. It's too late for both of us." And then he kissed her.

She tried to remember that he might very well be a potential murderer, but she couldn't. The solid warmth of his body through her bodice, the weight of him surrounding her and the determined assault of his lips drove all thoughts of suspicion from her mind. What had replaced fear and doubt was now a sweet longing for his arms to remain around her forever.

At first his kisses were soft and exploring. They teased her forehead, eyes, nose and neck down to the soft swell beneath her bodice. He even kissed the bandage of her wounded cheek with such gentleness that the touch seemed nothing more than the slight flutter of a butterfly's wing.

He nibbled at her mouth. "Raven," he whispered. "Kiss me the way I need you to. Kiss me as if you want me." And then his mouth crushed hers.

Raven obeyed, for she was powerless to do otherwise. Without hesitation, she willingly let her emotions go, and good sense went with them. As she sank into a delirious state of exultation, she slipped her arms around his firm torso until he was enveloped within her grasp. Then she began a deliberate and tantalizing investigation of taut muscles beneath the velvet warmth of his flesh. The thick pads of sinew forming his shoulders reacted to her touch by compressing, and his grip tightened on her. Further down, the tough, rigid cords running vertically down his trunk constricted in sensitive response to her delicate but deadly caress. But it was not until she had reached the small of his back that he begged for mercy.

"Please, Raven, don't." He breathed painfully

and then growled, "Damn," before losing control and sinking into her, pressing her even deeper into the straw.

She felt as if she had been plunged into a molten volcano. As one hand slid down her back, the other grasped the nape of her neck as he pulled her even closer to him until she thought she would faint from desire.

"Christopher," she whispered weakly. "Don't. If your feelings for me are not sincere," she gasped raggedly, "I'll die."

His mouth nestled by her ear, and she could feel him trembling. He raised up enough to kiss her lightly on the lips. "Don't tempt me, Raven," he muttered thickly, "because right now it's taking every ounce of resolve I have not to show you just how sincere I am."

She gazed up at him dreamily. "You were right earlier, you know. I was afraid. I was afraid of you touching me. Now I am afraid you won't."

She heard him catch his breath. "Dear God, Raven," he groaned, "how I've wanted to hold you like this. I want you so." His voice trailed off into a deep sigh.

The fire crackled, the storm raged, and time was forgotten.

Sometime later, a sudden calm flooded the room as the structure slowly blossomed with light. The storm was over. It had passed as quickly as it had come, and now the only sound heard was the musical peal of water dripping off the roof.

Christopher was the one to break the spell. He tore his lips from hers abruptly and buried his face in the crook of her neck, gasping for breath.

Reality had returned, but now everything seemed different. The threat of danger had disappeared. Life was sweeter, richer, more intense than before, and Raven's heart sang with joy because she knew Christopher loved her, just as she loved him. She sighed deeply, drunk with happiness, and stretched luxuriously beneath him.

He stiffened. "Don't," he moaned huskily. "Don't move, please."

A short time later, Christopher sat up and grabbed his shirt. He tugged the garment on and did the same with his boots. He stood up, looked down at her and held out his hand. "The storm is over, Raven," he said. "It's time to go home."

Chapter 8

When Christopher and Raven arrived back at Heathglade, everyone was waiting for them.

Flora met them at the front door, crying, "Oh, my poor lamb. Oh, my poor lamb," as Christopher set his charge down, still barefoot, in the entrance hall.

The others, hearing the commotion, piled through the parlor door and got their first glimpse of Raven. Her clothing, wrinkled and still damp, clung to her like so much wet laundry. Her hair was a mess; her face, hands and hem of her skirt were muddied, her feet bruised and devoid of shoes.

"She's all right, Mrs. Higgins," Christopher replied, running a hand through his own mussed hair, "although she's a little worse for the wear."

"My word," mumbled the major, coming toward them. "Are you certain she's not injured?"

"She's perfectly fine, sir. I assure you."

Flora took Raven by the shoulders and began heading for the stairs. "Come along, my dear. We must get you upstairs and into bed at once before you die of pneumonia."

"Excuse me, Mrs. Higgins," interrupted Christopher, "but before you do that, I'd suggest she have a good stiff drink. Brandy, I'd say, wouldn't you, Father? Besides, it's too late now to worry about pneumonia. If she's going to be sick, then the brandy will do her more good than dry clothes and blankets at this point."

"Absolutely," exclaimed the major. "Here. Bring her in the parlor."

They all filed back into the parlor, and Raven was made comfortable on the sofa while the major poured out the drinks. Julia and Camilla chose not to sit but roamed about the room casually, while Flora and Christopher settled into resting places.

Julia, as usual, was feverish with curiosity. "Well, what happened, for pity's sake? You've been gone for hours. What have you been doing all this time?"

Christopher had flung himself down in an upholstered chair facing the sofa, his legs stretched out in front of him. "Well," he began as his father handed him a glass of brandy, "as you can see, we got caught in the storm."

"My heavens, were you out in it all this time?" his sister shrieked.

"Only for a short time. Well, it was enough to get us drenched, wasn't it?"

"Well, don't just sit there, Christopher," Julia said. "Tell us what happened."

"There's nothing to tell, Julia. I found her just before the storm hit, and we took shelter at the old Coachman's Inn, or at least what's left of it. We waited out the storm there."

"How very convenient that you should be so close to sanctuary," Camilla commented silkily for the first time. She was smiling at Christopher pleasantly, but her eyes glittered with jealousy.

Christopher smiled back at her. "Yes. That was a piece of luck, wasn't it?"

Camilla turned her attention to Raven. "I must say, Miss Elliott, that was rather foolish of you to wander off alone like that. Surely someone had warned you of the dangers out on the moors. Whatever possessed you to do such an irresponsible thing?"

Camilla looked radiant. She wore a periwinkle blue muslin gown with gold detailing, the gold setting off her lovely hair, the blue accentuating her eyes. Beside her, Raven looked like a bedraggled street urchin. The contrast between Camilla's appearance and Raven's must have been remarkable, and Raven suspected Camilla had chosen to stop directly behind her for that very reason.

"It was foolish and irresponsible, but not deliberate," Raven replied, her cheeks burning with humiliation. "I had no intention of going so far, honestly. I suppose I just got lost in my thoughts and didn't pay much attention to where I was going. I'm just thankful Christopher came looking for me, otherwise . . ."

"Yes. Chris is a very thoughtful fellow, isn't he? And it was nice that the two of you spent some time alone. I'm sure it gave you both a chance to get to know one another a little better."

Christopher sat his glass down on the table beside his chair. "Yes. Well, I think Raven has had enough excitement for one day. Mrs. Higgins, why don't you take our adventurous little friend upstairs and put her to bed? I'm certain she's exhausted from her harrowing excursion and could use the rest."

"I think so too," Flora agreed. "Come along, Raven. It's time I got you out of those wet clothes." She took the glass from Raven's hand and helped her to her feet.

As they entered the hall, Raven heard Julia giggle. "What an amusing spectacle. My word, she looked just like a half-drowned little mouse pulled from a pond."

Strangely, Julia's unkind remark didn't bother Raven. She was too happy for anything to ever bother her again. Christopher had changed that. He had changed everything.

Once upstairs, Raven was dried off, dressed in a clean nightdress and put to bed. Flora had very nearly worn out her ears during the process, giving an ongoing verbal dissertation on the hazards of prolonged exposure to the elements. But soon Raven was settled in and left alone to revel in the exquisite pleasure of being in love.

How silly she had been to think that Christopher might have been the one who wanted her dead. How silly it was to think that anyone wanted her dead. Thank heavens she had gotten her perspective back. What had happened to her was simply an accident. Her first assumption had been right all along, and now there was nothing to fear at all.

She was served dinner in bed, followed by a nasty tasting draught cook assured everyone would ward off colds. After that, she was presented a good book from the library and given strict orders to get some sound rest. The book, *Emma*, by a popular new authoress, Jane Austen, promised to be a good one, but unable to concentrate on the words, Raven put it down after only a few pages and drifted off into dreams of love and happiness.

Late in the night, she was awakened by the mournful bellowings of Marigold. Raven quickly sat up in bed and lit her candle. Marigold sat in the middle of the room, blinking at her in boredom, and the wall panel was slightly ajar. There was no sign of Aunt Jessica, however.

To be truthful, Raven had almost forgotten about the passages within the walls because Aunt Jessica now used doors and hallways to traverse the house. Indeed, she was driving everyone crazy with her exuberance over suddenly being set free, and she darted about, trying to be everywhere at once.

Raven waited, expecting Aunt Jessica to appear at any second. After a few moments, Marigold stood up, bellowed at her once again and walked over to the wall panel. He nudged the partition open further, stepped through the threshold and turned around to stare at her patiently. It was an open invitation for her to follow if Raven had ever seen one.

She suddenly became wary. What if Aunt Jessica was sick or was somehow stuck in one of those passages? She slipped a pair of soft slippers on her sore feet, grabbed her candle and followed.

It was dark and musty inside the wall, but at least there were no cobwebs or sharp protruding objects for her to worry about. She plunged on into the darkness.

Marigold seemed to know not to go too fast. He would stop every now and then and wait for her to catch up. Raven didn't know what time it was, but she knew it must be very late because of the dead silence. Not a sound could be heard except for her own breathing and her soft shuffling footsteps on the stone floor as she made her way through the eerie passage.

Raven soon discerned that one way in the passage was always down, the other up, and Marigold was headed down. They would travel along one wall horizontally, then turn at the corner and meet a descending row of steep steps followed by another long horizontal passage.

They were on the first floor, moving down a level passage, when Raven caught sight of a ray of light shining through a crack in the wall a short distance in front of them. She calculated it to be the library and wondered who would be in there at this time of night. As she approached the luminous shaft, voices became audible.

"I don't care if he is your father. I hate the old fool! He's never liked me, you know. Why, he even blamed me for not loving Robert, as if I could help it."

Camilla! She was talking to someone, but who? Christopher? Julia? She crept closer to the light and peeped through the slit in the wall.

"Well, after all, you did marry him, Camilla. I don't think it was unreasonable for him to expect you to love your husband."

Christopher's left shoulder and the back of his head slowly appeared as he stepped into Raven's line of vision. Raven's heart began to pound. Why were he and Camilla meeting in the middle of the night? Had she accidentally stumbled upon a lover's tryst?

"You know why," Camilla cried. "I was still in love with you. And besides, Robert was so . . . so logical and practical and dull. I couldn't stand it, I tell you, I just couldn't stand it."

Christopher walked over to Camilla and took her in his arms. "Calm down, my love. If you don't stop frowning so much, you'll get all wrinkled and then I shall stop loving you."

Camilla jerked away from him and stalked about the room. "I'm beginning to wonder if you do now," she stormed. "You don't have to be quite so attentive with that wide-eyed little piece of baggage your father found, do you? And by the way, just exactly what went on between you and your blushing bride this afternoon out on the lonely moors?"

He caught up to her and kissed her deeply. "Absolutely nothing, my love. After all, how could anything happen when I love you so much? You know how I feel."

She pulled away and glared at him. "I'm not so sure. You seem to be enjoying the prospects of marriage just a little too much, as far as I'm concerned. And I'm still curious to know just what took you so long to rescue your little damsel this afternoon. You didn't, by any chance, take the opportunity to seduce her while the two of you were alone, did you?"

His face hardened. "We've been through this before, Camilla. Of course I am attentive toward her, and of course I seem happy at the prospect of marrying her. That is the plan, isn't it? Now, you know the only reason I'm marrying Raven is to please my father and get controlling interest in the company. But you already know all that. Lord, we've been over it enough, and you know there's no other way. I have to make love to her, otherwise she'll bolt. She's not stupid, Camilla. She's a very bright young lady, and if I don't give her a reason to stay, she'll leave and then all our plans will be for nothing."

"Fine. Let her leave. I want her to leave! Nothing is worth us being apart any longer."

"Oh? Not even all those silks and satins you are so fond of? Somehow I can't picture you draped in bombazine and liking it. No, this is the only way of getting what we both want."

"It's a way of getting what you want," Camilla snapped. "It's that hateful sugar plantation. You're obsessed with it. Oh, how I wish a storm would come and wash it and that whole despicable island away with it."

Raven couldn't listen any more. She turned around and fled back to her room.

It was a lie, her heart screamed all the while it was breaking. The kisses he gave her, the desire she thought he felt for her was all a lie. He didn't mean any of it. Her cheeks burned in humiliation as she remembered how shamelessly she had responded to his lovemaking. And then the tears came, the bitter and hopeless tears of a love suddenly obliterated in the wink of an eye.

The next morning Raven couldn't get up. She hadn't slept, of course, and her eyes were red and puffy from the endless hours of crying over a death far greater than the mere termination of life.

Of course, she knew the pain she felt was of her own making. When she had agreed to this fraudulent marriage, love or commitment had never meant to be a condition. Quite the contrary. Their marriage was to be only a ruse and only for six months, but yesterday, lying in Christopher's arms, she had forgotten that.

"I knew it," Flora lectured, as she propped Raven up with pillows. "Well, it's just what you deserve. Now you've gone and gotten yourself sick—and just before your wedding, too."

Raven's eyes welled up in tears at the mention of her wedding. "Flora, please," she begged, "just leave me alone. Just go away and leave me in peace."

Flora snorted. "Well, perhaps Mr. Chris can improve your disposition. He's coming up to see you after breakfast. He's concerned about your health even if you aren't."

Raven shot up out of bed. "No," she pleaded. "Flora, tell him I don't want to see him. Please. Just tell him I don't feel like company. I . . . I just can't. Not today."

Flora frowned and opened her mouth to say something, then seemed to change her mind. "All right, my dear," she said calmly. "You needn't get so upset. Now, lie back and rest. I'll be back now and again to check on you."

Two hours later, Raven heard her bedroom door creak open, followed by muffled footsteps. She closed her eyes quickly even though a constant stream of tears paraded down her cheeks and spilled onto her pillow. She didn't feel like dealing with Flora right now, and she hoped she would think her asleep and leave.

The sudden aroma of him jarred Raven's fragile control, and she felt as if an enormous dam was about to break inside her.

She felt the bed sag. He was sitting beside her, and her breathing became ragged as a fresh flow of tears began.

Christopher reached up and gently wiped away the tears before sliding his arms beneath her. "Raven, sweetheart," he whispered, "I know you're not asleep. Now, open your eyes, please, and tell me why you're crying. Whatever it is, I'll make it right. I promise."

Raven opened her eyes and stared at him with black lifeless orbs, dead as any corpse's. "Go away," she ordered, dully.

"Go away? Go away?" He grinned at her roguishly. "Not in a million years. I expect full compensation for the hell you put me through yesterday. I don't think you realize it, but you came within a hair's breadth of becoming my wife before you've had time to be my bride." He kissed her playfully on the lips. "Now, tell me what's so bad that it's causing all those tears."

Raven stared into his handsome, animated face and watched the dimples winking back at her as he spoke. Even now, knowing the cold, hard truth about his true feelings, his kiss still sent a burning desire through her.

"There will be no compensation for yesterday's folly," she said with surprising conviction. "Yesterday was a mistake. You know very well that that kind of intimacy has no place in our bargain, and that's as it should be."

He sat up, the smile gone. "You don't mean that, Raven," he said quietly.

From somewhere deep inside, she was gaining strength. "Of course I do," she replied adamantly. "Our marriage is nothing more than a business arrangement, or have you forgotten that? In six months, I shall leave and we will probably never see each other again. That's the way we both want it, isn't it? Now, it would be silly for us to run the risk of any complications."

His face became cynical, and an eyebrow shot up.

"Complications?" he sneered.

By now the tears had stopped, and Raven was amazed at how well she felt. That pride and stubbornness her father and Flora had always tried to quell had taken over. "Yes," she said nonchalantly. "Like children, for instance. What would we do if I became with child? Would we wait until the poor little thing was born and then split it down the middle?"

She observed a flash of anger in his eyes before he got up and walked over to the window. He lit a cheroot and stood staring out at the moors beyond the estate.

He's angry, thought Raven, because his little plan of enjoying the pleasures of wife and mistress at the same time have been dashed. Well, good! It's time he learned that not every woman was at his beck and call. Let him know what it's like to want and not be able to have.

Unfortunately, she suffered a little of that herself as she stared at his back.

Christopher never wore a jacket or cravat when at home. He apparently preferred the comfort and freedom of the loose-fitting shirts that were left open at the neck and with the sleeves rolled up just below the elbow. Today was no different. He had braced himself with a hand on the wall, and Raven's eyes drifted across the firm shoulder and arm muscles underneath the tautly stretched shirt. In spite of herself, she recalled the feel of those muscles as she had explored his bare torso the day before.

At last he spoke and jarred Raven out of her shameless musings. "I see you've thought this out very thoroughly, and you're quite right." He turned and looked at her. "Just tell me one thing. What were all the tears for?"

She shrugged. "It's nothing, really. I suppose it's just some sort of delayed reaction. After all, a lot has happened to me lately. My father died, I've been forced into an arranged marriage, I've been shot at, I've gotten lost in a wilderness and caught in a storm. I guess I just don't feel very much in control of things."

He threw the cheroot out the window. "You, Miss Elliott, are either very naive or very shrewd. In any case, you're quite mistaken. It seems you're very much in control." He walked out of the room without saying another word.

It was late afternoon before she saw him again. Raven had taken refuge in the library and had begun reading Miss Austen's book when he found her.

"Do you mind if I disturb you for a moment?" he asked, closing the door behind him.

Raven was curled up in an oversized chair by the window. "No, I suppose not," she replied stiffly. "Please come in."

Christopher walked over, confiscated the

book and checked the title. "Ahhh, I see you've discovered the talents of Miss Austen."

Raven couldn't bring herself to look at him but concentrated her gaze on the book in his hand. "Yes," she replied gravely. "She's very good, and I'm afraid her talent is habit forming."

He laid the book down. "Do you suppose you could suffer the withdrawals from Miss Austen long enough to take a walk with me? There's something I wish to discuss with you."

A mixture of pain and pleasure assailed Raven. Just the nearness of him sent her emotions out of control. It was too soon. The misery of wanting him and knowing she was not wanted in return was still too fresh, the wound too deep. "Could we talk another time?" she asked. "I'm sorry, but I don't feel like a walk just now."

He held out his hand to her. "I'm afraid I must insist, Raven. This is a necessity."

She took his hand, and they walked in silence until they reached the rose garden. She sat on a bench as he settled against the arched arbor over it.

He lit the now familiar cheroot and took a long draw on it. "I asked you out here because I needed to speak with you in private, and I didn't want to run the risk of being overheard. You know, with the walls having ears and all."

Raven closed her eyes in pain. "Yes," she whispered, "I know only too well."

He frowned. "What? I'm sorry, I didn't hear you."

"Oh, nothing. Please go on."

He picked a rose off the arbor and twirled it around in his fingers. "My father just informed me of something that I thought you had better be warned about."

"Warned about?"

"Well, maybe that's too strong a word. Maybe I should have said, prepared for. It's about a summer ball some close neighbors of ours give every year. It's the Carltons. Perhaps you've heard us speak of them?"

Oh, she remembered the name, all right. He'd escorted someone named Serena Faraday to a dinner party they were having the night she arrived. How long ago that seemed now. Then she was all fire and fury. And now? "Yes, I know the name," she mumbled.

"Well, this year it's scheduled for Friday, and of course we are invited."

There was a moment of silence, and Raven noticed he seemed uncomfortable.

"Was that what you wanted to warn me about, or is there something else?"

He handed her the rose. "No, there is something else."

"Well, what is it?"

He pulled away from the arbor and began pacing back and forth in front of her. "I guess I'm trying to find out how you feel about things, Raven. Between yesterday and the scene in your room this morning, well, I just need to know where we stand."

Raven began to feel defensive. "What does

that have to do with the Carltons' ball?"

He ran his fingers through his hair irritably. "Because, the Carltons have decided to hold the ball in our honor to announce our engagement."

"Well, that's very nice of them, but I still don't understand. Just what are you trying to say to me?"

He stopped pacing and snatched another rose, this time from a bush near the path. "The fact of the matter is that I'm a little unsure now whether or not you are willing to continue on with our little charade. If you aren't, then I need to know now, because I don't want to cause any embarrassment to the Carltons or my father."

"I see," she murmured.

He walked over and sat down beside her. "Look, Raven, I know this whole business is distasteful to you and we've gotten off to a bad start. If apologizing to you for yesterday will help, then I'll do so, although I think you should know I wouldn't mean it. I can't help being a man, Raven, and you're the kind of woman a man could drown in. Lord, I nearly died yesterday from wanting you, and you didn't help matters by responding the way you did."

Her cheeks burned with the memory of his desperate hunger for her and hers for him.

"I'm sorry," he sighed wearily. "I didn't mean to embarrass you. I'm just trying to explain what happened yesterday and find out if it has made a difference in our arrangement. I hope not."

Now was her chance to save herself. She opened her mouth, but the words wouldn't come. Why was it so hard to speak? Why couldn't she say what she desperately needed to say? Her mind kept shouting the right words to her, but her heart wouldn't let her say them. Somehow the very thought of being free of him brought a pain much worse than anything she could foresee in the future.

Surprisingly, when she responded, her voice was strong and noncommittal. "Don't worry," she replied with as much dignity as she could summon. "I intend to uphold my end of our bargain. And you don't have to apologize. Yesterday is gone and forgotten. It will never happen again."

After Christopher left her, there was a gnawing certainty within her that her last statement to him was glaringly inaccurate. She would never last the six months without becoming his wife physically. In frustration, she started toward the open moors, feeling those silken threads of destiny pulling her ever closer to destruction.

It was no longer a matter of if it would happen, but rather when it would happen. And what would the results be? Oh, she knew intellectually that Christopher's desire was only physical. Men were like that. They could make passionate love to a woman and not even know her name or care, but when a woman made love her heart and soul were involved. What would happen to her at the end of six months when it was over? Would she be able to walk away and still remain whole? She didn't think so. The price of her inheritance had suddenly become ruinous.

She was late getting back home. The sun, in its last stages of flight across the sky, now sat on the low horizon. She hurried across the lawn and cut through the rose garden. If she went up the backstairs, as she often did, she could save precious minutes and have the extra time she needed to change before dinner.

She rounded the corner at the back of the house, intent on her destination, and ran headlong into a swarm of angry hornets. The suddenness of the encounter startled her, and she uttered a strangled cry before taking evasive action. The two steps back saved her life. A huge stone, the size of a valise, came crashing down on the path in front of her and shattered on impact.

Several minutes later, Christopher and the major found her sitting beside the rubble, covered in stone chips and frozen into immobility. She was helped inside and taken to the salon where she was given exorbitant amounts of brandy until she was quite light-headed.

"But this is awful," blustered the major. "I mean, how could such a thing happen?" He roamed about the room, arms waving wildly. "That stone mason told me only last month that nothing needed immediate attention. He said there were several loose stones, but nothing that would constitute a threat. He said they were still quite stable. I tell you, I just don't know how this could have happened."

Christopher sat beside Raven on the sofa, forcing a third glass of brandy to her lips. He suddenly withdrew the goblet and set it down. "I don't know either, but I'm going to find out."

Before he could move, Joe Flannery, one of the handymen, appeared at the door looking pale and frightened. He held a metal rod in his hand.

"Ahhh, Joe, come in," the major said. "Well, what did you find, and what's that you have there?"

Joe shuffled into the room looking as if he would rather be anywhere else but there. "Well, sir, I don't rightly know what to say."

"Well, say something, man," Christopher ordered. "What did you find up there? Is the place falling down around our ears?"

"Oh, no sir," Joe stammered. "There ain't nothin' wrong with the stones."

Christopher glared at him. "Well, of course there is. One just fell off the roof and nearly killed Miss Elliott."

Joe swallowed hard, took a deep breath and plunged on. "Well, sir, the truth o' the matter is, it didn't fall off by itself. Someone kinda 'elped it along a bit."

"What?"

"That's the truth o' it, sir. Someone took this 'ere pole an' pried the mortar loose from around the stone and then tipped it over the edge."

Christopher's eyes narrowed. "What are you saying, Mr. Flannery? How do you know that?"

"Cause it's all still there, sir. There's a pile of mortar where they dug it out and this 'ere pole was layin' there beside it. Also, there's marks on the under stone that were made when they heaved it over."

Christopher got up, walked over to him and took the metal bar from his grip. "What is this?"

"It's used to prop the door open. On the roof, sir. Sometimes the door sticks if it slams shut. It's always up there, sir. It's supposed ta be."

Christopher turned to his father. "Will you stay with Raven till I get back? I want to go and have a look myself. And don't say anything about this to anyone until I've had a chance to see what happened."

He was gone for some time. When at last he did return, everyone had gathered for dinner. Flora sat on the sofa beside Raven. Julia and Camilla were at the piano playing nonsense, and the major had stationed himself at the fireplace.

Christopher walked into the room, tugging on his jacket. He exchanged a knowing glance with his father. "Sorry to be late," he said pleasantly. "Well, since everyone is here, we'd better go in to dinner."

It was as if nothing at all had happened.

Chapter 9

The next morning Raven went looking for Christopher. He had not been at breakfast, and she suspected he was avoiding her. For some unknown reason, he seemed reluctant to share the findings of his investigation on the roof, and she wanted to know why. When at last she found him in the study, she was furious.

He sat behind a messy desk, his feet propped up on the corner of it, with a pile of papers in his lap. He had a pencil gripped between his teeth and was frowning as he studied some figures scribbled on a piece of paper.

She slammed the door behind her. "Christopher," she muttered irritably, "just what is going on?"

He looked up and took the pencil out of his mouth. "What do you mean? Is something wrong?"

Raven marched over to the desk and shook a fist at him. "You know perfectly well something is wrong. Someone tried to kill me yesterday, and you sit there worrying about some silly numbers on a piece of paper. Why are you being so mysterious? What did you find out?"

He threw the papers in his lap on the desk and stood up. "Those silly numbers pay the bills around here, my dear, and nobody tried to kill you yesterday."

She stood there gaping at him as if he had turned green.

"Don't look so astonished. Surely you didn't believe all that rot Joe was telling us yesterday, did you?"

"Of course I did," she said, "and I still do."

He walked around the desk and took her by the shoulders. "Raven, be sensible. Now who on earth would want to kill you and why?"

She had had enough. She jerked away from him. "Will you stop treating me like some empty-headed schoolgirl? I'm not simple-minded. Someone tried to kill me yesterday, and it wasn't the first time."

Christopher's jaw locked, and he grabbed her arm. "Come here," he hissed between his teeth, and he dragged her out the study doors, across the terrace and down the steps.

"Let go of me," she ordered, trying to break his grasp. "Christopher, where are you taking me? I said, let go."

He didn't stop until they were in the garden.

"Now," he said, whirling her around, "what makes you think someone is trying to kill you?"

"What's the matter?" she spat hatefully. "Am I getting too close to the mark? Am I about to discover the truth?"

"What truth? Raven, what are you babbling about?"

She sighed wearily. "Oh, Christopher, I don't know what sort of game you people are playing here, but I'm not willing to die because of it. If you would just be honest with me, then maybe something could be worked out to prevent my life from being threatened any further."

"I don't know what you're talking about, Raven," he replied coldly, "but you've got to stop this. I know you're unhappy about our arrangement, but you're letting your unhappiness get the better of you. You're beginning to imagine things, things that aren't true."

"Oh, stop it," she stormed. "I've nearly been killed, Christopher. Twice! Please stop treating me as if I'm some hopeless lunatic." She stopped and took a breath, giving herself time to calm down. "Please just tell me the truth."

"What truth?" he asked angrily.

"The truth about you and Camilla, for one thing," she shouted back.

Christopher's jaw set, and his eyes issued a warning. "What about Camilla and me?"

She looked at him with a bravery she didn't feel. "I know you are in love with Camilla and she is in love with you and the two of you are having an affair. Why you are choosing to keep it a secret, I can't imagine, but I think the time has come for you to be open about it. Once your father realizes the way you feel toward one another, then you and Camilla can be married, I can leave and everything will be back to normal."

He had been holding her by the shoulders, but now he released her. He savagely stuffed his hands into his pockets and began to pace up and down the path. "I'm not in love with Camilla," he denied, indignantly, "and I'm not having an affair with her." He stopped then and turned to face her. "Where on earth did you get such an idea anyway? Has someone been spreading nasty little innuendoes in your direction perhaps? Because, if they have . . ."

Raven wanted to cry. He wasn't going to tell her. She knew she should confront him with what she had seen and heard in the library two nights before, but she couldn't. She didn't want to force him into a confession; she wanted him to admit it openly and freely. She desperately wanted him to prove himself to be the decent and honorable man she judged him to be, but apparently he wasn't going to give her that consolation.

"No one has to make suggestions to me before I notice the obvious. It's plain to see that my appearance on the scene has created unwelcome problems within the family. Even you, yourself, admitted I was an inconvenient complication."

The dark brown eyes searched her face. "If you will recall," he murmured seductively, "I also said it was a complication I was quite willing to take on."

Her heart jerked. Why couldn't she steel herself to hate him? "Yes," she answered shakily, "but is Camilla as willing?"

"Camilla has nothing to do with it."

Lies! The spell was broken, and she tore her eyes away from his hypnotic gaze. "It's no use, Christopher. This whole ludicrous scheme was impossible from the beginning, and we should have realized it would never work. I think it's best if I just leave before anything else happens to me."

"I don't love Camilla, Raven, and I'm not having an affair with her. I know you have not had an easy time of it since you arrived, what with these silly accidents and all, but you've let your imagination completely run away with you."

"Do you call being shot at and having a stone heaved over on you imagination? Don't you understand?" she shouted. "Someone is trying to kill me!"

All the anger seemed to drain out of him, and he sighed wearily. "Raven, please," he muttered, "just leave it alone. Please!"

"I can't, Christopher," she replied softly. "Things have gone too far. When I came here, I thought I'd only be here a few days, just long enough to untangle my inheritance and then leave. But it didn't work out that way. Somehow

I've become a pawn in some dangerous game you people are playing, and now my life is in danger."

Christopher scrutinized her for a moment before reaching for her hand. "Let's get away from here for awhile. I need some fresh air, and so do you. Let's go for a ride."

All the way to the stable she kept reminding him that she didn't know how to ride, but he insisted there was a horse in residence even an infant could master.

At the stable, she was put on a sleepy little gray mare named Prissy, and Christopher took a beautiful bay named Polly. Mr. Bridges was asked to inform the house that they would be gone for the day. Then Christopher pointed them toward Dunsford.

They ambled along for some time without speaking, and Raven knew Christopher was brooding. She glanced over at him several times and noticed he was always looking straight ahead but wasn't seeing anything. He just rode along in deep concentration, staring at nothing. She thought he was in some far off place, when he broke their uncomfortable silence abruptly.

"Raven, how much do you think you know?"

The question, issued as a challenge, rattled her. "I think something is very wrong at Heathglade. I've felt it from the beginning. There are too many secrets. Everything seems false as if all of you are waiting for something to happen."

"And what do you think we are waiting for?"

She shook her head. "I don't know, but it has something to do with Camilla. She seems to have some sinister power over all of you, and no one seems to care or be able to do anything about it. That's why I've decided to leave. I couldn't live under those conditions."

Christopher stopped unexpectedly and slid out of the saddle. He helped her down, and they walked over to the side of the road where he deposited her on the top of a rail fence. He stood in front of her and gripped the top rail on either side of her.

"I don't want you to leave, Raven. I think you know that. I don't know what's happened between us, but something has made you suddenly withdraw from me. The other day during the storm, you felt something for me—I know you did—but now everything has changed and you want to run away. Why?"

Raven shook her head, but he raised a hand to stop her. "Deny it all you please, Raven, but remember, I was there. I know. You wanted me as much as I wanted you, and the hardest thing I've ever done was not make love to you right then and there. I should have. Believe me, if I had, you would be clamoring for our marriage right now instead of making excuses to run away from it."

Raven sat there, her face burning with shame. "What happened between us was a mistake," she mumbled.

"Oh no," he said, "the mistake was me not ensuring the necessity of our marriage."

"And what of Camilla?" Raven asked stubbornly.

Christopher glared at her. "There you go again," he muttered. "For God's sake, woman, will you never listen and comprehend what I'm saying? Camilla has nothing to do with us."

"She does," Raven screeched. "You just won't admit it because you're in love with her. Christopher, open your eyes and see what she is doing. Camilla is in complete control of everything and everyone at Heathglade—you, your father, Julia, Aunt Jessica and, yes, even me. That's what I mean when I say that something is terribly wrong and that I have to leave."

Christopher took a deep breath before sighing heavily. He picked up her hands and kissed them. "Very well," he uttered wearily, "I suppose I might as well admit it. There is something wrong at Heathglade, very wrong, but Raven, I can't discuss it with you. I won't. That's where your trust comes in. I need you to stay, Raven. I need you to be patient and trust me until I can get this mess cleared up."

She looked at him. The deep brown eyes sparkled in the reflected sunlight, but his expression was serious and troubled.

Should she trust him? Could she? After all, her very life would depend on that trust. Her head told her no. Everything he had said or done from the very beginning had been a lie, especially where Camilla was concerned, and yet she wanted desperately to believe in him.

"You're asking a great deal of me, Christopher," she replied quietly.

He slipped his arms around her waist and kissed her softly on the neck. "Yes, I suppose I am," he whispered.

"Don't, Christopher, please. If you want me to stay, then I will. But that doesn't alter the fact that I know about you and Camilla."

He pulled away from her. "You haven't been listening to a word I've said, have you?" he replied in helpless frustration. "Now, for the last time, I am not in love with Camilla, and I am not having an affair with her. I happen to be in love with you, you silly little twit. If you would only pay attention, you would see that."

She watched the sunlight, filtering through the trees, dance across his dark head. She shook her head sadly. "No, Christopher. What I see is you and your father using me as a cat's paw in some sort of ghoulish game. That's why I was brought here, isn't it?"

When Christopher blanched, she knew she had, quite by accident, hit upon the truth.

He went to stand beside her, resting his forearms on the fence, and began to examine the meadow behind them. He looked suddenly tired. "Very well, Raven," he sighed. "Yes, I suppose it was that way in the beginning."

"Damn you," she muttered and jumped off the fence, but he caught her arm before she could take a step.

"You haven't let me finish," he growled. "In

the beginning, yes. As soon as you arrived and I
learned about you, I saw you as a way of
reaching a goal that's very important to me.
Instantly I recognized you as a perfect weapon.
You see, things weren't going well and I was
running out of time, but then, out of nowhere,
you walked into our lives. It was as if fate had
suddenly stepped in and sent me the aid I
needed, just when I thought all was lost. But that
was then. Now it's not that simple."

Fate! He used the word fate! The word reverberated in her brain and stirred a memory. She
remembered back to what seemed a lifetime
ago when she also felt the gentle intrusion of
fate into her life. At the time she thought it the
result of feminine whimsy. Even the major's
suggestion that she was destined to save his son
went misinterpreted as fanciful melodrama.
How wrong she had been, how utterly wrong.
She had never had a choice. None of them had a
choice—not Christopher, not the major, not
Camilla. They were all as hopelessly caught up
in the silken threads of destiny as she. She also
recalled the feeling of everyone acting out characters in a play, and now she understood why. It
was true, except they didn't know it. They were
like puppets, each one performing a prescribed
role that would eventually conclude in a predes-
tined ending. How simple, and yet how hopeless.

She sighed in resignation. "Oh, but it is," she
whispered weakly. "Nothing has changed, has
it? I'm still here. I'm still that perfect weapon in

your hideous little war of wits, aren't I? And not even the threat of me possibly losing my life is going to change that, is it?"

"One thing has changed greatly, Raven. I've fallen in love with you. That changes everything. But I can't stop now. I'm too close. It's a matter of honor, you see, family honor."

As the memory of him holding and kissing Camilla flashed through her mind, Raven stiffened. Love and honor! How flippantly he used those words—and how disreputably!

She pulled out of his grasp. "It seems, sir, that you fall in love all too easily and all too often."

"And just what is that supposed to mean?" he challenged.

This couldn't go on. She hated deception wherever she found it, and she especially abhorred being a party to it. At some point, one of them had to force the truth out in the open. It was the only way all of them were going to get through this muddle. Still, she had to give him one more opportunity to exercise some of that honor he claimed to espouse.

"You know, Christopher," she began, toying with the leaves at her feet, "I've been very patient. I've given you every opportunity to be honest and forthright with me. But no, you will lie and deceive to the bitter end, won't you?"

Christopher threw his hands up in frustration. "For God's sake, woman, will you stop being so . . . so female and just tell me what you're trying to say? Now it sounds as if you're attacking my integrity. If that is the case, then please be specific. Don't make me have to decipher the rumblings in a feminine brain. It's too exhausting."

Both temper and eyes flashed. "You hypocrite!" she hissed. "You speak of honor but practice something quite different." She paused long enough for him to assimilate her meaning and then plunged on. "I know, Christopher. I witnessed that lovers' quarrel between you and Camilla the night you rescued me from the storm. The two of you were in the library, and I heard everything you both said. Now tell me again that you are not in love with her, how the two of you are not lovers and, let me see, oh yes, how you have no wish to marry her."

Christopher looked as if she had slapped him, and then his temper erupted. "And just where were you?" he demanded.

"In the wall passage."

He swore. "Eavesdropping again!"

"I was not," she shrieked defensively. "I was following Marigold. He . . . Oh, never mind."

He stepped in front of her and pinned her against the fence. "Raven, just how much did you see and hear?"

Her eyes glittered defiantly. "Enough to know that you and Camilla are in love and that the affection you showered on me was nothing more than a distasteful task you felt you had to perform in order to trick me into staying."

At first, Raven almost felt sorry for him. He had the look of a helpless fox about to be pounced upon by a pack of angry hounds. But only for a moment. Then he glared at her. It seemed the fox had some fight left. "So that's it!" he hissed between clenched teeth. "I've been going crazy trying to figure out what could have caused such an abrupt change in your attitude toward me. Now I understand. You saw Camilla and me in the library that night and you believed it." He began to laugh. "No wonder you treated me with such aversion the next morning." He took her in his arms and kissed her soundly. "Lord," he muttered against her lips, "what a relief. I thought you were serious about not wanting anything to do with me."

Raven tried to escape his grasp. "I do believe it, Christopher, and I am serious. Now please let go of me."

"But it's not true, Raven," he argued impatiently. "If you would just listen to me and try to understand. What you saw and heard is a lie. It's just a deception. It doesn't mean anything."

"A deception," Raven repeated with a sneer. "Just like our marriage. Just like our little scene in the storm. Just like my accidents." She placed her hands on his chest and tried to push him away. "I'm sorry, but there are just too many deceptions for my addled female brain to keep straight."

She slipped past him and went to mount Prissy, unaided. "It doesn't matter, in any case," she finished flippantly, "because I will be leaving in six months so whatever is between you and Camilla is your own affair." She broke into a convulsive giggle. "Excuse my poor choice of words, but somehow the pun just seems appropriate in this instance."

Christopher stood for a moment looking like a thundercloud about to burst, and then he grabbed Polly's reins and swung into the saddle. He said nothing more.

Surprisingly, the rest of the outing went very well. They continued on to Dunsford, ate a light meal at the inn and then strolled about the town, window-shopping. Christopher did his best to be accommodating, and Raven tried her best to forget, just for the day, that he was in love with Camilla.

They arrived back home in time for afternoon tea which was pleasant enough, at least in the beginning. The topic of conversation centered on the wedding and the upcoming ball at the Carltons. Since Raven had no wedding gown of her own, it was decided that she would wear Christopher's mother's gown. To Raven's amazement, no one, not even Julia, seemed to mind her doing so. If anything, everyone seemed to be going out of their way to be pleasant and accommodating, but that in itself was enough to make her uncomfortable.

Halfway through tea, they were involved in a discussion concerning the choice of flowers to be used in the family chapel, when Aunt Jessica belatedly joined them. Her appearance turned out to be the beginning of a disastrous finale to tea.

"Yes, well, roses are nice, of course, but I don't know if we should depend upon them,"

Camilla was saying. "This is the beginning of the stormy season, you know, and if we should have a heavy cloudburst, the roses could be spoiled."

The door burst open and Aunt Jessica bustled into the room with great excitement, her face and hands smeared with grime. "Oh, my dears," she announced breathlessly, "I've discovered the most delicious treasure and in such an unexpected place, too."

Christopher, standing at the window, turned and chuckled. "Aunt Jessica, you're a mess. What on earth have you been doing? It looks as if you've been grubbing around in a cemetery."

She ignored him. "I tell you it's marvelous. And Marigold, the smart fellow, found it."

"Found what?" Raven asked.

"My treasure, of course. Oh, I tell you that Marigold is a wise one. Just look at him."

Marigold was up on the corner table, sniffing wistfully at the decanters of liquor.

"The only thing that hairy tosspot is capable of finding is alcohol," Camilla jeered.

"That's not true," Aunt Jessica said. "He was down there looking for vermin."

Flora squirmed in her seat. "Down where? For heaven's sake, Jessica, tell us before we all die of curiosity."

"Down in the wine cellar. Did you know there is a hidden room down there? It's full of stuff, you know, old trunks and boxes of papers. And Roger," she turned to her brother, "there are even some of Michael's things in there. I know because I recognized them."

"Who's Michael?" Raven asked innocently.

"Michael was a young man employed here several years ago," the major replied. "He disappeared though, and it's a shame. He was a good worker."

"But what happened to him?"

The major shrugged. "I don't really know. I always thought he was happy here—at least he appeared to be—and then one morning he was gone. It was all very strange. He apparently left in the middle of the night and didn't even collect his wages."

Flora's nose twitched. "It was a woman, you mark my words. When a man jumps up and leaves good money behind, you can bet a woman has something to do with it."

Everyone chuckled, and Raven happened to glance at Camilla. She was sitting there, paler than usual, and looked frightened.

"You have no business prowling around down there," she hissed. "I mean, it's no place for a lady. It's dirty and unwholesome and you could get hurt."

Normally, Aunt Jessica withered under Camilla's commanding presence, but not this time. Raven watched as Aunt Jessica's eyes locked onto Camilla, her expression openly defiant. "I'll prowl any place in this house I choose to."

Camilla sprang from her chair. "This is ridiculous," she shouted. "Roger, are you going to allow her to root about in the bowels of this house as if she were some demented mole?"

"My dear Camilla," the major said, "I can't see any harm in Jessica exploring the premises, especially since it gives her pleasure. After all, it is her home every bit as much as it is ours. Let her enjoy herself."

"And I suppose you would allow her to run through the streets of Dunsford naked, if she enjoyed it." Camilla turned to Christopher for support. "Christopher, are you going to allow this kind of bohemian behavior?"

"I am not master in this house, Camilla," he replied stoically. "My father is. And if it's acceptable to him, then it most certainly is to me."

Camilla stared at him in shocked disbelief. She obviously expected Christopher to support her, but when he didn't, she simply had no choice but to accept the edict from her superiors. Suddenly she seemed to remember herself. She cleared her throat and pulled herself up. "Excuse me," she said calmly. "I must be tired. If you don't mind, I believe I'll go up and lie down for a while."

As Camilla left, Aunt Jessica cackled. "My, my, so many secrets. Now, let me see, how does it go? Oh yes, now I remember. 'Oh, what a tangled web we weave, when first we practice to deceive.'" She blushed prettily. "Sir Walter Scott, you know."

Julia had been unusually quiet during Camilla's outburst, but now she came alive. "I think you're all horrid," she cried, jumping up. "All Camilla was trying to do was make Aunt Jessica behave in a more refined manner. And you, Christopher, how could you be so hateful to her when you know you're in love with her?"

"Stop it, Julia," Christopher snarled. "One more word, just one more word and I'll give you a tanning you'll remember into your dotage."

"Ohhh," his sister shrieked and then ran, sobbing, from the room. "You'll be sorry, all of you. Just you wait."

The major dragged out an oversized handkerchief and wiped his forehead dramatically. "Mercy," he mumbled, "what do you suppose all that was about?"

Christopher, staring at the closed door Julia had just slammed, frowned. "I wonder . . ."

At two o'clock in the morning, Raven stepped on the catch and the wall panel in her room popped open. She had to see what was so important about that room in the cellar. Camilla's reaction to Aunt Jessica's discovery of the room appeared to be too vehement to be just an innocent objection. No, fear had spurred Camilla into that overzealous outburst, and Raven wanted to know what could instill such fear into someone as self-assured as Camilla.

She stepped inside and started down the passage. She didn't know for certain, but Raven was willing to bet the passage went all the way down to the cellar.

She wasn't mistaken. At the very end of the passage, a door waited to be opened. She triggered the latch and stepped out into the wine cellar.

The air, musty and heavy with the smell of stale liquor, assaulted Raven, and her stomach lurched slightly. She stood there for a moment, allowing her eyes to become acquainted with the dimness. Soon she could make out rows and rows of wine racks, some full, some almost empty, but all elaborately draped with a thick coating of cobwebs. They completely filled a cavernous room resembling one of the chambers in the infamous catacombs of Italy.

A muffled noise at the far end of the room startled Raven, and she jumped back in the shadows. She heard the thump again, this time accompanied by a flickering light bouncing off the walls. Raven quickly put out her own candle and crept closer to the sight and sound of someone in stealth.

The grate of rusty hinges reverberated through the cellar and then the light faded before a large shadow raked across Raven's body. A momentary silence prevailed, and then a female's voice groaned as if the owner was performing some weighty task. There were sounds of objects being moved about and then more groans. Raven crept even closer to the mysterious activity.

She was concentrating on the commotion in front of her when Raven heard the familiar click of the wall panel behind her. Someone else had arrived. She darted around the closest wine rack and huddled in the shadows.

A dark figure passed her.

"Find anything?"

Raven recognized Christopher's voice. She

heard a startled gasp, and then Camilla's voice, shrill and frightened, answered.

"Christopher! What . . . what are you doing here?"

"I might ask you the same question, being as how you thought it was so distasteful down here."

Camilla laughed nervously. "Yes, well, I . . . I suppose I was just curious. You know, I wanted to see what Jessica had thought was so interesting."

Christopher snickered. "At two o'clock in the morning? Come now, Camilla, aren't you carrying curiosity just a bit too far?" He walked into the room, and the voices faded into murmurs.

Raven huddled there for what seemed like hours, then light filled the room once more. They were coming out.

"But why can't I wait for you?" Camilla whined.

"Because I may be here awhile. I want to look through those boxes. There may be something important in them, especially in all those papers. And while I'm here, I might as well see what all we've got down here. Who knows? I may find some vintage bottles of wine that we know nothing about."

They passed Raven.

"But, darling," Camilla complained, "I want to stay. Maybe I could help. With the both of us searching—"

"Absolutely not! You're going straight up to bed. Now."

"But Christopher, I—"

"No buts, Camilla. It's unpleasant down here, and you might catch a cold. Now, do as I say . . . No, not that way. Use the stairs."

Raven heard them climb the cellar stairs, and then the door closed. She remained frozen. He was coming back.

The footsteps grew louder until they were directly in front of her. "All right, little rabbit, you can come out now."

Cold and frightened, she came out of the darkness. "How did you know I was here?"

Christopher laughed. "Because you stick out like a beacon in that white nightdress. Lord, even a blind man could have spotted you hopping about down here like a little white rabbit looking for its hole."

"Do you think Camilla saw me?"

His face turned grim in the candlelight. "No. I'm afraid she had other things on her mind besides looking for you."

Raven shivered. "Christopher, what was she doing down here?"

"I've no idea, but then I might ask you the same question. Just what are you doing down here skulking around in your nightdress?"

She shrugged. "The same thing you are. I wanted to know why Camilla got so upset when she discovered Aunt Jessica had been down here. Her reaction was so peculiar."

Christopher was pulling absently on his bottom lip, lost in concentration. "Yes, it was, wasn't it?"

"Well, let's go see," Raven suggested enthusiastically. She started around him.

"Ohhh no, little rabbit," he said, stopping her. "You're staying out of this. You're going right back to bed where you belong."

"But Christopher . . ."

"Why do women always argue with their biggers and betters?" he interrupted. "Now, come along. Besides, there is nothing to see. I know because I was in there, remember?"

He gently but firmly guided her back to the wall. "Well, something was in there," she argued. "What was it?"

He stopped at the wall and relit her candle. "There's nothing in there except a large trunk, several boxes, a bed and a table."

Raven searched his face in the candlelight, her eyes large with fear. "Christopher," she whispered, "I'm afraid. Something is very wrong about Michael's disappearance, isn't there?"

He leaned over and kissed her softly. "Go to bed, little rabbit. Whatever happened to Michael has nothing to do with you. Now go." He turned her around and gently pushed her through the opening.

Once inside, she turned and looked at him, her eyes still frightened. "Christopher? Michael's things. Were they there, too?"

In the candlelight she saw his jaw tighten. "Yes, little rabbit. Michael's things were there. All of them."

Chapter 10

The morning of the Carletons' ball arrived in magnificent splendor. By now, early September, everyone feared the weather would change for the worse and spoil the annual event marking the end of the summer season. They shouldn't have worried, for the day bloomed warm and sunny.

Raven woke to the usual sound of the quarreling sparrows beneath her window. She rolled over and smiled. Apparently even sparrows had problem marriages, she mused. She threw off the covers and began dressing for the day.

By the time she got downstairs, Christopher and the major were already at the table, discussing business over half-eaten plates of eggs, ham, steamed kidneys and scones.

"Yes, but if we cut our production," Christopher was saying, "how will we meet our orders to the Yanks?"

"Oh, bother the Yanks," blustered the major. "Let them grow their own sugar. They were cocky enough in Seventy-Six when they said they didn't need us any more. Well, let them do without us now."

Raven, at the sideboard dishing up her plate, heard Christopher chuckle. "You're skinning the wrong cat, sir. You know very well that the Yanks are the most lucrative market we have. If we lose their business, it'll hurt us more than it will them. Lord, they're too close to the market. They'll just buy from another independent supplier, and they'll still have their sugar, someone else will have the profit and we'll have our arrogance."

Raven quietly sat down at the table and listened intently.

"Yes, but blast it, Christopher, what you propose is utterly insane," the major said. "Why, it would be financially disastrous for us to suddenly have to pay wages to field workers. Not only would it eat up our profits, it would cut into our capital. We'd be ruined in a month."

"I disagree," Christopher argued. He turned to Raven. "I know. Let's put the proposition before an unbiased observer and see what she thinks."

Raven put her fork down. "Oh no," she said hastily. "Why I don't even know what you are talking about, and besides, I don't know anything about business."

"Quite right," blustered the major. "Anyway, you know very well that women have no sense when it comes to business. Commerce falls into a man's realm of expertise which is why men are in charge of such matters."

"Rubbish," Christopher countered. "You're just afraid of an honest and impartial opinion." He shoved his plate back and lit one of the slender cigars Raven now identified as being part of him. "Now, here is the dilemma, Miss Elliott. We have a major labor problem in Barbados. For years now, our slave laborers have been unhappy with their lot in life. To prove it, they have revolted, sabotaged things and in general created a lot of fuss and feathers over the status quo. Lately it has gotten to the point where it has interfered with our production demands. Do you follow me so far?"

She blinked at him innocently. "If you mean the slaves you use to work your sugar cane fields are revolting, then yes, I understand that."

"Excellent. Now, Miss Elliott, I have never liked slavery. I believe, and I am sure you will agree with me, that it is a degrading practice. It crushes the human soul and is against every rule of civilized behavior, both ethically and morally. Therefore I think we should liberate our fellow human beings and offer them wages in return for their labor. Now, my father believes that such a folly would bring financial disaster to the Mallory holdings. What is your opinion?"

Raven sat for a moment in silence. Christopher was right, of course. Slavery was wrong.

But should she voice her views? The major had just expressed a well-known fallacy still flourishing within the male ranks. However intelligent, a woman's opinion on any subject still carried very little weight in a world run by men.

"Well?" Christopher asked, breaking into her thoughts. "What is your feeling on the subject? Surely you have a viewpoint."

She shoved her plate back and rested her arms on the table. "I believe it is wrong for any one human being to force another into doing their bidding simply because they have the power to do so. Unless a person is allowed to perform a deed out of his own free will or desire, it will be shoddy and far less rewarding to both the giver and the receiver."

"Well said," Christopher exclaimed. "That is exactly my point. If we give them their freedom, the will to choose for themselves, and offer them a legitimate wage, we will have happier workers who will take pride in their work and therefore increase their production volume which in turn will increase our profits."

"Nonsense," the major snorted. "Sounds like bloody anarchy to me."

"Don't you believe it," Christopher said. "Our government is heading in that direction and has been for some time now. You just wait. Before long slavery will be outlawed. It's just a matter of time."

"Bah," the major said. "I thought you were a smart man until now. Oh, I'm not saying slavery will never end, but we'll never see it in our time.

Why, the world's economy couldn't withstand such an outlandish system."

After that, both men seemed to forget her and argued back and forth for a while until Christopher finally put an end to the debate by standing up.

"Well, sir, I wish you would think about it. Times are changing, and we must change with it. If we don't, we will be left behind smothering in the dust of progress." He walked over to Raven, took the teacup out of her hand and pulled her to her feet.

"Where are we going?" she asked.

He smiled. "Riding. You and Prissy still haven't mastered the talent of teamwork, but with a little practice I see a potential for success." He winked at her. "That is if Prissy's back and your . . . er . . . stamina hold out."

As they reached the door, Camilla appeared, looking lovely in a lavender dress. Just once, Raven muttered to herself, I'd like to see her in one of Aunt Jessica's throwaways.

Christopher, however, didn't seem to notice the stunning appearance of his sister-in-law as they skirted past her. "Morning, Camilla," he uttered absently. "The scones are delicious this morning." Then they were out the door and into the hall.

Prissy was not at all excited about this sudden interest in riding. She eyed Raven mournfully as Mr. Bridges saddled her and even tried to balk when Christopher, pulling her patiently but persistently, dragged her into the morning light.

"Lord," Christopher muttered, taking Polly's reins from Mr. Bridges, "I can't imagine why my father still keeps that indolent nag installed here."

"Shame on you," Raven scolded. She walked over to Prissy and nuzzled her nose. "I like her," she murmured.

"You would," Christopher chuckled as he swung up onto Polly's back.

Mr. Bridges helped Raven mount the lethargic little mare, and soon they were riding out of the yard at a snail's pace with Christopher trying to control Polly's enthusiastic energy to match Prissy's sleepy gait.

Raven liked Prissy's docile temperament because it suited her own riding skills; Christopher was another matter. Why he had chosen her to accompany him on his morning ride was a mystery to Raven. He was used to a much more spirited ride than she could accommodate. Camilla, on the other hand, was an expert horsewoman. She could ride like the wind, and Raven had often watched with a certain begrudging admiration as they flew over the countryside. But this morning Christopher had deliberately rejected Camilla, and Raven wondered why.

As they rode out of the yard, she decided to find out. "Christopher, why did you intentionally shun Camilla this morning?"

He glanced at her, surprised. "I have no idea what you're talking about."

"Oh, yes you do. You know perfectly well that Camilla expects to ride with you every morning. She looks forward to it. Yet you brazenly walked out with me and left her standing there. Why?"

"I didn't want to ride with Camilla this morning. Besides, I thought perhaps you might enjoy an outing. Was I wrong?"

"No, you weren't wrong," Raven replied truthfully. "It's just that I think what you did to Camilla was demoralizing and, what's worse, you knew you were doing it."

He frowned. "She'll recover."

A flood of anger washed over Raven. He really was an insufferable man! Why was he deliberately causing Camilla misery? Surely he must know this subtle snub would only inflame her already jealous nature. In spite of her dislike for Camilla, Raven felt sorry for her. It must be terrible for her to stand by and watch the man she loves court and marry another woman. Christopher knew that, and yet he had intentionally fanned her insecurity just now. Why? "I should think you would be a little concerned about Camilla's feelings, that's all," Raven replied with a disapproving note in her voice. "I know I am."

Christopher snickered. "You don't have to worry about Camilla's feelings. She manages quite well."

Raven's ire began to bubble up. "You're using me to hurt Camilla, aren't you? That's why I'm here, isn't it?"

"No, Raven, that's not why you're here."

"She's in love with you, Christopher. Why are you deliberately causing her misery?"

He reached out, grabbed her reins and stopped both horses. "There are no hidden motives in my actions, Raven," he replied roughly. "I chose to go riding with you this morning because I want to be with you, not Camilla. I am not in love with Camilla and haven't been for some time. If she is in love with me, then that is her misfortune. As far as I'm concerned, it came several years too late." He eased back into the saddle. "Now, let's forget Camilla and see if we can manage to persuade Prissy to stretch her legs a bit." He nudged Polly in the flanks, and she moved forward at a gentle trot, forcing Prissy to follow suit, however reluctantly.

Actually, Prissy did quite well. She managed something between a brisk trot and a slow gallop for several minutes before they were forced to slow down because of a hedgerow. Christopher gave Prissy's reins back to Raven and led the way into the brushy barrier.

Raven, still thinking about Camilla, suddenly remembered their expedition the night before. "Christopher, about last night, did you find anything?"

He was in front of her and pulled a low branch aside for her to pass. "No. There was nothing to find."

"But there had to be," she insisted. "Did you look carefully?"

"Of course I did. Lord, I didn't get to bed till almost four this morning. I spent the whole time digging through that moldy old trunk, and there simply wasn't anything worth finding."

Prissy was dragging her feet, and Raven nudged her impatiently until they were alongside Christopher. "Then what was Aunt Jessica so excited about? I mean, she was in a fever over her discoveries."

Christopher laughed. "Yes, well, Aunt Jessica has a rather odd view of what's valuable and what's not. You know an object's value is very subjective and depends entirely upon the person assessing its worth. I suppose, for her, it was a windfall."

"What was?" Raven demanded. "For heaven's sake, are you going to tell me or not?"

He chuckled pleasantly. "My, my, such flagrant inquisitiveness is not becoming in young ladies. Oh, all right. For your information, I spent the better part of an hour digging through mounds of old dresses and knickknacks that I swear must have dated back to the Renaissance. Knowing Aunt Jessica, she took one look at them and reckoned she had access to an unlimited new wardrobe. I swear, I can't imagine why families keep all that old junk lying around."

"Well, how about papers? Were there any papers in the trunks?"

"Sure. Tons of them, mostly in the boxes, though. But they weren't anything important. Just junk, you know—diaries, records of births, receipts for purchases—that sort of thing."

Raven couldn't contain her curiosity a minute longer. "Christopher, Michael's things. Last night you said they were there. All of them. What did you mean?"

They had cleared the hedgerow and were now in a meadow with a small brook cutting its way through the middle of it. Christopher dropped Polly's reins and slid out of the saddle. "Let's sit here a minute. Polly and Prissy could stand a break from this tedious business, and so could we."

He helped Raven alight, and they sat down beside the brook and allowed the horses to drink.

When they had settled comfortably, Raven prodded him. "Well? What did you mean?"

Christopher was stretched out and propped up on one elbow, plucking blades of grass absently. "Just what I said. Everything was there."

The implication caused Raven's eyes to widen. "Everything?"

"Everything. All his clothes, at least I assume they were his. I mean, I don't know how much he had, but it couldn't have been much. There were two pairs of pants and two shirts, a jacket, some personal linen and, oh yes, a Bible. It was given to him by his mother. There was an inscription inside, so I know it was his."

Raven swallowed even though her mouth was dry. "Christopher," she said shakily, "that means he never left."

He sat up. "Not necessarily. I know he was planning to leave."

"How do you know that?"

"Because everything was neatly rolled up in a knapsack and shoved under the bed. No, he definitely was leaving, but why he didn't take his belongings, I don't know. Maybe he just decided they weren't worth taking."

Raven didn't believe that for a moment. She knew Christopher was deliberately trying to minimize what was fast becoming a deep mystery with malevolent undertones. "What I want to know," she asked eagerly, "is what were his things doing in that room? Surely he didn't live down there, did he?"

"Lord, I wouldn't think so. It's just a storage room, you know. There are no windows since it's below ground, and it's dark and musty. No, I can't imagine anyone living down there. Not by choice, anyway."

Raven frowned. "Christopher, what was he like? Was he young or old?"

He threw a handful of grass up in the air in frustration. "How should I know? I never met the man. He was gone before I got here. Anyway, what difference would that make?"

"I'm not sure," she mumbled.

"Oh, look," he said irritably, "we could speculate about this for a hundred years. The man is gone, and that is that." He rose and held out his hand to her. "Come along. I'm exhausted. I'm planning on going home and resting for the remainder of the day. Tonight is that wretched ball, remember, and we have to be at our best."

He helped her to her feet, but she was still frowning. It was the Bible. No one would go off and leave something so personal as a Bible, especially one given to them by their mother. It would be an unnatural thing to do. And why were his clothes found in a dark and dingy storage room that no one would visit with any regularity?

"Hey," Christopher called, interrupting her thoughts. "If you don't stop frowning like that, by tonight you'll look like my grandmother, and then what will people say? Now, wipe the gloom off that pretty face or you'll get wrinkles."

Wrinkles. The man was obsessed with wrinkles! First Camilla and now her. Apparently he didn't like for any of his women to be facially marred. Raven reached up and instinctively touched her damaged cheek. If wrinkles on a woman's face were unappealing to him, she could well imagine how he felt about bullet wounds.

As if reading her thoughts and wishing to prove her wrong, Christopher seized her hand, pulled it from her cheek and kissed the angry scar softly. "Is it still painful?" he murmured.

His nearness sent her into a panic. "No, no," she stammered. "I don't know why I did that. Just habit, I suppose." She pulled her hand out of his and went to mount Prissy on her own.

Christopher walked over to her. "Do I notice a sudden frost in the air?"

"Certainly not," she replied haughtily.

"Well, tell me, will this fictional coolness thaw out by tonight, do you suppose?"

Raven looked down at him intently. "This little charade is very important to you, isn't it?"

"Is that what you still believe it is, Raven? Just a charade?"

Her cheeks reddened and she looked away. "Don't worry, Christopher. Tonight I shall play my part admirably, whatever I believe. I shall be your adoring and affectionate bride-to-be, as planned."

As soon as the words were spoken, she nudged Prissy into her second slow gallop of the day.

Late that afternoon, Raven sat at her dressing table applying a thin coat of rice powder to the ugly gash cutting its way across her cheek, at the same time trying to control an attack of nausea. The flutter in her stomach testified to her nervousness in handling Christopher's prospective show of affection toward her. She knew he would offer an amorous display since there would be an abundant audience expecting it, and that part of the ruse delighted her. The problem would be in her reaction. Whatever happened, she must never allow Christopher to discover her true feelings for him.

Satisfied with the application of powder, she put the puff down and turned to give her ball gown a close look.

Hanging on the wardrobe door, the beautiful ice-blue gown resembled a misty waterfall, with the frothy material, soft and filmy, floating about in the soft breeze coming in through the window. Tiny crystal beads of blue and white sparkled about the deep scooped neck, topping off the tight bodice. The skirt flared out in yards and yards of soft ruffles stacked in three tiers. The dress had been the last purchase she had made before her father's death, and she remembered feeling guilty about the extravagance at the time. Now she was glad she had been so reckless.

"If you don't stop daydreaming and get into your dress, you'll be left behind," Flora scolded, as she drained the bath. "You've been sitting there an age just staring into space. What's the matter with you? Are you not feeling well?"

Raven gave the soft swirls of a delicate and feminine hair style one last pat before she rose from the dressing table. "I'm fine, Flora. I guess I'm just a bit anxious about this evening. After all, Christopher and I will be expected to behave as if we are mad for each other, and that's going to be a little difficult with Camilla constantly in the background."

Flora chuckled and set down the pail of bathwater she had just retrieved from the tub. "Oh, I wouldn't worry too much about that paper doll if I were you. When Mr. Chris sees you in that dress, he won't know there's anyone else around."

Raven stepped into the first of her petticoats. "Flora, what difference is a dress going to make? He's in love with Camilla."

Helping Raven climb into the three remaining petticoats, Flora snorted. "Rubbish! Oh, I know you believe that nonsense. Ever since you witnessed that disgusting scene from the window, you've convinced yourself that he's completely dotty for her. Well, he's not. I've been keeping a close eye on him, and I'm telling you he's far more interested in you than he is in her."

Raven carefully removed her gown from its hanger and handed it to Flora. She had not told Flora of the scene in the library she had witnessed between Christopher and Camilla and had no intention of doing so. Her pride wouldn't allow it. That humiliation she meant to keep to herself. "You don't know what you're talking about, Flora," she muttered as she disappeared under the billowy folds of the skirt.

A few moments later, she stood before the mirror, giving herself a final critical inspection.

She began with her hair. The ever-present tendrils, spilling free of their confines, softened the attractive Grecian hair style Flora had painstakingly sculpted. Two combs, studded with blue and white crystal beads and trailing tiny blue ribbons strung with the same beads, gave a finishing touch to the work of art. Powder, rouge and lip paint were perfection. The dress, molded to her delicate figure, spilled gracefully down to tickle the blue satin slippers on her feet, encircling her in a soft blue haze. Try as she would, Raven could find nothing amiss in her appearance.

Flora stepped up behind her. "Oh, my dear," she whispered breathlessly, "you're a picture, for sure."

Raven felt like crying for she knew it didn't matter how lovely she looked. Christopher's heart belonged to Camilla. "Thank you, Flora," she replied sadly.

She collected her coordinated gloves, reticule and shawl, blew Flora a kiss and walked out of the room.

The sound of laughter from below drifted up into the upper hall as she started down the stairs, and then she heard a door open.

"Never mind, I'll go see what's keeping her." It was Christopher. He reached the stairs and put a foot on the bottom step before he looked up and saw her standing on the second floor landing.

Ironically, he was dressed in blue also, only a shade or two darker than her gown. His jacket and trousers, tailored to his frame with the precision of an artisan, merely emphasized his dark good looks as did the immaculate white silk cravat puffed slightly beneath his square chin.

As their eyes met, all thoughts of Camilla left Raven's mind. Standing at the foot of the staircase, the man she loved waited for her, and tonight was their night.

She refused to hurry. Christopher stood staring up at her as she slowly descended each step until she was level with him. She never said a word. She simply slipped her arms around his neck and kissed him softly but thoroughly. "Do you suppose," she whispered as she nibbled at his lips, "this is good enough to fool everyone, or should I try harder?"

"Oh, shut up," he growled and hungrily took her in his arms.

The sound of the major calling him broke Christopher's concentration long enough for her to speak. "I believe your father wants you," she sighed.

"Let him wait," Christopher replied hoarsely. "Let the whole bloody world wait."

She continued to tease and torment his lips with her own. "That isn't a very nice thing to do," she whispered.

He kissed her savagely. "Oh, Raven. Dear God," he moaned, "you'll pay for this."

The major's voice, this time louder, allowed her to slip out of his arms and dart into the salon.

"I'm sorry to be late," she said breathlessly. "I hope I haven't made us tardy."

The major, in pearl gray evening clothes, looked up from his pouring of another brandy. "My word," he uttered in genuine appreciation, "if you did it was worth the wait. My dear, you look ravishing. All of you ladies do."

Camilla and Julia sat on the sofa. Camilla did indeed look ravishing. She wore a deep rose taffeta gown that complimented her exquisite figure and blond complexion with maddening

219

results. Julia, as befitting her age and status in society, wore a traditional white muslin gown, but a small concession had been made in the form of yellow ribbons gracing the top of each shoulder and one large one cascading down the back of her dark auburn hair.

Christopher had come back into the room and was just recapturing the glass of brandy he had left on the mantle when his father proposed a toast.

"Christopher, my boy, I think we should drink a toast to the bouquet of lovely blossoms we are escorting tonight."

Christopher raised his glass. He managed to catch Raven's attention, and their eyes met and held. "By all means," he murmured.

The major, feeling extremely gay, issued an elaborate toast to the ladies.

After the toast had been saluted, Camilla decided to take the reins of conversation and shift it in a more feminine direction. "Your dress is quite lovely, Miss Elliott," she said politely. "Is it from London?"

Raven smiled. "Yes, it is, and thank you. I think it's lovely too, but I'm afraid it can't compare with yours. Why do I get the feeling that, if your gown could speak, it would do so with a decidedly French accent?"

This time Camilla smiled. "What a keen eye you have, Miss Elliott. Yes, it is from Paris. I'm afraid it was terribly extravagant of me, but I just couldn't resist it. There is a little shop in London that specializes in French designs. Perhaps you've heard of it? It's called La Parisienne Royale."

Raven knew the boutique, nestled among a group of outlandishly expensive stores on Bond Street. "Yes, I know of it, but I've never ventured inside."

Camilla's eyes glittered maliciously. "What a pity, Miss Elliott. You know, I believe a woman's appearance is an indication of her self-esteem, and she therefore should seize every opportunity to look her best."

"Oh, I agree," Julia gushed. "And your dress really is the loveliest thing I've ever seen." She turned to Raven. "It's just a shame you're in the same color as Christopher—and so pale, too."

Christopher frowned. "What's wrong with it? Actually, I think we're quite handsome together."

Julia smiled hatefully. "Well, yes, you both look very nice, but let's face it, Christopher, she will simply fade away next to you. I mean, who will notice her?"

Raven watched as Christopher's jaw hardened. "I will notice her, Julia."

Raven knew Julia was trying to spoil their evening by provoking Christopher into a bad mood, but she refused to allow that to happen.

"Well, I hope that is the case," she said hastily. "I'm afraid I'm a bit nervous about being the center of attention tonight, and I would just as soon be overlooked as much as possible."

"Well, you certainly won't be overlooked by me," the major exclaimed. "I intend to secure as many dances as I can manage, although I shall probably be standing in line most of the evening for the privilege."

"And what about me?" Christopher interjected. "Does the prospective groom not have any claims on the evening?"

Camilla smiled. "Not tonight, I'm afraid. But don't worry, you'll be kept quite busy this evening dancing with all the fair maidens whose hearts you are about to break."

"Oh Lord," he muttered.

"Don't worry," Camilla said, "I promise to rescue you from time to time."

Everyone laughed, but Raven didn't fail to notice the gleam in Camilla's eyes when she made her offer.

Chapter 11

Two carriages were necessary in order to comfortably transport the ladies with their billowing ball gowns to the festivities. Christopher and Raven occupied the first, while Julia, Camilla and the major followed in the second.

The September night was enchanting as they moved down the country lane bordered by large trees, their branches overlapping above them, forming a lacy arbor. Only the air, a bit cooler than the evenings before, subtly announced the change of season, but the moon, large and full, still hung in the cloudless night sky, bathing the landscape with a silver-blue luster, as if summer were just beginning.

Christopher sat across from Raven, and she watched the dappled shadows dance across his face as he studied her thoughtfully.

At last he spoke. "What will you do, Raven, when you leave?"

Up until now, both she and Christopher had carefully avoided any reference to their fraudulent commitment since their argument on the day they had spent in Dunsford. Why he chose to open the subject at this particular time, she couldn't fathom.

She frowned. "I don't really know. I suppose Flora and I will settle someplace where it's quiet and peaceful. Why?"

He shrugged. "I'm just curious, I suppose. I somehow assumed you had definite plans."

They rode on in silence for awhile before he spoke again. "You said someplace quiet and peaceful. I would expect a girl like you would prefer the lights and gaiety of city life."

Raven looked at him in amusement. "You mean because I was raised in London? Well, I probably would have if I had never come here, but now London, or any place like it, is the last place I would go back to."

"Does that mean, then, that you like it here? I mean, the country and the monotony of country life?"

"Oh, but it's not monotonous at all," she exclaimed. "It's lovely here, and there are plenty of things to do. Believe me, life in London can become quite tiresome. Oh yes, it's busy and hectic, but it's all so meaningless. I mean, you can become quite exhausted doing things that have no real value."

"Well, how about your friends? Won't you miss them?"

The smell of wild honeysuckle filled the carriage. "No," she stated with shocked awareness. "I only have one friend, true friend that is—Alicia, Alicia Morebridge—and she has been married for two years. They have a baby now, and she is so busy with her new life that we haven't been as close as we used to be. My other acquaintances are exactly that, just acquaintances."

"Then why leave?"

She felt her face flush. "I don't think it would be very wise of me to stay," she mumbled.

"Why? Think about it for a moment. Being married to me wouldn't be such a hardship, you know. You would have a nice home, all the frills and trifles you could ever want. Why, you could buy out that French shop Camilla was talking about if you chose to, although it would probably put a substantial dent in my wallet," he finished sourly. "And I promise not to beat you. Actually, I would probably spoil you rotten."

Her heart began to ache. "I've told you before that material things are not very important to me."

Christopher looked completely relaxed except for two things. He sat with an arm draped across the back of the seat, but when she looked closely, Raven noticed both his jaw and his fist were flexing in unison.

"Yes, so you did," he replied. "Very well, what would it take for you to stay?"

"Christopher, please," she sighed. "You have Camilla. Why on earth would you want me to stay? I'm sorry, but I just don't understand what you want from me."

He took out a cigar, lit it leisurely and took a lazy draw on it. Raven watched, spellbound, as the silver-blue haze drifted off into the night. "You know exactly why I want you to stay, and you know perfectly well what I want from you. Now, I can offer you a lot, and you would be safe and protected for the rest of your life."

"I know all of that," she replied miserably, "but that isn't enough. Don't you understand? What I want out of marriage, you could not give me, and I can't imagine a marriage without it."

He snickered. "Would that one ingredient you feel me incapable of giving you, by any chance, be fidelity?"

She didn't answer.

"So," he murmured, "we're back to that."

Again she didn't respond. Raven just sat there, busily playing with the fringe on her shawl.

Christopher took another long draw on the cheroot and flicked the ashes out onto the roadside. "Do you honestly believe I would marry you if I were in love with Camilla?" He chuckled hatefully. "Dear God, your opinion of me must border on the obscene if you believe I could marry one woman while I am in the midst of carrying on a torrid affair with another."

"Oh Christopher, please!" Raven sighed. "It happens all the time."

He swore. "It doesn't happen to me. Why

can't you just trust me and believe me when I say what you saw and heard isn't what you think it is?"

The fires of pride and temper were beginning to flare inside Raven. Did he really expect her to believe him after she had witnessed him with Camilla? After overhearing his pledge of love to her and watching the passionate kisses and embraces they shared? Not by half! She looked at him mutinously. "Then you tell me what it really is," she demanded.

He threw the cigar away. "I can't," he snapped. "You're just going to have to trust me."

"Why? Why should I? You've already admitted you're using me for some obscure purpose, and it has almost gotten me killed. And it still may. Yet you won't explain anything. You won't even tell me who or what I should be afraid of."

Suddenly, the carriage veered off the main road, and they slipped past an impressive stone entrance, its iron gates thrown open.

The turn into the Carlton estate put an abrupt end to their conversation and sent Raven into a fit of nervous primping. She fussed over her hair and dress, patting at them. "Christopher," she asked shakily, "do I look all right? I mean, am I presentable?"

His white teeth, nestled between the dark slashes of dimples, glistened in the moonlight. "If you looked any better, I'd have to take you home. As it is now, I'll have to fight off every man in the place."

She looked at him nervously. "Yes, well, next

to Camilla, I fade in comparison. I just don't want to embarrass you, that's all."

Christopher was watching her intently. "Believe me," he answered drily, "embarrassment is not the reaction you should be worrying about."

The Carltons turned out to be a very nice couple. They were both in their mid-forties and quite unassuming. Sybil Carlton was aging very gracefully. She had light brown hair, soft brown eyes and still maintained a very respectable figure. David Carlton was slightly overweight, of medium build and had laughing blue eyes. They greeted Raven with genuine pleasure, and presently Raven was quite relaxed, chatting comfortably with Sybil.

Before long, the guests started arriving, and the next hour or so was spent in the receiving line, being introduced to the neighborhood gentry and then mingling with her new acquaintances.

Dinner went well. Approximately 40 people were in attendance but everyone was seated comfortably, and the festive atmosphere was heightened by the gentle roar of numerous conversations going on at the same time.

At ten o'clock, the members of the orchestra took their places and the ball began.

Christopher was playing his part well. He never drifted more than a few feet away from her, his conduct toward her that of an ardent and attentive fiancé. When she wasn't holding onto his arm, his was either gently wrapped around her waist or casually draped about her shoulders. That was the case now as he leaned down to whisper in her ear, "Well, Miss Elliott, are you ready? This first dance is only for us. Now remember, smile and pretend that you are in love with me, if only for one night, and please be careful where you step. I don't wish to marry a girl who tramples upon my feet."

Before she could answer, he pulled her out on the floor as music flooded the room.

Halfway around the room, he smiled down at her. "Well, Miss Elliott, I'm impressed. You dance very well."

"Thank you," she replied nervously. "So do you."

As Christopher guided her about the floor, she tried to glimpse the expressions of their attentive audience, but they were only a blur as he whirled her round and round.

"Can you tell yet how we're doing?" she asked, at last. "I mean, is everyone watching and are they suitably impressed?"

Christopher glanced around the room as they danced and chuckled pleasantly. "Oh, they're watching all right, and believe me, we're making an impression."

"Yes, but what kind of impression? Is it good or bad?"

The dimples danced. "Well, let me put it this way. All the ladies are whispering behind fluttering fans, speculating on the number of children we will have and who they will look like. They're probably also wondering what kind of hostess you will make. And the men?" He raised an eyebrow. "Well, never mind what they're thinking. Let's just say they would love to stick a knife in my back and take my place."

She blushed prettily. "I believe you're exaggerating just a bit."

"Don't you believe it," he muttered drily. "I know that look well."

Soon after, the dance ended and the ball began in earnest. Her first dance was with a Mr. Cambridge. He was Christopher's godfather, she was informed, and understandably a close personal friend of the major's. Mr. Cambridge was a delightful gentleman, displaying a charm and wit belying his 60-odd years, and his command of the dance floor was remarkable. During the promenade around the floor, Raven noticed Christopher dancing with Sybil. Camilla was partnered with David while Julia had been captured by a darling young man, a good foot taller than herself and with bright red hair.

Next came a Mr. Billingsly. He raised fine thoroughbred horses for breeding and racing. He was fiercely committed to marriage and to prove it was the father of ten children. Raven couldn't help wondering if the ten children weren't the result of him setting an example for his horses, or the other way around. For this dance, Christopher was coupled with Camilla, and Julia was with the same young man as before.

After that came a Mr. Forbes, Mr. Cambridge again, the major and then some French count named Montrachet. He was visiting one of the invited families and immediately began a grand seduction until David rescued her.

As the evening progressed, she lost track of names and faces. She did not, however, lose track of Christopher. He danced with Camilla a total of three times, which she thought was excessive. Of course he danced with others, but his choosing Camilla so often nettled her.

Raven was dancing with the ardent count for the third time when Christopher finally claimed her.

"Damn," he muttered, trying to dodge the crowd on the floor. "May I ask who that fervent admirer of yours is? I swear, every time I looked up you were dancing with him. Just who the devil is he anyway?"

Raven smiled up at him sweetly. "Well, I'm surprised you even noticed or remembered I was here since you seemed to be so enthralled with Camilla."

Christopher swerved to miss an enthusiastic couple with flaying arms. "Oh, don't be idiotic, and for heaven's sake, don't let us get on that tiresome subject again. I'll have you know I've been doing my duty like the gentleman I am. Lord, I've danced with every old crone and every homely daughter in the place. They all trampled on my feet. Some issued open and indecent advances to me, and the matriarchs of those very same shameless young ladies very nearly deafened me with advice on the subject of marriage and a man's duty to it. Don't condemn me for seeking respite in the form of Camilla. Lord knows, I couldn't get close to you."

She glared at him. "Liar. You didn't even try. Oh, you may bluster and complain all you like, but you don't look very bruised to me."

"Well, it's all very easy for you. All you've had to do was smile sweetly and receive lavish compliments. You haven't had to listen to the male's view on the subject, since we poor devils aren't allowed to have one."

Raven looked at him in astonishment. "Oh, you think not? Listen, I've had to endure an endless parade of men with knowing smiles and a gleam in their eyes that illustrated quite plainly just exactly what they considered a woman's duty was."

Christopher's eyes swept over her seductively. "Now there's some wise counseling."

All at once, he grabbed her arm. "Come on, let's get out of here. I've had enough of this mingling."

He pulled her out of the crunch and through the open doors leading out onto the terrace. Several large tubs, containing hefty specimens of gardenia, jasmine and something resembling little yellow stars, stood strategically about, giving anyone a choice of secluded nooks to hide in. Christopher chose the nearest niche, between a gardenia bush and a pot of little yellow stars. He backed Raven into the corner and trapped her there.

"Now," he said huskily, "this is for me and I don't want any arguments." The velvet touch of his lips prevented any response from her own.

Little did he know she had no intention of arguing. The minute his body crushed her against the wall, she felt herself melt. Without an ounce of shame, she reached for his waist and slid her hands up under his jacket before trying to grasp the whole width of his back in her two small arms. As she reached his shoulders, she pressed her nails, ever so slightly, into the firm warm flesh beneath the silk shirt and left a trail down his back as she brazenly pulled him closer to her.

A sort of silly insanity settled over Raven. She forgot about Camilla and about Christopher being in love with his brother's beautiful widow. Tonight he loved her. Every caress was genuine, every kiss a true expression of love and desire meant for her and her alone.

He moaned painfully. "Oh Lord," he gasped. "Raven, please don't do that."

"Why not?" she whispered between kisses. "I thought this is what you wanted me to do."

Two young ladies about Julia's age were coming in from the lawn and stopped long enough to eye the two lovers. They giggled childishly and hurried on into the house.

Christopher propped his elbows against the wall of the house, still pinning her there, and began a slow assault on her senses with delicate caresses from her shoulder to her ear. "Marry me, Raven," he groaned. "Marry me and live with me and spend the rest of your life with me."

"Excuse me for intruding."

The sound of Camilla's voice jolted Raven. The innocent dream of loving and being loved vanished as quickly as a whiff of smoke in a gentle wind.

Camilla stood a few feet away, watching their tender scene. Raven couldn't tell whether she had heard Christopher's desperate plea or not, but one thing was certain—Camilla was extremely angry.

"I'm sorry to break into such a private scene," Camilla apologized stiffly, "but David wishes to toast the happy couple and sent me to look for you."

Christopher hadn't moved. He still faced the wall and looked as angry as Camilla. "Thank you, Camilla. Tell David we'll be there in a moment."

She didn't move.

"I said we would be there in a minute, Camilla," Christopher repeated, roughly.

The rustle of her skirts told them when Camilla had left. Raven tried to extricate herself from his hold, but Christopher stopped her. "Not yet," he said tensely. "I want to talk to you."

His face, deep in shadow, hovered only a breath away from hers. "What is it?" she asked, shakily. "Is there something wrong?"

He kissed her hungrily. "Yes, damn it, yes," he whispered. "It's this stupid game we're playing. I want to call off our bargain, Raven. Now."

She took a deep breath. "What do you mean?" she asked tremulously. "I don't understand."

He had his mouth next to her ear, and she could hear his ragged breathing and feel the hammering of his heart. "I can't go through with this, Raven. I can't be married to you and not have you in my bed."

A sort of emotional paralysis set in. What was he saying? Was he telling her to go? Had he decided that having a superficial wife, as well as a mistress, was more of a complication to his scheme than a help? Or had Camilla's growing jealousy been a factor in his decision?

"Are you asking me to leave?" A whisper was all Raven could manage.

Christopher's arms seemed to devour her. "No!" he moaned. "Dear God, Raven, I think I would die if you left. I love you so. Can't you see that? It's this pretend marriage that I can't take. I want you as my wife, as a real wife. I want to make love to you, have children with you and grow old and dotty with you."

Raven tried to pull away. "Please, Christopher," she begged, "don't do this to me."

He let go of her and took a step back. "It's still Camilla, isn't it? You just can't believe me."

"I want to believe you," she cried, "but I can't forget what I saw and heard."

"Raven, please! I've already explained that to

you. I have no love for Camilla. I haven't had for a long time." He reached up and stroked her wounded cheek. "It's you I want, not her."

"Then why the scene in the library?"

"Christopher, for heaven's sake. Everyone is waiting for you." This time it was Julia, and she wasn't about to be dismissed.

With a sigh, Christopher admitted defeat. "Very well, Julia, we're coming." He took Raven's arm. "We're going to finish this discussion later."

Raven returned to her engagement ball in a delightful yet tumultuous state. She danced, she talked, she drank to her health and happiness, but it was all a blur. Was it possible he could be telling the truth, she kept asking herself? Was he really in love with her as he said? He had been so convincing. The look in his eyes, the tone in his voice, the sensation of his touch when he held her, all carried the nuance of truth, a nuance so fragile that it would be impossible to feign.

"Do you mind if I intrude upon those heady thoughts of yours?"

Several minutes earlier Raven had quietly slipped behind a potted palm in the corner of the room. She thought she was well hidden, but David Carlton's voice behind her proved her wrong. Startled, she turned and smiled at him. "Oh, Mr. Carlton, I'm sorry. I'm afraid I didn't hear you."

He chuckled. "I know you didn't, and please call me David." He handed her a glass of champagne. "I've been watching you, you know, and

I have to admit that your face has been a study in perplexity."

She looked surprised. "Oh?"

He flushed slightly. "Look, my dear, I know it's none of my business, but you don't look the part of a happy bride. If you would rather not talk about it, then please feel free to put me in my place. If, however, you would like to discuss your dilemma, whatever it may be, then I'm your man. Now, what's it to be?"

Raven looked into his friendly round face. The blue eyes gazed back at her questioningly. She sighed. "Oh David, I suppose I'm just a bit unsure of myself these days. I don't know how else to explain it."

"Ahhh," he commented, "I think I can. It's Camilla, isn't it? You think, maybe she and Chris are, well, involved with each other. Is that it?"

Raven gaped at him.

"Uh huh. Well, I thought so." He took a sip of champagne. "Well, we all have wondered that from time to time." A young couple skirted past them as David took her arm. "I tell you what. Why don't we take a pleasant stroll in the moonlight and let me show you one of our gardens? It's Sybil's pride and joy, and besides, we'll have more privacy there."

Outside in Sybil's prized garden, David and Raven sat down on a stone bench. "Now, let me see. Oh yes, we were discussing Camilla, weren't we?"

"David," Raven interrupted, "he's in love with her. I saw them, you see. They were, well . . ."

"Rubbish!" David cried. "I'm sorry, my dear, I don't know what you saw—nor do I care—but I can't accept that. Camilla may be beautiful and tempting for a man, but she's well, I'm sorry to say it, but she's completely selfish and quite unlikable. No, I'm sorry, but Christopher would never fall in love with anyone like that."

"He did once," she murmured.

"Oh yes, I know all about that, but that was a long time ago when he was young and foolish. Christopher didn't really know her then, but now he does." He sighed and shook his head. "I really hate to admit this, my dear, but we men, when we are fresh and untried, tend to be quite an imprudent lot. We dash about grabbing at every pretty bauble along the way without stopping to wonder at its real worth. Oh, it's pleasant enough for awhile, but then at some point we receive a nasty blow that cures us of that inane tendency and begin to realize the value of quality. That's where you come in, young lady."

Raven shook her head adamantly. "You don't understand the circumstances surrounding our marriage. If you did, you wouldn't say that."

"I don't have to know anything. You forget, my dear, I'm a man and I can see. When Chris looks at you, I recognize that look for what it is. I tell you, the man is all but drawn and quartered."

"Who is?" Christopher asked, coming into view.

"Sybil's gardener, I'm afraid," David replied comfortably. "She's found mold on two of her prized rosebushes, and she's out for blood."

"Well, I'm sure that's all very interesting, but what the devil are you doing out here with my fiancée? What's the matter with you, man? Have you no honor?"

In the moonlight, Raven could see David grinning. "Apparently not," he replied as he rose from the bench. "Well, if you will excuse me, I'll go see about my guests. Perhaps the two of you would care to root about for further evidence of mold, or perhaps . . . something else?"

As soon as David was out of sight, Christopher gently enveloped her. "I would prefer something else," he murmured against her lips, "but I suppose we would get just as dirty."

"You are a shameless lecher," she scolded softly.

"Not at all," he whispered between teasing kisses. "I'm in love. Now," he continued, "are you going to marry me in earnest? Are you going to be my true wife, my companion through thick and thin, my friend? But most of all, will you be my love?"

Without hesitation, she answered, "Yes."

"Do you love me, Raven?"

"I have loved you from the beginning, and I will love you all my life."

Almost an hour passed before they rejoined the festivities.

By two o'clock Raven was exhausted. She had danced until her limbs were weak from fatigue, and she needed a few minutes of peace and quiet to reflect upon what she finally had allowed her heart to believe. She had just finished her third dance with the stately Mr. Forbes when she slipped out the terrace doors.

She ambled along the length of the terrace, discreetly ignoring the occasional young couple embracing in the shadows, Julia and the redheaded youth among them. She smiled. How lovely life was now. The music was more beautiful, the fragrance of jasmine and gardenia sweeter. The night air was fresher and was permeated with the promise of rain. Colors, sounds and smells. All the senses seemed so much more acute when one was blessed with love.

"Oh Christopher, darling, I can't stand it."

Raven froze in front of the open doorway. The voice, soft and plaintive, was Camilla's. Like someone hypnotized, Raven turned slowly toward the darkened room and gazed at the couple inside.

"Hush, my love," Christopher crooned as he held her in his arms. "Please. You mustn't do this."

Camilla clung to him desperately. "But darling, the wedding is only a week away. How can I be anything but miserable, thinking of you making love to her? I tell you, I hate her!"

Christopher held her at arm's length. "If I stood it, so can you, Camilla. How do you think I felt, knowing my own brother had married and was making love to the woman I yearned for? At least you know I don't love Raven. I didn't have that privilege."

Camilla clung to him once more. "Oh, stop it, please! You know I never loved Robert. I only married him to hurt you, and now you're trying to hurt me. I know it."

Again he held her away. "That's not true, Camilla. You know I love you." He sighed. "Oh, I don't know. Perhaps, if you had not married Robert, we might have had a chance. But now . . . ?"

Camilla threw her arms around him. "Oh Christopher, my darling, it isn't too late. It isn't! But we must make our chance happen. We've been through too much not to have everything turn out our way. I've done things, made sacrifices, taken risks, just so we could be together. I can't stop now. *We* can't stop now."

"And just what would you have me do, Camilla? You say you've done things, made sacrifices and taken risks. Well, I'm sorry but I haven't seen any evidence of that. It seems to me you've always enjoyed a very pleasant existence from where I stand. You've managed to reside in a fine home, you've been able to continually adorn yourself in fine silks and satins, and you've had a bevy of servants waiting to do your slightest bidding. Now, where are all of these loathsome sacrifices you've made in my behalf?"

"Oh, don't be nasty to me, darling," Camilla whined. "Let's go away, Christopher. Forget about your father and that sniveling little bride of yours. She could never make you as happy as I can."

Once again Christopher held her away at arm's length. "And just what would we live on? You know everything I have is tied up in the family holdings. Are you willing to take to begging in the streets to earn our bread?" He snickered scornfully. "I didn't think so. No, Camilla. My father wants me to marry Raven, and that's the way it's going to be."

At that moment, Christopher raised his head and recognized Raven standing in the doorway. Their eyes met and held for a moment before Raven turned slowly and walked back toward the sounds of music and merriment.

Chapter 12

At 2:45 their carriage pulled away from the Carltons' doorstep accompanied by the ominous rumblings of thunder off in the distance. Overhead, the once bright moon now competed for space in the sky with an ever-growing accumulation of angry clouds of moisture being pushed along by the mounting wind. But even the promise of a full-blown torrent couldn't match the black mood Christopher was steeped in.

"I don't suppose it would make any difference to you if I said what you saw didn't mean anything," he growled as they pulled out onto the main road.

A sudden gust of air blew a dark wispy curl across Raven's injured cheek. She reached up and pulled the tendril away. "No," she replied frostily.

He leaned forward. "I meant what I said earlier, Raven. I don't want to be married to you if I can't have you for my wife."

"I'm not simple-minded, Christopher," Raven responded, her voice strangely indifferent. "I heard you the first time."

"Well?" he asked impatiently. "Where does that leave us? Does that mean you are still willing to have a true and binding marriage? I mean, no silly pretense, no six months' time limit, no separate bedrooms?"

Raven pulled her filmy shawl closer around her. "It means," she said quietly, "that I have no intention of marrying you at all. Tomorrow morning, I shall write Aunt Charlotte and make plans to leave as soon as possible."

He sat back and stared at her angrily. "Are you so certain she'll have you? I've heard she's a rather singular person. What if she doesn't want to be intruded upon?"

Raven smiled with certain knowledge. "Oh, she'll want me, all right. She's wanted me ever since I was born."

A strained silence followed while Christopher lit a cigar. When he was satisfied it was well-lit, he asked casually, as if the subject bored him, "How much is your inheritance, Raven?"

"I don't really know, exactly. Mr. Feeny said something about fifty thousand pounds. Why?"

"Because I'll double it if you will agree to the marriage and live with me as my wife for six months. Then at the end of that time, you will be free to go and have a settlement of one hundred thousand pounds over and above your inheritance."

She stared at him in disbelief.

"Think of it, Raven. Think what you could do with a hundred and fifty thousand pounds. If you invested the funds wisely, you could do anything you wanted, anytime you wanted and for as long as you wanted, and you would never run out of money. You would be wealthy in your own right. Now, don't tell me that doesn't appeal to you."

Raven wished he had struck her. It would have been less painful. As it was, Christopher had placed her on the same level as a harlot, albeit an expensive one.

She began to tremble. "Why, Christopher? Why are you treating me this way? Isn't it enough that you've completely humiliated me by forcing that silly schoolgirl confession of love out of me?"

He tossed the cigar away with the flick of a finger and chuckled. "You know why, Raven."

She reached out to slap him, but he grabbed her hand in mid-swing and pulled her over on top of him.

"I would do anything," he murmured huskily, "pay any price, face any obstacle, to have you, and that's the truth of it."

A vicious burst of lightning lit up the sky just as his lips touched hers, and the wind, already whipped up to a frenzy, began to tear savagely at the trees. Leaves, swirling and dipping about them like demented butterflies, showered down on them.

She began to struggle in an effort to break his grasp. "I hate you," she cried hysterically. "Let me go. Please. Just leave me alone."

Christopher's arm around her waist tightened, and he reached up with his free hand to seize a fistful of black curls. Hairpins and combs fell away, releasing a flood of dark curls to tumble down about her shoulders in riotous freedom.

"It's too late for that, Raven," Christopher whispered. "You know that, and so do I. Don't you think I've seen the love in your eyes even before you spoke the words? Oh no, you're in love with me every bit as much as I am with you, and there's absolutely nothing we can do about it."

She began to cry. "No!" she sobbed. "Please, just let me go. All I want to do is leave here."

Christopher, still grasping her hair in his fist, shook her head roughly. "Stop it, Raven," he growled. "I've had enough. There'll be no more talk of you leaving. Do you hear me?"

Raven focused tear-filled eyes on his furious face. "Let me go, Christopher," she whimpered. "Just let me go and let's be done with it."

He kissed her softly. "I'll never let you go," he replied, his voice thick with desire. "Not now or ever. Through fair means or foul, whatever the cost, I intend to keep you."

"Please, Christopher," she begged weakly, "let me up. I'm very uncomfortable this way."

He released her, and she raised up to sit back down across from him.

Christopher watched her settle back in the seat. "Do you suppose we could have the semblance of a rational discussion now?"

A flash of lightning once again cut through the darkness, and Raven shrugged. "I don't see we've anything else to discuss. You've made it exceedingly clear that you intend to force me into a loveless marriage just to satisfy some lascivious whim in that male ego of yours."

"Well, I'll say one thing for you," he said between gritted teeth. "You're tenacious, if nothing else. Once you get an idea in that brain of yours, nothing can sway the notion." He leaned forward. "Just what sort of fool do you think I am, Raven? Just imagine, if you can, the intricate machinations that having a wife and mistress living in the same house would require. Do you think any man in his right mind would attempt such an arrangement?"

Raven looked at him with cool detachment. "Certainly. It's quite common, and you know it. How else do you explain the remarkable number of comely maids suddenly leaving good employment amongst whispers concerning their master's masculine prowess? Coincidence?"

Christopher slumped back in the seat. "I wouldn't know about that," he sighed in defeat.

"I only know the thought of such an unwholesome coterie sends terror through me, and I would rather face the hounds of hell before participating in such an arrangement."

"Then let me go," she suggested quietly. "Let me go before something dreadful occurs—and it will, Christopher. Even I see that. Camilla is becoming more and more desperate, and I am the reason for her unhappiness. But you know that. So why are you insisting that we continue on with this farce? You don't love me. You love her. Just let me go."

The lightning had increased. Almost an incessant series of flashes surrounded them, and Raven could see the stony expression on Christopher's face. "No," he stated with grim determination. "It no longer matters whether you believe me or not. You're staying. You consented to our marriage, and you're going to honor that pledge, Camilla or no Camilla."

Raven's eyes widened with speculation. "You're using me to feed Camilla's insecurity in the hope that something will happen, aren't you? But what, Christopher? What is so important that I may end up dying for?"

Christopher took out another cheroot, lit it and took several long draws on it before he answered. "I've asked you once. This time I'm telling you. Stay out of it, Raven. Whatever is about to happen has nothing to do with you, and I want it to stay that way."

"Christopher," Raven pleaded helplessly, "that's not true. You and your father have gone out of your way to make me a part of it. Someone is going to get hurt. Don't you understand?"

Christopher's response was lost in the wind. The first few drops of rain began to spatter down on them, and the carriage suddenly lunged forward in a mad dash for home.

The next morning Raven awoke to the sound of torrential rain beating against her window. She sat up and looked in the direction of the sound. From inside her bleak and murky room, she barely made out the sheet of rain sliding down her window, and she thought wistfully of the family of sparrows beneath her window. She hoped they were fairing all right.

A soft rap on her door sent her plunging under the covers. "Come in," she called grudgingly.

Flora bustled into the room carrying a breakfast tray and set it down on a table near the window. "Well, it's about time you stirred. Do you have any idea what time it is?"

"Go away, Flora," Raven groaned from beneath the covers. "It's too gloomy to get up."

Flora walked over to the fireplace and began lighting the kindling. "Well, apparently everyone in this house is suffering from the same fatal dose of laziness. What on earth happened last night that everyone should be so laggardly?"

Raven rolled over and yawned. "Nothing, Flora. It was just a very late evening, and everyone is tired."

"Yes, well, it's a good thing I've still got some

life about me. Otherwise nothing would ever get done around here." She walked over to the bed and pulled the covers back. "Now there's no use hidin' under those covers any longer. It's time you were up. Besides, cook made some new concoction for breakfast. They're called crêpes, ya know, and they're from France. They have to be eaten right away or they get leathery."

Raven sat up and smiled. "Flora, crêpes are not new. They've been around quite awhile."

Flora snorted. "Well, they're new to me, but I can't say much for 'um. It's like eatin' a bunch of feathers. The more you eat, the more you wonder where breakfast is."

Raven giggled. "That's the Welsh in you. You were raised on the kind of breakfast miners need to keep them going."

Flora sniffed indignantly and started for the door. "Well, apparently I still need it since I'm still hungry. As a matter of fact, I'm going downstairs right now and fill up on something substantial."

After she left, Raven reluctantly rose to begin the day. She ate breakfast in front of the fire and then dressed in a soft woolen gown, the color of garnets. The weather had turned cold during the night, and she huddled next to the fire, soaking up the warmth emanating from the crackling blaze. Once she got up to search the leaden sky for any indication of a break in the downpour but was disappointed. The day promised to be bleak and dismal, and so, with nothing else to do, she went back to the fire and curled up to finish Miss Austen's book.

She had lunch downstairs but ate alone. Camilla and Julia were ensconced in their rooms, and Christopher and the major were locked up together going over some report for the bank. Flora, of course, was too busy with Mrs. Bagly, the housekeeper, to stop for lunch. Apparently Flora had managed to find a Welsh breakfast substantial enough to allow the skipping of the noon meal.

After eating a light lunch, Raven returned to her room in a state of depression. The cold permeated the house, and the rain continued its stubborn assault with maddening monotony. In forlorn resignation, she returned to her nest in front of the fire with another book she had confiscated from the library. This time the book was a collection of works by Voltaire.

Raven was well into *L' Indiscret* when Aunt Jessica interrupted her in the middle of an amusing scene.

Aunt Jessica stumbled into the room, barely missing Marigold beneath her feet, gripping a jewelry box rusty with age.

"Oh, my dear, how very convenient of you to be free just now." She came over to Raven and fell down on the footstool as her feet became entangled in her long skirt of orange velvet bordered with bright blue ribbons.

Raven fought to stifle a gasp as she took in the dear soul's apparel. *Wherever does she get them?*

Christopher's aunt managed to right herself in a sitting position and then handed the jewelry box to Raven. "Just look at what I found, my dear."

Raven couldn't help but smile. "Aunt Jessica, you haven't been prowling around down in the cellar again, have you?"

Aunt Jessica giggled. "We've been snooping again, Marigold and I, and look what we found." She reached over and pried open the lid. "Just look," she crooned.

Raven did gasp this time. Inside was a collection of the most atrocious jewelry she had ever had the misfortune to look upon. "Oh my," was all she could think of saying.

Aunt Jessica, on the other hand, squealed in delight. "Isn't it the most marvelous find?" She leaned over and whispered softly, "But don't tell Camilla. She would be so angry if she knew we were still treasure hunting."

Raven began fingering the hideous trinkets. "Aunt Jessica, why do you suppose Camilla is so against you searching the wine cellar?"

Aunt Jessica cackled with glee. "She's afraid," she said covertly.

"Of what?"

Aunt Jessica leaned forward. "Secrets," she whispered. "She's afraid I'll discover her secrets."

Raven's spine began to tingle. "What secrets, Aunt Jessica? What sort of secrets could she have in a wine cellar?"

Raven watched as the elderly woman draped

herself in a gaudy strand of beads with child-like enthusiasm. "Oh, like papers, for instance."

Raven tried to hide her impatience. "Aunt Jessica, what kind of papers? Do you know what they are?"

"No," she sighed, fingering the beads. "But Chris wants them, and she's hidden them. Of course, there also are other secrets down in the cellar."

A crash behind them caused Raven to whirl around. Marigold, climbing around on her bed-side table, had knocked over her night candle, and he was about to do the same thing to the bottle of brandy Aunt Jessica had brought her the night after she had been shot. On their previous visits to Raven, both Aunt Jessica and Marigold had enjoyed nips from the bottle, and Marigold wasn't about to let the habit go neglected.

Raven got up, poured his saucer full of the potent liquid and set it on the floor before pouring Aunt Jessica a glass and giving it to her.

"Ohhh," Aunt Jessica crooned happily. "How very thoughtful of you, my dear." She swallowed the full glass in one gulp. "Ahhh, that was lovely. Just the thing."

Raven sat back down, replaced the jewelry box in her lap and picked up an enormous ring, the center of which was the head of a dragon. She slipped it on her finger. "Aunt Jessica," she began, "about those papers, do you have any idea why Christopher wants them or why Camilla has hidden them?"

Aunt Jessica, tugging on a string of metal beads caught in a tangled mess in the box, suddenly threw them down and grabbed a monstrous bracelet encrusted with pieces of yellow and green glass. "Ohhh," she exclaimed breathlessly. "It matches my brocade."

"Yes, yes," Raven muttered in frustration. "Now, about the papers . . ."

Aunt Jessica suddenly stood up. "I'm sorry, my dear, but Marigold and I must leave you now. You see, I really must go and try this on with my brocade. It's the very thing I've needed. I just know it."

Several minutes later, Raven lit the bruised but intact candle from her bedside table and headed for the wall panel. Christopher had said there were boxes and boxes of papers in that mysterious room in the wine cellar. Was the paper that Camilla was hiding from Christopher among them? Would she know it if she saw it? Somehow she thought she would.

She stepped out into the cool darkness of the wine cellar and made her way to the obscure little room at the far end. The door stood ajar, and Raven hurried in and lit the lamp sitting on the table next to the bed.

Aunt Jessica had been here, all right. The place was a mess. The heavy trunk in the corner was open with all sorts of debris hanging out of it. If Camilla came down here again she would take one look at the mess and know Aunt Jessica had been prowling again.

In an effort to save Aunt Jessica from an

unhappy scene with Camilla, Raven began to stuff the overflow back into the trunk. Underneath one section of the overhanging paraphernalia, Raven found a small pile of dirt dug out from between the blocks of stone making up the floor. Apparently Marigold had been in attendance and had tried to root out some hapless vermin escaping under the trunk, although Raven didn't know how. The trunk sat flush with the floor. Nonetheless, she skillfully scraped the dirt back into place and patted it down firmly with her slipper before turning her attention to the stack of boxes on the bed.

Raven worked for about an hour, sorting through papers of every description, stacking them in categories. The diaries and journals she dismissed as unimportant since Aunt Jessica had implied the paper or papers Christopher sought were separate entities. But the logbooks were only a small part in the collection of documents saved for posterity.

She had half her upper body buried in one of the boxes, trying to retrieve a receipt stuck to the bottom when Christopher's voice startled her. Raven straightened up and dropped the carton as if it were on fire.

"Raven," he barked, "what in the devil are you doing down here?"

She turned around and looked at him guiltily. "Oh, Christopher. Uh, I was just, uh, well . . ."

"Answer me," he ordered.

Raven's eyes flashed. "I was trying to help

you," she spat. "I thought if I could find the papers Camilla is hiding from you, then maybe this silly game of cat and mouse we're playing will end before somebody gets hurt."

He sprang across the room and grabbed her arm. "How did you find out about those papers, Raven?" He began to shake her. "Tell me, damn it. Tell me what you know."

Raven aimed for his chest and pushed him away as she wrenched free of his grip. "Let go of me!" she commanded. "How dare you speak to me that way."

"I'll speak to you any way I please. And if necessary, I'll have you locked in your room until you learn to obey orders."

"You wouldn't dare!"

Christopher smiled confidently. "Oh, wouldn't I?"

The look on his face told Raven he meant it, and she raised her chin haughtily. "Very well," she replied regally, "I'll leave you to scavenge on your own and may you not have a minute's luck with your endeavors." She grabbed her candle and turned for the door.

"Just a moment," he demanded, halting her retreat. "You haven't answered me, and you're not leaving until you do."

She turned back to face him.

"I want to know how much you know about those papers, Raven, and I want to know who told you about them."

"I don't know anything about them, really," she admitted with grudging honesty, "other than you want them and Camilla has hidden them."

"Who told you that?"

"Aunt Jessica."

"My word," Christopher muttered helplessly. "This whole business is beginning to turn into a carnival." He ran a hand through his hair. "And just how did she find out about them?"

Raven smiled. "You know Aunt Jessica better than I do, Christopher. Need you ask?"

He sighed wearily. "No, I suppose not. Between her treks through those bloody passages and her snooping . . ." He frowned. "I wonder," he said wistfully, "if she knows all of it."

Raven happened to glance down and noticed one of the papers had fallen off the bed. She bent down to pick it up when something shiny entangled around the leg of the bed caught her eye. Raven deftly retrieved the object and slipped it into her pocket before rising. "Well, if that's all you want of me, I'll be going."

Christopher, still lost in his thoughts, never noticed her departure.

Raven left through the cellar door and made her way up the stairs to her room. Had she retraced her steps through the passage, perhaps she would have had a sense of warning as to what she was about to find.

When she opened her bedroom door, a cold draft hit her. Raven looked in the current's direction and discovered the wall panel in her room stood open. She walked over, closed it and turned around.

For a moment, Raven couldn't believe what her eyes relayed to her brain. Next to her bed, Aunt Jessica lay sprawled on the floor, an empty glass in one hand, the bottle of brandy in the other. Beside her, Marigold sat, calmly washing his face.

"Aunt Jessica?" Raven called cautiously and hurried toward her. "Aunt Jessica, are you all right?"

As soon as Raven touched her, wild hysteria took over. She screamed as if the gates of hell had opened up. Aunt Jessica, dressed in her yellow and green brocade, complete with the offensive bracelet, was dead.

Raven lost all sense of reality until Flora slapped her roughly across the face, shocking her into silence. Until then, she had been screaming the whole time but hadn't realized it.

"Stop it," Flora shouted, shaking her violently. Then she bent down and inspected the crumpled corpse at their feet. "Dear Lord," she gasped.

By now, all the servants had rushed to the scene, and Flora took immediate command. "Lizzy, go find the major and Mr. Chris. Mary, get to Mr. Bridges and tell him to go for the doctor and notify the constable. Mrs. Bagly, we're going to need quite a lot of strong tea and some smelling salts. All the rest of you clear out but stay close by."

Minutes passed, perhaps hours. Raven didn't know. She sat in a chair across from the grisly scene and watched in detached stupidity as a sea of faces came and went.

She was finally jarred out of her stupor by the sound of Christopher's voice. By then, Aunt Jessica had been removed and the room was empty except for herself, Christopher and a man Raven had never seen before.

"Raven," Christopher called gently. He knelt in front of her. "This is Constable Wicks. He needs to ask you some questions. Do you think you can manage that?"

She nodded sluggishly.

Constable Wicks matched Christopher's pose. "Miss Elliott, when did you see Miss Mallory last?"

Raven reached up and wiped away the tears sliding down her cheeks. "About two hours before I found her," she choked out.

"And where was that?"

"Here. In my room."

"Why was she here?"

"She . . . she came to show me a treasure she had found. It wasn't anything, really, just a rusty old jewelry box full of trinkets."

"Did you leave her in here?"

"No. She left. You see, she found a bracelet, the bracelet she had on, and she wanted to see if it matched the dress we found her in." Raven began to sob softly. "I guess she put them on and came back to show me. I . . . I don't know."

"Miss Elliott, did you know the brandy on your bedside table was full of arsenic?"

Raven looked at him as if he had suddenly gone mad. She shook her head. "Arsenic? Oh, no, that is impossible."

"I'm afraid, Miss Elliott, that it is so. Dr. Lamb has stated there was enough arsenic in the brandy to kill several able-bodied men."

Raven began to tremble violently. "But that can't be," she mumbled, her voice dry and rasping. "Both she and Marigold had some before they left. It was perfectly fine, and so were they."

Constable Wicks frowned. "Did you also have a drink, Miss Elliott?"

She shook her head adamantly. "No, no," she responded with growing agitation. "I don't like it. It's too strong. The only reason I have it is because Aunt Jessica gave it to me, and she and Marigold usually have some every time they visit me. I'm sorry, Constable Wicks, but the doctor must be mistaken. It couldn't have been the brandy."

"There is no mistake, Miss Elliott. As you can see, most of the brandy spilled when Miss Mallory fell, but what was left in the bottle was quite potent."

Raven's head began to throb, keeping pace with a burring noise in her ears. "No," she argued vehemently, "there was nothing wrong with the brandy, I tell you . . ." She stopped and caught her breath. "Unless it was another bottle. Yes, that's it! It must have been another bottle, not the one on my bedside table."

Constable Wicks held up an empty bottle of

brandy. Do you recognize this bottle, Miss Elliott?"

Raven sighed in relief and smiled. "Yes," she answered exuberantly, "that's it. That's the bottle that was on my night table."

"How do you know that, Miss Elliott?"

"Because," she replied, "the label is torn. See? Marigold did that. He was always clawing at it, and he scratched the label."

Constable Wicks shook his head sadly. "I'm sorry to hear that, Miss Elliott, because this is the bottle we found in Miss Mallory's hand and this is the bottle that was poisoned."

The sound of an altercation out in the hall interrupted the constable's interrogation.

"See here, my good man, you can't just . . ." The door flew open, and Raven watched a mop of unruly blond curls march into the room above the back-stepping, arms-flaying, blustering major.

"Raven," Jeremy called excitedly, "what the blazes is going on here? This idiot tells me there has been a murder here and you are confined to your room. Are you all right?"

Raven leapt from the chair and rushed toward her gallant rescuer.

Jeremy, flushed with excitement and feeling quite the hero, brushed the major aside as if he were a bobbing cork in a pond just in time to catch Raven in his arms.

"Jeremy," Raven cried, clinging to him desperately. "Aunt Jessica has been murdered, and the constable thinks I did it."

The room suddenly began to roar with everyone trying to talk at once. Bodies began to mill about. The major, trying desperately to gain control of the chaos, merely added to the confusion until Constable Wicks finally asserted his authority.

"Quiet," he shouted, and the room fell silent. "Now, sir," he said, addressing Jeremy, "just who might you be and why are you here?"

Jeremy, still holding Raven, held out his hand and shook the constable's hand. "My name is Jeremy Frasier, sir, and I've come to take my fiancée out of this mad house."

Constable Wicks' eyebrow rose, and he turned to Christopher. "I'm afraid I'm a bit confused, Mr. Mallory. I was under the impression that Miss Elliott was your fiancée."

Christopher stood there looking grim. "She is," he growled. "This young whelp is merely a friend of Miss Elliott's from London. As to why he is here, I haven't the faintest idea."

Constable Wicks turned back to Jeremy. "Well, Mr. Frasier, perhaps you would be willing to enlighten us as to the reason for your apparently unexpected appearance on the scene."

Jeremy drew himself up to imperial heights. "With pleasure, my good man. To put it bluntly, I have come to save Miss Elliott from a hateful and contrived marriage to this . . . this gentleman." Jeremy waved an imperious hand toward Christopher. "You see, I have just discovered that Miss Elliott is being forced to marry this scoundrel because of a stipulation in her father's will, a stipulation, I strongly suspect, Mr. Elliott was coerced into making. Now, I have already asked Miss Elliott to marry me, and I have come to take her back to London and save her from this despicable scheme."

"Mercy," the constable replied, fanning himself with his hat. "I must applaud you, sir, for your gallant attempts to save Miss Elliott from such a terrible fate as you describe." He turned to Christopher. "As for you, Mr. Mallory, I have to admit you certainly had me fooled. Why, I never for a moment suspected you of being a scoundrel capable of such despicable schemes. I always thought you to be a gentleman of the first water."

Christopher, standing apart from them, continued to glower at them. "Oh, Constable Wicks, you don't know, by half, what I'm capable of."

The constable chuckled. "Well, it looks as though all our capabilities are going to be put to the test, doesn't it? Some more than others, apparently." He turned back to Jeremy. "As I was saying, Mr. Frasier, I appreciate your efforts, but I'm afraid your daring rescue of Miss Elliott must be postponed for the moment. You see, however inconvenient, murder takes precedence over chivalry, and that means that Miss Elliott must remain in residence until we have this foul deed cleared up."

"You see?" Raven cried, still clutching Jeremy. "They all believe I killed poor Aunt

Jessica. But I didn't! I swear it! I loved her. She was good and sweet and kind to me. Why would I?"

"Please, Miss Elliott," Constable Wicks interjected, "you must not become so overwrought that you misinterpret my words. Besides, I don't believe I ever even suggested such a possibility, did I, Mr. Mallory?"

"Certainly not!" Christopher grumbled in disgust.

"No, no, Miss Elliott," soothed the constable. "I don't believe for one minute that you are the murderer. No, indeed, I believe you were the intended victim."

Chapter 13

Two days later, the morning of September 17, 1817, dawned cold and bleak. A fine mist hung in the air like a thick gray curtain, causing the handful of mourners standing among the headstones in the Mallory family cemetery to huddle together in chilly defense against the weather. Each of them stood patiently in icy misery, listening to Mr. Holms' words. The task was difficult since the vicar's soft and plaintive voice often rambled off the subject and frequently became lost in a sudden gust of frigid wind.

The only outsiders present for the somber occasion, besides Raven and Jeremy, were Constable Wicks and the Carletons. As Raven glanced around at the meager number of witnesses, her heart broke. So few present, she lamented to herself, to bid the final farewell to such a gentle and endearing soul. There should be more to say good-bye.

When, at last, the rites were concluded, the gloomy group returned to the house to mark the day's passing by indulging in muted murmurs, spiced tea and cakes, and endless hours of quiet reflection.

Jeremy stayed on, and Raven was grateful for his company. For once, he behaved with a solemn maturity befitting the circumstances. His quiet and attentive presence helped her get through the wretched time both before and after Aunt Jessica's funeral.

In the days that followed, neither the weather nor the spirits of the morbid inhabitants of Heathglade improved. The major moped about, looking tired and disheartened, Christopher seemed angry and aloof, and Camilla and Julia remained quiet and unresponsive. Raven most probably would have fallen into one or more of those states had it not been for Marigold. No one seemed to realize that he had lost his best friend and companion, and his grief gave Raven something to focus on.

From the day of Aunt Jessica's death, Marigold hadn't moved from the spot where Raven had found him. He would lie there motionless for hours and then begin to howl pitifully. Raven knew he was mourning his loss, and she tried to keep him supplied with a saucer of brandy in an effort to boost his spirits, but he refused to drink it now. The only concession he made was to sleep with Raven. Every night, at some point, she would be awakened by his jumping up on the bed and trying to nestle close to her. She would take him in her arms and snuggle him in the crook of her body. Only then would he drift off into a peaceful sleep.

It was a week before the pall over Heathglade finally lifted. The insistent sun eventually broke through the dismal clouds, promoting the semblance of life to return to the melancholy group vegetating within its walls.

As Raven walked into breakfast on that first sunlit morning, the sounds of happy chatter greeted her.

"Raven," Julia gurgled merrily, "I hope you don't mind, but Camilla and I are stealing Mr. Frasier away from you this morning. We're taking him on a grand tour of the countryside."

Raven, at the sideboard, smiled at the happy change in her colleagues. She picked up a plate and began to fill it with a variety of edibles. "I think that is a lovely idea, Julia," she replied pleasantly, "and I heartily approve since I'm sure Jeremy will enjoy it very much."

"Of course," Julia continued, "I'm certain Mr. Frasier will find our rural delights rather dull compared to the daily splendors of London."

Jeremy, sitting beside her, put down his fork. "My dear Miss Mallory," he exclaimed with polished practice, "how could you even think such a thought? What with two lovely escorts such as you and Mrs. Mallory, you could take me to the dullest place on earth and I should feel as if heaven itself had been laid before me."

Christopher, at that moment, choked on a mouthful of scone. As she took her place beside him, Raven leaned over and asked with feigned gravity, "Are you all right?"

He glared out at her from under his napkin. "I'm fine," he grumbled. "I'm just finding breakfast a bit hard to swallow this morning."

Julia, thankfully, was too engrossed in Jeremy's charms to even notice her brother's theatrics, much less catch the double meaning in his words. Instead, upon receiving such a lavish compliment, she turned a most charming pink, and Raven smiled to herself. Jeremy might never be popular among his masculine peers, but he certainly had winning ways with the ladies.

After breakfast, Jeremy and his two decorative guides were off, Christopher and his father retired to the study, and Raven returned to her room. She had started crocheting a shawl several weeks earlier and only needed a couple of more hours' work before the wrap, made of soft lamb's wool, would be completed. Done in a shell design, she thought the project her best effort. She had planned to give it to Flora for Christmas and had had a devil of a time creating the gift in secret.

Just before noon, Raven had attached the last

strand of fringe to the shawl when Lizzy appeared with a message that Raven was wanted in the study.

She answered the summons promptly, entered and closed the door behind her.

Christopher sat at the messy desk scribbling furiously on a piece of paper. He finished, threw the pen down and stood up. "I've just finished the last note to our neighbors canceling our wedding," he announced blandly. "I've discussed the matter with my father, and he agrees that under the circumstances a wedding following so closely behind a tragedy would be in poor taste, to say the least."

Raven nodded in mute agreement.

He lit one of the slender cigars and looked at her skeptically through a blue haze of smoke. "I see you have no objection."

"No," she answered quietly.

"Would your complacency in such a decision have anything to do with that oily little popinjay we now have cluttering up the place?"

She glanced at him, slightly irritated. "If you are referring to Jeremy, the answer is no. Besides, what on earth would he have to do with it?"

Christopher walked around the desk. "Sit down, Raven."

When she had done so, he braced himself against the desk in front of her. "It just seems that you and good old Jeremy have developed a rather close affinity for one another since his arrival, and I was just wondering if perhaps you might be entertaining notions of returning with him to London.''

Raven looked up at him in surprise. "Why would you think that?''

"Well, it appears to me as if this sterling white knight of yours has suddenly appeared at a most advantageous moment. Now, I don't think for one moment that you are not intelligent enough to recognize such an opportunity as a way of escaping the distasteful situation you find yourself in." He took a long draw on the cheroot and blew the smoke out. "Can you honestly say you have not been entertaining such a notion?''

"Certainly not," Raven snapped. "Jeremy is just a friend, a very good friend. You know that.''

Christopher chuckled. "Oh yes, that is plain to see, but I've seen alliances spring up between people with far less foundation than friendship. But then, perhaps you are nourishing something a bit more substantial than friendship for Mr. Fraiser. Say love, for instance? If that is the case, then the possibility of a marriage between the two of you would not seem beyond the realm of possibility.''

"Say what you mean, Christopher," she demanded. "If you are asking if I plan to run away with Jeremy and marry him, the answer is no. I do love Jeremy, but not in the romantic sense. He is like a beloved brother to me. In reference to the closeness we have shared lately, it was because I needed someone." She sighed. "Honestly, without him these past few days, well, I don't know what I would have done. He was there when I needed an anchor, and I shall always be grateful to him for that."

Christopher glared at her. "And what about me? Was I nowhere about?"

"No!" she answered angrily. "Since Aunt Jessica's death, you've been surly as an old bear. You've been hateful and nasty and barely civil to anyone."

Christopher stomped over to the fireplace and threw the cigar into the flames. "Did it ever occur to you that I might have some problems of my own?"

"You've got problems!" she shouted and sprang from the chair. "For heaven's sake, Christopher, I am being forced to marry a man who is openly making love and conspiring with another woman. On top of that, someone is trying to kill me, and I can't leave. I have to sit here and act as a target while you . . . you stalk about the place in a foul mood because you and Camilla are playing hide-and-seek with a bunch of silly old papers which you can't find."

"That's not what I'm worried about, you foolish little chit," he shouted back. "I'm trying to figure out a way to protect you while you dance attendance to that insufferable, little, wet-nosed fop."

Raven whirled around and headed for the door. "If all you wanted was to inform me of the wedding cancellation and to insult my friends, then I'll be going."

"Just a moment," Christopher commanded.

"There is something else. Tonight you and I have been invited to the Carletons for dinner. Wear something special, a favorite dress perhaps, and pack a valise with enough clothing to last several days."

She stopped and turned around.

"It's all right. I've cleared everything with Constable Wicks. We feel that you should have a respite from the tension here, somewhere where you can relax and get some rest. You'll be staying with the Carletons for awhile."

Raven felt a wave of relief sweep over her. The thought of safety and a few days of peace sounded heavenly. She nodded and fled the room.

At 6:30 that evening, she and Christopher pulled away from Heathglade. This time, Christopher had wisely ordered an enclosed carriage since the sky, angry and turbulent, once again promised a downpour.

Sitting next to Christopher in the dimness of their enclosure, Raven felt his eyes studying her intently as they moved along in silence. She had dressed in her favorite gown, the dusty pink muslin trimmed in white lace. The gown was completely inappropriate for this time of year, and she began to worry about his not liking her choice, but he had said to wear her favorite, so she had.

"What are you thinking about?" she asked, when she couldn't stand his gaze any longer.

He blew a cloud of silver blue haze upward. "I was just thinking how beautiful you are now and wondering how much more beautiful you will be in fifty years."

Just getting away from the house had lifted Raven's spirits, but now Christopher's extravagant compliment made her completely forget about the inappropriateness of her dress. She felt absolutely light-hearted and smiled. "Aren't you being rather optimistic? It is men that become more handsome with age. Women just become old and wrinkled, and I seem to recall you have an aversion to wrinkles."

His eyebrow shot up. "I do?"

"Yes. I remember you said something to me once about becoming wrinkled. I knew you didn't like them because you had mentioned wrinkles to Camilla the night I spied on the two of you in the library. I remember wondering at the time how you felt about bullet wounds." She reached up and brushed her now bandage-free cheek.

Christopher leaned down and placed a gentle kiss on the angry red streak across her cheek. "Believe it or not," he murmured, "it's one of the most sensual sights I've ever had to struggle against."

His voice, soft and caressing, sent that well-recognized tingle of desire through her. "Christopher," she pleaded softly, "please tell me that everything is going to be all right."

The only light visible in the carriage came from the lanterns mounted upon the outside. Soft and muted, it filtered through the window and bathed his face in a twilight glow. "Everything is going to be all right, little moppet. Sooner than you imagine. Just trust me a little while longer, that's all I ask."

She leaned back into the lush seat and relaxed. Why did she believe him? What was it about him that made her cling to his promises and reassurances after finding them lacking so many times in the past? The answer was simple, of course. She loved him. In spite of his back-door affair with Camilla and his unscrupulous coercion to possess her, she loved him.

They arrived at the Carletons' just as the storm broke. Heavy banks of thunderclouds sent vicious bolts of lightning slashing across the sky, and as they stepped out of the carriage, the rain began.

"Come in, come in," David called out as they rushed through the front door. "My word, it looks like we're in for it, doesn't it?"

Christopher, removing Raven's cloak, frowned. "Yes, I'm afraid it does. I feel sorry for the poor farmers. If this keeps up, their crops are going to wash away before they get them harvested, if they haven't already."

At that moment, Sybil floated out into the hall from the salon looking lovely in a gown of pale green silk overlaid with matching lace. "Oh, there you are." She smiled pleasantly. "We were beginning to worry about you. Please come into the salon and warm yourselves." She walked up and slipped her arm through Raven's. "Raven, my dear, you look enchanting. Now, come along, there's someone I want you to meet."

"Sybil," Christopher interrupted, "I wonder if I might have a private word with Raven before we join you. Would the parlor be acceptable?"

Sybil gave him a scolding look. "Christopher Mallory, don't tell me you haven't, as yet, told her about tonight."

David took his wife's arm quickly. "Now, now, Sybil, this is none of our business. I'm certain Chris has his reasons, and we shouldn't interfere."

"Yes, but David," Sybil grumbled as her husband dragged her toward the salon, "the poor girl deserves to have some advance notice, for heaven's sake."

David opened the salon door and gently pushed his wife inside. "Please, pay no heed to Sybil's prattle. It's the female in her, you know." And then he threw up his hands in a gesture of frustration. "Unfortunately, they all suffer from it, God bless them."

Once they were alone, Raven turned to Christopher. "Christopher, what's all this about? Who am I supposed to meet? And why didn't you tell me?" She looked down at her dress, horror expressed on her face. "If I had known someone else would be attending, I would have worn something more appropriate."

Christopher took her by the shoulders. "It's our parish priest, Father Sinclair. He is here to marry us, Raven. Tonight."

"What?" she gasped. "But . . . but I don't understand. You just told me the wedding was canceled."

"The public wedding, yes. But there's no reason why we can't have a private one. Now, David and Sybil have agreed to be our witnesses, and you like them, don't you?"

"Well, of course I do, but—"

"Well, that's it then. Listen, Raven, we were going to be married in three days anyway, so why not now?"

"But Christopher, why? I mean, it's . . . it's so sudden! And your mother's dress, Christopher . . . I haven't got it." She looked down once more at the woefully inappropriate muslin. "I can't be married in this!"

Christopher took her face in his hands and kissed her gently. "Do you love me, Raven?"

She began to tremble from the sheer closeness of him and recognized the absurdity of trying to lie. "Yes, but . . ."

"No buts," he interrupted. "The dress doesn't matter. I love you, Raven, and you love me. That's what counts. I want our wedding to be peaceful and private. It's the only wedding I ever plan to have, and I don't want its importance marred by a bunch of outsiders turning it into a carnival." He took her by the hand. "Now, come along. Tonight is for us alone."

Within the hour they were married in the Carletons' salon. The quiet ceremony was performed before a glowing fireplace and surrounded in candlelight. To Raven, it was a wedding dreams were made of. Father Sinclair, a big bear of a man with golden hair and beard, glowed with pleasure as he guided them through their vows. Afterward, he proclaimed the rights of marriage his second favorite duty, the first being the christening of little babies or little souls of God, as he called them.

During the nuptials, his deep vibrant voice washed over Raven like a soothing balm, and for the first time in her life, she felt the presence of pure, unreserved, unequivocal love.

After the ceremony, the Carletons served champagne. A round of happy toasts were issued to the bride and groom and then everyone filed into the dining room for a sumptuous wedding dinner.

That evening was Raven's first taste of profound happiness. After dinner had been completed, the wedding party settled back in the salon and the remainder of the evening was spent in pleasant conversation among genial company. Sitting on the sofa, wrapped in Christopher's arms, Raven felt safe and wanted. She had married the man she loved in a beautiful and reverent ceremony among valued friends in a safe and protected atmosphere. For awhile, Heathglade, Camilla and all their troubles were forgotten.

At 10:30, Father Sinclair began his farewells to his hosts and the bride and groom. He was interrupted by the sound of a disturbance in the hall. An imperious knock came next. Then the door suddenly burst open before David had a chance to respond.

Graves, the Carletons' butler, stood in the doorway looking distraught. "Excuse my abrupt entrance, Mr. Carleton, but there is an emergency message for Mr. Mallory. It can't wait."

Christopher sprang from his seat beside Raven. "What is it, Graves?"

"I'm sorry, Mr. Mallory, but it seems your father has suddenly become quite ill and your presence at home is urgently requested."

"What happened?"

"The messenger didn't say exactly. Something about his heart, I believe. He's waiting for you outside to take you back."

Raven jumped up from her seat, but Christopher stopped her. "No, Raven, you stay here. There's nothing you can do, and I'll feel better knowing you're here with David and Sybil. Besides, you need to get some rest."

"But Christopher," she cried, "how can I do that knowing the major is so ill?"

Christopher was already halfway across the room. "Has a doctor been sent for?"

"I believe so, sir. They said—" The door closed and left Graves' sentence unfinished.

Immediately a comforting hand settled on Raven's shoulder. "You musn't worry, my dear," Father Sinclair said soothingly. "God, in his infinite goodness, will take care of the major." He turned to David. "If you will excuse me, Mr. Carleton, I think perhaps I should follow Mr. Mallory. I might be needed there."

"Of course, of course," David replied, and he hurriedly escorted the priest from the room.

Later that night, Raven sat alone in front of the fire in the room that she and Christopher were to have shared. She felt isolated and desolate. As she stared into the flames, Raven couldn't help feeling that Aunt Jessica's demise and now the major's possible death were her fault. If she had never come here, would all this misery have happened? She didn't think so. However unintentional, her arrival had set into motion a series of events that spelled disaster for all of them.

The hours ticked by slowly. She paced back and forth in that lonely room wondering what was happening. Was the major dead? Was he all right? Was it only a false alarm?

Just before dawn, Raven couldn't stand the waiting any longer. She had to get back to Heathglade, and she couldn't wait for Christopher to send for her.

She dressed quickly in the warmest thing she'd brought, an emerald green wool gown with a high neck and long sleeves. Then she stole downstairs to retrieve her cloak hanging in the hall.

She stepped out the back door just as the first pink rays of morning began to soften the sky and made her way to the stable. Once there, Raven knocked gently on the stableboy's door. Presently the door opened sluggishly, and a very sleepy young man, about 17 years of age, peered through the opening.

"Excuse me for waking you," Raven apologized, "but this is an emergency. I am a guest of the Carletons, but something has happened. I must get home immediately. Could you saddle me a horse?"

The boy scratched his head drowsily and nodded without saying a word.

Twenty minutes later the boy helped Raven into the saddle. "Thank you," she said, "and please tell the Carletons I'll return the horse as soon as I can." Then without waiting for a reply, she dug her heels into the mare's flanks, and they thundered down the drive.

Raven never gave a thought to her lack of riding skills. She simply hung on and let the horse have its head. In no time at all, she and the horse were one. They flew through the early morning light like jockey and racehorse until they galloped full tilt into Heathglade's yard. She slid off the horse and handed the reins to a startled Mr. Bridges.

"Mr. Bridges," she asked breathlessly, "how is the major?"

"Don't know fer sure, Miss. The doctor is still here, though."

She nodded absently and then raced for the house.

Raven burst through the back door and found Mrs. Bagly standing over the teakettle on the stove. "Mrs. Bagly, how is the major? He isn't, isn't . . ."

"No, Miss," she said kindly. "But it's that close. It's his heart, Miss. He and Mrs. Mallory were in the study last night when he had some kind of attack."

"Is Mr. Mallory with him?"

"No, Miss. The doctor made him go to bed several hours ago. The major was resting comfortably, ya see, so there was no need for him to be stayin' up."

"Has the doctor been with Major Mallory all night?"

"Not quite, Miss. I believe he's restin' himself just now, but you don't have to worry none. Mrs. Higgins is watchin' the major so there's no need to fret."

Raven felt suddenly exhausted and sighed. "Thank goodness, everything seems to be under control." She walked over and slumped down in a chair by the work table. "Oh, Mrs. Bagly," she moaned, "it's been a horrendous night, hasn't it?"

The housekeeper took the boiling teakettle off the fire and poured the steaming liquid into a silver teapot. "Aye, that it has, Miss. Seems like ill fortune has found a new place to dwell."

"I feel like this is all my fault, Mrs. Bagly. If I hadn't come here, none of this would have happened. After all, everything was fine until I came along. And then?"

Mrs. Bagly's snort sounded remarkably similar to Flora's. "Don't you believe it, Miss," she replied setting a fresh cup of hot tea in front of Raven. "This hasn't been a happy home since Mrs. Mallory came into it."

Raven's blood began to race. "Mrs. Bagly, you said Camilla was with Major Mallory when he had his attack. You don't suppose . . ."

Mrs. Bagly sat down beside Raven. "I don't know, Miss. All I do know is that they were locked up in there together, and all of a sudden Mrs. Mallory came running out saying the major had had a fit of some kind. I tell you, Miss, it was awful. But, thank heavens, Mr. Frasier was here. He handled everything and got the major upstairs."

Raven took a healthy gulp of tea. "Mrs. Bagly, does the doctor know what caused the major's attack?"

"Well, he said it was most probably caused by the strain of Miss Jessica's passing. He hasn't been well for some time, you know. We just never knew what it was."

Raven finished her tea and then went upstairs to change. During her flight home, her skirt had gotten wet and soiled from the mud kicked up by the horse's hooves, and her hair was a mess.

She washed up, put on the same garnet wool dress she had worn the day Aunt Jessica had died and tied a ribbon around her free-flowing hair before going to check on Christopher.

She knocked softly on his door and got no response. She knocked again and still heard nothing. Finally, she opened the door slowly and peered in.

The room, with its drapes drawn tightly, sat bathed in complete darkness except for a faint glow coming from the fireplace. She crept in and closed the door behind her. She stopped and listened until she heard Christopher's deep breathing, then she tiptoed over to the fireplace and placed several more small logs on the fire before turning around.

When movement off to the side of the room caught her attention, she looked in that direction just in time to see and hear the wall panel snap shut.

She gasped. "Who's there?" she asked shakily.

Her words awakened Christopher, and he sat up abruptly. "What is it?" he asked in alarm. "Is it my father? Has something happened?"

"I'm sorry," Raven apologized, coming toward him. "I just came to see if you were all right and then I put some logs—"

"Raven?" he asked in amazement. "What on earth are you doing here? I thought you were at the Carletons'."

As she approached the foot of the bed, something caught on one of her slippers. She bent down to pick it up. When she raised up, Raven held a lilac silk robe in her trembling hands. She recognized it as Camilla's.

"What is it?" Christopher asked curiously. "What have you got there?"

Raven tore her tortured eyes from the flimsy robe and stared vacantly at Christopher. He sat there, naked from the waist up, his bare chest glowing in the firelight. Beside him, the spare pillow was rumpled and the covers were messy and thrown back. He had not been alone.

Christopher looked at the robe and then followed Raven's concentration to the empty space in the bed beside himself. Everything—the robe, the rumpled pillow and mussed sheets—

suddenly registered. He blanched. "Dear God," he whispered.

Raven threw the robe across the bed and bolted for the door. She felt herself wanting to scream but fought back the urge. If only she could get to her room. There she could exorcise the devils that tormented her soul, where nobody could witness the wretchedness of her pain.

"Raven, stop!" Christopher sprang from the bed and grabbed her as she darted past him. He flung her down on the bed to trap her there with the weight of his own body. "Don't believe it, Raven," he snarled between his teeth as he fought against her struggles.

She began to writhe like a crazed animal. "Let me go," she shrieked. "Please, just let me go."

Christopher began shaking her. "Listen to me, damn it. I'll be damned if I let this ludicrous misunderstanding spoil our happiness." And then he kissed her savagely.

Raven, exhausted from no sleep and now drained from a pain so intense as to be unbearable, quit fighting. She simply went limp and began to sob like a helpless little child.

Feeling the tension leave her body, Christopher released her lips just enough to speak. "Raven, listen to me. I know it looks bad, but it isn't true."

She shook her head slowly. "No," she whimpered hoarsely. "No more lies." She moaned painfully. "Ohhh, I loved you so. I believed you and trusted you. How could you do this to me after making me believe you loved me, too?"

He wrapped his arms around her and squeezed her to him as he kissed the area just below her ear. "Oh Raven, I do love you," he groaned. "Dear God, surely you don't believe I could bed another woman on our wedding night."

The thoughts his words evoked caused her stomach to lurch, and she began to struggle again. "Please," she begged. "Let me up. I'm going to be sick."

He raised up enough for her to push him away, and she scrambled to her feet just as she began to gag. Her feet touched the floor, but her legs had no strength in them. She sank slowly to the floor as a thick blanket of fog blinded her.

Chapter 14

An oppressive headache awakened Raven. She opened her eyes and found her own familiar bedroom ceiling staring down at her. It was a comforting sight, for here she felt safe and protected from the harsh truth awaiting outside the sanctity of her room. Here she could hide from the hideous reality of Christopher's betrayal and nurse her wounded heart in peace.

She lay there, remembering every sickening moment before she had fainted, until tears blurred her vision. She wiped them away briskly, took a deep breath and tried to sit up. The painful protest of tender stomach muscles prevented the attempt from being successful. Raven felt as if she had swallowed broken glass, and she eased herself back down. Seeking to relieve the discomfort, she rolled over and came face to face with Christopher's stormy brown eyes.

He sat in a chair beside the bed, watching her angrily. "Are you ready to have a sensible talk now?" he asked.

Raven rolled over with her back to him. "No," she replied in a dull monotone.

"I'm not leaving until we have this out, Raven."

"Please, Christopher," she mumbled, "I don't feel well. Just go away."

"Look, Raven," he replied wearily, "I know how the evidence must look to you, but it simply isn't true. I don't know how that robe got in my room. I swear to you, I was in my room alone."

"Go away," she repeated.

"No," he snapped angrily. "Not until you believe me. Lord, woman, I was sound asleep. You saw that."

She rolled back over and their eyes met. "I saw her leave, Christopher. She was still there when I walked in. Now go away and leave me alone. I don't feel well, and I don't want to hear any more lies."

He turned pale. "That witch," he hissed. "Don't you see, Raven? It was nothing but a mean, despicable trick. She wanted you to believe we had been together, so she planted the evidence for you to find."

Raven's stomach began to churn, and she sat up and put her feet over the side of the bed. "Christopher, please," she shouted, "I'm tired and sick and . . . and . . ." Her head felt as if it were about to burst, and she reached up to rub her aching brow with shaky fingers.

Christopher reached over and picked up a glass from her bedside table. "Here, drink this," he ordered. "The doctor said you would most probably have a headache when you awoke."

She took the glass and downed the fluid, but as soon as the contents hit her stomach, it rebelled and she had to fight to keep the liquid down.

"Stomach still giving you trouble?"

She nodded.

"I'm sorry," he replied. "I wouldn't think there was anything left to cause a problem."

Raven looked at him, slightly embarrassed. "I was sick, then?"

"I'm afraid so." He reached over and took the glass from her. "How do you feel now?"

She shrugged.

Christopher was watching her closely. "I love you, Raven," he murmured. "I know you don't know me very well—and believe me, I'm no saint—but I could never have done what you're accusing me of. I do have some honor in me, and, believe it or not, I meant every vow I made to you last night—including fidelity."

"Christopher, please," she moaned, "it's too late. I've seen and heard too much, and last night simply verified what my mind already knew." She sighed helplessly. "When I first saw the two of you together in the library and overheard your scheming, I should have realized how things were. I suppose, deep down, I did, but I wanted so much to believe otherwise that I let you explain it away. Then, at the ball, when I saw the two of you together, well, by then I was so in love with you that I was unable to recognize the indisputable proof in front of me. But that has all changed now. You've given me no choice but to see things as they really are, and now that you have, please don't make the situation any more unpleasant than it already is."

He sat in silence for a moment. "What are you going to do, Raven?" he asked at last.

She shook her head. "I don't know. I can't think straight right now."

He shifted in the chair. "My father is asking for you. Are you going to tell him?"

An expression of horror settled on her face. "Oh, Christopher," she breathed, "I've been so caught up in my own unhappiness, I'd forgotten about the major. Is he going to be all right?"

"I don't know," he replied grimly. "The doctor doesn't either. He's gravely ill, Raven, and the doctor says if he has any upsets, anything at all, it could kill him. That's why I'm asking you not to say anything to him about our problems." He chuckled, the sound harsh and cynical. "You know, you complained to me once that you didn't feel very much in control of anything, and I told you then you were wrong. You have always had an immeasurable amount of power over us and never more so than now." He leaned forward. "At this moment, Raven, you have the power of life and death over my father, and I have to know what you're going to do with it."

The potion the doctor had left for her must have been a miracle drug because Raven suddenly felt better, or perhaps it was that dreaded temper working wonders of its own. Whatever the cause, Raven rose to new heights of indignation.

"You know, you really are the most hateful man I have ever encountered," she hissed. "How dare you imply that I would do anything to cause any more damage to your father's health? I'm not simple-minded!"

"Raven, please," he muttered impatiently, "this is not the time to quibble over your misinterpretation of my meaning. Right now, my father's health should be what we are concentrating on, not my poor choice of words. Can't you understand? I just don't want you to say anything that will cause him any shock or distress."

"You insufferable toad!" she said. "You're not concerned about your father's health, not a whit. You're just afraid if I tell him about you and Camilla, he will deny you that precious control of the Mallory finances you and Camilla are so worried about."

Christopher's face turned stony except for his eyes which glittered with a dangerous warning. "You know, for a tuppence, I'd take you over my knee and whale the daylights out of you for that remark." He stood up abruptly and started for the door. "If you would just stop and think about it, Raven, you would realize that if all I wanted was the control of our finances, then his demise would be more important to me than his recovery." He stopped at the door and turned back to her. "And incidentally, for your information I've had complete control of our finances for some time now. I've had it since Robert's death, three years ago."

Raven sat on the side of the bed regretting her words as he slammed the door behind him.

She really hadn't meant the hateful things she had said to him, and she certainly didn't believe them. She had just wanted to hurt him. It had been a reflex to the pain she felt because the truth of the matter was, regardless of what he had done, she still loved him. It seemed that disease she had been so certain she could recover from earlier now had proved fatal.

After a few moments, she got up slowly and walked over to the mirror to see if she looked as wretched as she felt. She did. Her face bore the ravages of pain and sickness. Her eyes, dark to begin with, had deep shadows under them, and the effect emphasized the pallid tinge to her complexion. She sighed. It would take the skill of a magician to repair last night's damage.

She bathed her face in cool water. Then she applied a generous coat of rose oil to the sooty shading under her eyes before adding a layer of rice powder. After that, a stiff brushing of her hair and a change into a royal blue mohair gown transformed her into a human **being** once more, if only externally.

An hour later, she opened the major's bedroom door and peered in cautiously. Flora, sitting beside the major's bed, rose from her chair and motioned for Raven to come in as she quietly prepared to leave them in privacy.

Once at the bed, Raven leaned over to get a good look at the major. Her breath caught in her throat. Lying there so ominously still, she barely recognized the robustly healthy gentleman she had come to love. Pale and drawn, he had aged 20 years since the last time she had seen him. The silver ring of hair was still there, but now the slightly florid complexion had faded into a pasty shade of yellow, and his lips, as well as his hands, had a bluish cast to them. He looked terribly ill.

He heard her gasp and opened his eyes. "Oh, my dear," he mumbled weakly, "you have come at last."

Raven picked up his hand and kissed it. "Please, Major, you mustn't try to talk. You must save your strength so you can get well."

He shook his head slowly. "No, my dear, what I have to say to you is important, and I must say it now."

Raven continued to hold his hand but eased down in the chair beside the bed. "Very well, but if I see you becoming tired, I shall leave."

He chuckled. "Very well, my dear. Already issuing dictates, I see." He paused and looked at her, smiling. "So, you at last have married my son."

Tears welled up in her eyes, and she nodded. "Yes," she whispered.

He sighed as if in great relief. "I cannot tell you how happy that makes me and how grateful I am that he has found you. He loves you, you know."

"Does he?" she asked tremulously.

"Oh yes, he does. Oh, I know at first he denied his feelings to you. You both did." He grinned. "My word, it's been a delight watching the two of you discover what William and I suspected would happen if the two of you ever met. But now that you have found each other, you mustn't let anything destroy the love between you. Love is a precious thing, my dear. Embrace it, abide in it and fight to keep possession of it, for there are those that would like to see it spoiled."

"Yes, I know." Her voice sounded strained.

He frowned. "I'm too late, aren't I?" he asked sadly. "Something is wrong."

Raven shook her head adamantly. "No, no. I'm just worried about you, that's all. Everything else is just fine," she lied. "I promise."

"You can't fool me, my dear. You don't look like a new bride. You look as if your heart is broken." He began beating the covers with a feeble hand. "She's done something, hasn't she? Oh, why didn't I send her away long ago? I should have, regardless of the consequences."

"No, no," Raven cried. "Please, Major, it's just been a harrowing night, that's all. I didn't get

294

much sleep last night. Well, none of us did. It's just that we've been worried about you."

He hesitated a moment and then closed his eyes. Raven thought he had drifted off to sleep, and she sat with him awhile, still holding his hand, until her back began to ache from the uncomfortable position she was in.

She rose from the chair and began taking her hand from his when his eyes opened again and he gripped her hand tightly. "Take care of him, my dear. Do not allow her lies and schemes to damage your future together. Promise me."

She nodded. "Yes," she whispered, "I promise." And then she bent down and kissed him on the forehead. "You must rest now," she commanded gently. "I want you to get well, and so does Christopher."

The major patted her hand. "Oh, I intend to. I can't possibly leave this life with things the way they are. That would be most cowardly. No, I must put them right before I go. I must see that you and Christopher have a chance at happiness." He smiled up at her. "Now, run along, child, and don't worry about me any longer. Everything is going to be all right."

Once out of the room, Raven felt a desperate need for fresh air. The rain had stopped during the night, but the ground was still wet and soggy, so instead of going out, she went up.

As she headed up the stairs, she agonized over the major's health. What would happen to him when he realized that everything was not all right and never would be? Would he suffer a relapse? He was so certain that Christopher loved her. What would become of him when he discovered his fondest wish would never be anything more than just that?

When she reached the roof, Raven found the door propped open. She stepped out and looked briefly at the clear, crisp countryside washed clean by the night's rain. Everything looked so fresh and unsoiled. If only her heart could feel that way. If only . . . The sound of muffled voices behind a nearby gable caught her attention, and she wondered if work had begun on the loose stones edging the roof. Curious, she headed for the sound and walked around the corner of the abutment only to stop short.

"Of course, darling, I'll tell her anything you like."

Christopher and Camilla stood facing each other. Camilla was smiling up into his face as he held her by the shoulders.

Raven whirled around to leave but Christopher saw her. "Raven," he shouted sternly, "stay where you are." He dragged Camilla over in front of her. "Now," he said roughly, "we're going to have some truths spoken." He gripped Camilla with one hand and took hold of Raven with the other. "Tell her, Camilla," he hissed and shook her roughly. "Tell her what really happened last night or, so help me, I'll do you damage."

"Darling, please," Camilla whined. "You don't have to be so violent. After all, I've already agreed to tell her, haven't I?" She turned to Raven and smiled. "It's true, Raven, what he said. I did play a nasty little trick on you." She turned back to Christopher. "Now, I've confessed. Can I go now?"

"Stop it, Camilla," he snarled. "Tell her, damn it. Tell her exactly what you did."

"Oh, very well," Camilla sighed wearily. "I went into Christopher's room last night and mussed up the covers next to him and then deliberately left my robe for you to find." She turned back to Christopher. "There, darling, I told you I would say it right, didn't I?"

Christopher lost control and grabbed Camilla by the throat with both hands. "You miserable little witch," he spat. "You've deliberately made it appear to be a lie."

Raven began beating on him. "Christopher, stop it," she yelled. "Stop it, I said. Please. You're going to hurt her."

He suddenly released Camilla as though she were a hot poker, and she staggered backwards, coughing. "I'm sorry, darling," she sobbed. "I tried to tell it right. Didn't I say what you wanted me to?"

Christopher glared at her murderously. "Get out of my sight, Camilla," he wheezed between gasps of breath, "and stay away from me, or so help me, I'll finish the job of wringing your detestable neck."

Camilla took his advice and bolted for the safety of the open doorway.

Raven looked at Christopher, her eyes dull and lifeless. "Please, Christopher," she replied quietly, "it just doesn't matter anymore."

He reached over and took her face in his hands. Their eyes met. "Don't say that, Raven," he murmured. "It'll never be over until you believe me. I'm not going to lose you, Raven, not because of her."

She pulled away from him. "Don't you see?" she said jerkily. "Last night when you made love to Camilla, it was you who destroyed everything —you, Christopher, not Camilla. The choice was yours to make, and you made it." She began to cry softly. "Oh, Christopher," she whimpered, "just a few short hours ago, I loved you so and was happy beyond my wildest dreams because I thought you returned my love. But I was such a fool, wasn't I? I believed my love was enough for you and that was my folly because now there is nothing but a terrible emptiness within me, and the pain far exceeds the punishment for my foolishness. So please, just don't make it any worse for me by trying to continue the lie."

Christopher opened his mouth to speak, but before he could reply, she turned and fled from the roof, leaving him alone in the deceptively cool sunshine.

The next day Raven's belongings were moved into the bedroom next to Christopher's, but the adjoining door separating their rooms remained locked. Every evening she heard him come in followed by the usual sounds of retiring. Occasionally she would be awakened by the muffled sounds of pacing late in the night. Once, he rapped softly on the door and called her, but she refused to answer. After that, he left her alone.

The next several days passed quietly. The major seemed to be gaining strength, and he began eating better and sleeping less. Raven spent most of her time in his company. She would read to him or occupy his mind with light conversation while she concentrated on various sewing projects. Once in a while, she would serve as his secretary and write letters for him. All in all, the arrangement was beneficial to both of them. It provided the major with constant supervision and prevented her from coming into contact with Camilla or Christopher.

Christopher, of course, spent his days taking over the management of the Mallory finances, a job Raven was certain he enjoyed, and they saw very little of each other.

What Camilla was up to, Raven had no idea, but Julia and Jeremy were becoming quite an item of interest. According to Flora, romance was in full bloom, and the whole countryside had been watching breathlessly as the dashing Jeremy courted the fair Julia with the flair and polish for which he was famous.

One afternoon into her second week of hibernation in the major's room, Flora relieved Raven and insisted that she go for a walk to get some fresh air. She finally agreed, but only reluctantly. So, at a little after two, Raven donned her bonnet and cloak and slipped out the back door.

She had almost reached the first rise leading out onto the moors when she heard her name being called. She turned and saw Jeremy scampering up the grade behind her.

"Ya-hoo, Raven. Wait up," he called. He finally made it up the slope and stood panting for breath.

"Jeremy, what on earth are you doing here?" she asked pleasantly. "Where's Julia?"

"Oh, she's washing her hair or some other foolish nonsense you women do."

"But what are you doing out here? You're no outdoor enthusiast."

"Well, for one thing I've come to see if you're still alive. I saw you from my bedroom window, and I thought if I joined you maybe we could have a talk. Gad, Raven, I've barely seen you since your marriage. Where have you been hiding?"

She laughed. "I haven't been hiding, silly," she lied. "I've just been busy looking after the major. I'm sorry if it seems I've deserted you. It's just been a hectic time. Besides, I understand you haven't been exactly bored without me." Raven took his arm, and they started down the back side of the slope. "Now, tell me," she asked coyly, "what's this I hear about you and Julia?"

Jeremy stopped. "I say, Raven, that Julia is a bit of all right, isn't she?"

Raven giggled. "I don't know. Is she?"

He turned slightly pink. "Well, yes, she is, rather. Oh, I know she's a bit saucy, and there are some men that don't like that sort of thing. But I do. That's what I like about her. She certainly keeps me on my toes, I tell you."

They began to walk again. "And you like that also?"

Jeremy assumed a solemn expression. "Yes, I do," he answered gravely. "I've decided I need a girl who can keep a tight rein on me. That's been my trouble all along, you know. I've never had limits. That's why I've never grown up."

"Hmmm," Raven murmured, "this sounds serious, Jeremy. Are you so sure you're ready for such a sobering change as maturity?"

He laughed. "Sounds ridiculous, doesn't it? Me, Jeremy Frasier, suddenly becoming concerned with such mundane things as nesting materials and putting nuts up for the winter. Ugh. Sounds absolutely ghastly, now that I think about it."

Raven couldn't help but smile. "It sounds as if you're in love, Jeremy. Are you?"

He laughed nervously. "Yes, well, I guess I am. It seems to be the only logical explanation for my rather odd behavior, doesn't it? I mean, I can't sleep, I don't have much of an appetite, and I seem to wander about in a most pleasant daze all the time."

"Jeremy," Raven cried, "you really are in love. Tell me, have you mentioned anything to Julia about these so-called feelings of domesticity?"

"Heavens, no. It's way too soon for that. Anyway, Julia has invited me to stay on for a while and Chris has graciously extended the invitation, so there's time enough for that. After all, we barely know each other, and besides, maybe these deranged symptoms will simply fade away like a bad cold. They have before, you know."

Raven was no longer listening. She stopped. "You say Chris extended the invitation?"

"Certainly. Didn't he say anything to you?" He grinned. "My word, Raven, I know newlyweds are in a world of their own, but don't the two of you ever talk about anything?"

Raven began to walk again in an effort to hide her embarrassment. "Well, things have been in such a turmoil, what with the major's illness and Christopher having to take over for his father that, well, we haven't had much of a chance to talk about anything."

"You know, Raven, now that we're on the subject, I have to admit to you that I was wrong about Chris. At first, I didn't like him at all. I thought he was a bit pompous and stiff-necked. But he's turned out to be quite a nice chap, and I like him very much."

"Apparently so," she mused, "since he's climbed the ranks from scoundrel to Chris in a mere two short weeks."

"Gad, Raven, you're not going to hold that against me, are you? And anyway, you ought to know by now what a terrible judge of people I am—well, most of the time, at any rate."

"Most of the time?"

He shivered dramatically. "It's that Mrs. Mallory. I mean, she's a bit of blight, isn't she? I'm sorry, Raven, I know she is your sister-in-law and all, but I never did like her." He shook his head. "I don't know. She's just got a predatory quality about her that causes my spine to tingle, and now that she's taken to skulking about the place, well, she makes me positively skittish."

Once again Jeremy had caught Raven's attention. "Predatory in what way, Jeremy?"

"Well, how should I know? If I knew that then she wouldn't make me so uncomfortable, would she? She's getting some of it back though. Chris seems to be able to make her dance to his tune."

Raven's heart began to ache. "Yes," she mumbled. "Camilla is quite fond of Christopher. I imagine she would do just about anything to please him."

Jeremy snickered. "Fond, my eye. She's terrified of him! She skulks about the place, creeping around corners and hiding in shadowy nooks, trying to avoid him. But occasionally they do meet, and when they do, he gives her a look that would frighten Lucifer himself and she scurries away like a panic-stricken rabbit."

Raven frowned. "Are you sure, Jeremy? I mean, you said yourself you're not a very good judge of character. Maybe the same shortcoming could be applied to situations. Maybe you've just misinterpreted their exchange to a peculiar set of circumstances you weren't aware of."

Jeremy shook his head adamantly. "No, no. When I walked in on them once, he was threatening her with violence if she didn't remove herself from his presence. She very nearly knocked me down running from the room. No, I think it's safe to say that he abhors the sight of her and she is terrified of him. The only explanation I can come up with is the possibility that he blames her for the major's illness. She was with him when he had his attack, you know, and there's been talk amongst the servants."

Raven nodded. "Yes, I know," she responded, remembering Mrs. Bagly's vague implication.

"It really is a shame that no one likes her, at least no one except Julia," Jeremy continued. "But drat it, Raven, it's her own fault, I say."

Raven scarcely heard Jeremy now. Her mind was busy analyzing Jeremy's speculation. Was it possible that Christopher blamed Camilla for his father's attack? If so, then that would certainly explain the strange behavior Jeremy had witnessed.

A short time later, when they turned for home, their conversation drifted back to Julia. Raven listened with as much concentration as she could muster, but in the back of her mind she kept trying to piece together the evergrowing parts to a complicated puzzle.

Could Camilla be responsible for the major's sudden attack? Camilla knew very well that if the major were out of the way, Christopher would inherit everything, and then there would be nothing standing in the way of Christopher and her marrying—nothing, that is, except Raven. But from Camilla's standpoint, if she were desperate enough, that could be remedied. After all, if there was no Raven, there would be no wedding and no wife. That would account for the attempts on Raven's life although she still couldn't figure out how Camilla had managed the shooting. The falling stone was obvious. She had simply waited until Raven walked by and then heaved the stone over the edge. The poisoned bottle of brandy was certainly meant for Raven, only poor Aunt Jessica had found it first and had died in her place. Yes, all the pieces fit. The only problem was, Raven kept escaping death. After three attempts, maybe Camilla had decided to switch victims for a while. With the major being her most obstinate obstacle, perhaps she had decided to concentrate on eliminating him and then, at a later date, disposing of the last hateful impediment to her goal, Christopher's wife.

The more she thought about it, the more grotesquely simple it all seemed. Furthermore, knowing Camilla's desperation and determination, such a bizarre scheme began to have a sort of demented sense to it. The only thing that didn't make sense was Christopher's role in all of this. If she could figure all of this out, surely he had done the same thing, but for some reason he refused to intervene. Why? Was his ambition so great that he would stand by and allow murder to take place? Raven couldn't believe that. She wouldn't! Then there was the mystery of those papers Camilla supposedly had hidden. What were they, and why were they so important to Christopher?

By the time they reached home, Raven knew

how precarious her life was. From now on, every step she took, every bite of food she put in her mouth was a potential threat to her life, and there was no one capable of protecting her. Christopher couldn't . . . or wouldn't. Flora would be more hindrance than help. The major was as vulnerable as she, and Jeremy was . . . well, Jeremy. No, she was on her own against a determined killer, and Raven's only weapon against such a formidable opponent was her wits.

Chapter 15

The third week of October announced
the arrival of a bitter winter. The days
became frigid with frequent showers of
sleet resembling shards of glass soon replaced
by a gentle but steady powdering of large, fluffy,
snowflakes.

The countryside had taken on a lovely look of
enchantment, what with its dense crystal cloak,
and sometimes at night when the moon shone
bright, the normal winter scene of day would be
transformed into what appeared to be millions
of diamonds floating atop a silver-blue sea. But
even so, Raven often found herself peering out a
foggy window, wishing for the lazy summer days
gone by.

By now, Marigold had given up his grieving
station in Raven's room and had taken to follow-

ing her around just as he had Aunt Jessica. This meant that most of his time was spent in the major's room holding down a place of honor on the bed.

This morning, Raven was, as usual, standing by the major's window gazing out at a fresh blanket of snow when Marigold appeared beneath her feet and began bawling for attention.

The major, with his steady improvement, had taken to sitting in a chair by the fire. He noticed Marigold's curious behavior and chuckled. "Better pay attention to him, my dear. Looks as though he wants something."

She turned from the window and bent to pick him up, but he darted away from her and went to sit by one of the wall panels where he began to scratch at it tenaciously.

"What do you suppose that is all about?" Raven asked.

The major sighed with sadness. "Well, I'm no authority on felines, of course, but it looks as though he might be missing those excursions he and Jessica used to take with such relish through those ghastly passages." He feigned a cough. "Bloody bit of nonsense, if you ask me. I never could understand her obsession with them."

Of course he couldn't, thought Raven. He was never aware of Camilla's evil mental subjugation of his poor sister.

She walked over and scooped Marigold up in her arms. "Of course, that's it," she murmured. "To be perfectly honest, I'd completely forgotten about the passages, but naturally Marigold wouldn't. After all, those trips were a major part of his life for quite a while." She put her face down to nuzzle him, but he began to squirm until he broke free and jumped down, only to begin clawing at the wall once again.

"Better let him go, my dear. He seems adamant about it, and what harm can it do? It might even be good for him. Give him some exercise, if nothing else."

Raven tripped the latch, and the panel popped open. Marigold immediately stepped into the passage. Instead of continuing on, however, he stopped, sat down and called mournfully for Raven to follow.

"Well, don't just stand there, my dear," the major said. "With an invitation so graciously put, how could you possibly refuse?"

"Oh, no sir," Raven declined. "I couldn't possibly leave you alone. Why, if you needed something, there would be no one here with you."

"Nonsense," the major replied. "What could I possibly need? Just look at me. I'm settled in a comfortable chair with a good book, and I'm bundled up like an explorer ready for the arctic. Besides, Mrs. Higgins should be bringing my lunch shortly, and it's obvious he wants to show you something or at least requires your presence. Now run along. You've been cooped up in this room for far too long. It will give you a break from this tedious business of taking care of a crabby old man."

A few minutes later, Raven had followed Marigold to the wine cellar.

As soon as she released the latch and the panel swung open, Marigold darted out into the darkness. Raven wasn't nearly as adventuresome, and she eased herself more slowly down the rows of wine racks until she reached the storage room. The door was still open, and she walked in and lit the lamp from her candle.

Nothing had changed. There was the stack of empty boxes on the foot of the bed, just where she had left them, along with the piles of papers she had been categorizing when Christopher had ordered her to leave. The large trunk still sat in the corner, its top open, but the contents had been stuffed haphazardly inside. Everything appeared to be as it had before. Nothing had been touched or moved.

Marigold's whining interrupted Raven's inspection, and she found him clawing feverishly at the base of the trunk once again. She watched him as he stopped and sniffed his way around the outside of the trunk until he found another likely spot whereupon he renewed his scratching efforts.

Raven walked over and bent down beside him. "What's the matter, Marigold? Are you still trying to capture that elusive prey you missed before?"

He ignored her. Instead, he began a high-pitched bawl and increased his clawing endeavors with renewed vigor.

Raven could see that he was almost beside

himself. She tried to lift the trunk but it was too heavy, so she took a firm grip on its top edge and pulled the cumbersome receptacle away from the wall. He immediately scurried to the back of the trunk and started a new campaign from the rear.

Raven watched in bewilderment as he frantically tried to dig under the trunk. Then an idea struck her. Perhaps the object of his quest was inside the trunk rather than underneath it. She unloaded the chest, spilling its contents out on the stone floor but found nothing unusual. Disappointed, she began to replace the articles.

The aroma of cigars and Christopher's masculine cologne filled Raven's nostrils. She knew he was standing in the door.

"Still scavenging for secrets?" he asked.

The sound of his deep vibrant voice sent a mixture of pain and pleasure through Raven. She turned around to look at him nervously. "No," she answered shakily. "It's Marigold. He seems to be in a frenzy to catch something, and I was simply trying to aid his efforts."

Christopher leaned against the doorway, his arms folded across his chest. As usual he had on the loose fitting, white silk shirt that draped his frame with such alluring appeal. With her eyes, Raven could follow the outline of his broad shoulders and the solid muscles forming his arms beneath the sheer fabric. The sight teased her senses, and she felt that all too familiar wave of longing sweep over her, a longing, she reminded herself, she must learn to get over.

He pulled away from the door and came toward her. She sat on the floor in front of the trunk, and he reached down and helped her to her feet. "I went looking for you in my father's room, and he told me you and Marigold had gone exploring. Tell me, just how long have you been down here?" he asked, promptly releasing her.

She felt oddly disappointed and shrugged. "Not long. Why?"

"Because you're cold."

She had dressed in the same garnet dress she had worn the day Aunt Jessica had died. The gown was made of wool and had long sleeves, but even so, the lush fabric hadn't been enough to prevent the cold from permeating its thickness. As if to verify his observation, she shivered. "Yes," she agreed, "I suppose I am although I hadn't been aware of it until now."

Christopher reached down and grabbed a handful of moldy garments. He threw them in the trunk. "What on earth are you doing down here, anyway? I thought you were dedicated to the care and rehabilitation of my father. At least, you've certainly thrown every waking moment into that lofty endeavor."

At once she felt defensive. Was he criticizing her for leaving his father unattended? "I'm afraid it's Marigold's fault," she replied sheepishly. "He lured me down here to witness this arduous game of cat and mouse." She suddenly looked puzzled. "At least, that's what I think he's doing. What did you wish to see me about?"

Christopher slammed the lid. "I need your signature." He faced her. "I thought you would like to know, I've finally gotten around to writing Mr. Feeny. I've notified him of our marriage and instructed him to take the necessary steps required for the processing of your inheritance. It will require your signature though."

Raven had completely forgotten about her inheritance. "Oh, yes," she mumbled. "I suppose it would, wouldn't it? Is it upstairs?"

"Yes. I left the papers with my father."

"Yes, of course," she stammered. She turned to leave. "Well, I guess I'd better go and . . ."

"Just a moment, Raven."

Raven noticed a certain terseness in his voice, and she slowly turned back to face him. "Was there something else?"

"Is it always to be this way between us, Raven?" he asked quietly.

Raven feared any private contact with Christopher for this very reason. That's why she had gone out of her way to avoid him these last few weeks. "Please, Christopher, under the circumstances, I . . ."

He walked over and took her by the shoulders. "Are we to spend the rest of our lives avoiding each other with never a word between us?"

She concentrated on the buttons on his shirt. "No," she sighed. "As soon as I receive my inheritance, I'll be leaving and that will be the end of our association. Until then, I think it's best if we try not to cause any more pain to one another than is necessary."

313

"Come here," he grumbled and led her over to the bed where he sat down beside her. "Is that what you really believe, Raven? Do you honestly believe in your heart that I could be so callous as to hurt you that way?"

She sprang from the bed. "No, no," she muttered. "I don't think for one moment that you are a cruel or deceitful person." She turned and faced him, her eyes pleading. "I know you didn't do it deliberately. You just couldn't help it. You love her, Christopher, and you always will." She began to wring her hands. "Oh, don't you see? I never should have come here. It was wrong of our fathers to play God. You can't force one person to love another just because you perceive it to be beneficial or expedient. Love doesn't work that way."

He stood up and took her in his arms. "Maybe not," he sighed, "but I fell in love with you, just the same. And you fell in love with me."

She slipped out of his arms. "That isn't enough, Christopher," she cried. "Oh, I believe you love me, perhaps a little, but Camilla will always have a place in your soul. If I didn't love you, then maybe it wouldn't matter. But I do, and because I do, that knowledge would destroy me. Can't you understand?"

He reached up and took her face in his hands. "I understand a lot of things I didn't understand before, one being what a bloody fool I've been, expecting you to believe mere words when all about you the overpowering evidence seemed to imply the reverse. Now, come back and sit down. It's time you knew the truth." He took her hand and led her back to the bed where he set her down once again.

Instead of joining her, he stood before her and lit a cigar. "In the past few weeks," he began, "I've been doing a lot of thinking, and I've come to the conclusion that I've expected too much of you. Hell, if the situation had been reversed, I wouldn't have believed you either, not for a second. Lord, I would have killed the son of a . . . the gentleman in question." He started to walk about the room aimlessly. "You've always been wrong about Camilla and me." He chuckled maliciously. "Lord, if you only knew how much I loathe that woman you'd see how ludicrous this whole situation is." He stopped pacing and looked at her earnestly. "She's going away, Raven. I've talked to my father, and we're sending her packing. I've given her three days to be out of this house or else I throw her out."

Raven gasped. "But why? I mean, why now?"

"Because the threat she's holding over us can't compare with the damage she's causing by staying." He threw the cigar down and ground it out with his boot before resuming his aimless walking. "Oh, Raven, I thought by pretending to be in love with her I could somehow get my hands on that blasted confession. You see, we were safe as long as she thought there was a possibility of her marrying the Mallory heir once again. I mean, she would have to be crazy to kill the golden goose, so to speak. And then there was my father. It meant so much to him not to have the family name sullied that I was willing to try just about anything."

Raven interrupted him. "Christopher, what threat and what confession? What are you talking about?"

He ran a hand through his hair in an irritable gesture. "Robert's confession. Oh, Raven, I don't know where to begin. The gist of it is, Robert embezzled a lot of money from our various companies. Apparently he did it in an effort to keep up with Camilla's lavish spending sprees. I suppose, when he finally realized there would be no end to it, he wrote out a confession, listing the amounts he had taken from each company and included a letter admitting his guilt. Those were the secret papers Aunt Jessica babbled to you about and those are the papers I've torn this house apart looking for."

"But Christopher, what difference does it make? I mean, I know he did wrong, but it was the family business after all. Who would care? In essence, he only stole from the family, didn't he?"

"Oh, Raven, if it only concerned the family, that would be one thing, but we have stockholders, for heaven's sake. Do you have any idea how that kind of information, if made public, would affect our credibility as a safe and competant company for investments? Why, if that confession ever becomes public, every stockholder we have, and there are hundreds, will be breaking down our door, demanding their money. And if that happens, we'll be out of business within a week."

Raven paled. "Christopher, you can't let that happen. Can't you reason with her? I mean, maybe she would take a settlement. You know, offer her a generous amount of money in exchange for the confession."

"Lord, woman, don't you think my father has already tried? Oh, no, she wouldn't have any of that. And why should she, when she can have a steady income for life? Why do you think she's still here?"

Raven shrugged. "I . . . I assume because she is in love with you," she murmured hesitantly.

"Oh, yes, there's always that, isn't there." He sneered. "Well, I'll tell you the real reason. It's because she's been bleeding my father out of twenty thousand pounds a year since Robert's death just to keep that confession private, and she would never drift too far from an eternal fountain of money like that."

"Yes, but if you asked her," Raven suggested eagerly, "maybe she would take the offer. After all, Christopher, she's in love with you. Maybe—"

"Ahh, that's another little macabre twist to this sordid business," he muttered. "I couldn't ask her because, up until this morning, Camilla didn't know I knew about the confession or that she had it. In that, we've both been walking a tightrope, so to speak. Had she known, she would have undoubtedly used it as a bargaining tool in which to force me to marry her. And it would have worked, if you hadn't entered the picture. But that was her fatal mistake. She waited too long and was afraid to use the one weapon she had to force me into marriage. She was uncertain, you see, of how I would react to the knowledge of her extortion. She couldn't take the chance of telling me about it because she feared, if I ever found out about it, I would do exactly what I did."

"What did you do?" Raven asked, her voice barely audible.

"I simply told her everything. I told her why I came home when Robert died. My father had written to me about Robert's confession and what Camilla was up to. I told her the only reason I pretended to love her was to get possession of that confession and then I intended to throw her out when I got it. I took relish in explaining the depth of my hatred for her and the revulsion I had for myself for ever loving her to begin with."

"Oh, Christopher," Raven breathed, "you shouldn't have done that. Now she will certainly use that confession against you."

"Let her," he snarled. "I told her to take the bloody thing and do her worst because I didn't give a damn—and I don't. That's the reaction she feared, you see. Heavens, we started out with nothing once. We can do it again. Besides, being penniless is a small enough price to pay for ridding ourselves of that worthless piece of baggage."

"But Christopher, why have you done this now? After all that's happened, why now?"

He walked over and sat down beside her. "Because I'm tired, Raven," he sighed wearily. "I'm tired of living a lie, of watching people's lives damaged or destroyed and all under the name of love. It's ironic, isn't it, how many kinds of love there are in the world and how they effect the people who suffer from them?"

"I don't understand what you mean," Raven whispered.

"No," he groaned, "you wouldn't. You've only known the pure, pristine variety that we read about in story books, but even that can be distorted until it wreaks havoc on everyone concerned. Now, you take the kind of love I feel for my father, and his for me. Because of our desire to protect the other from any unpleasantness or worry, neither of us bothered to tell the other what we were doing. He thought I really was in love with Camilla, and because he had already witnessed one son destroyed by her, he contrived to marry me off to you before I succumbed to Camilla's charms. That's why you were brought here. What he didn't know, of course, was the depth of my hatred for her and that my perceived interest in her was only a ruse to possibly gain possession of that blasted confession in order to save him from the humiliation and financial ruin that is sure to come. You see now how love, even with the best of motives, can complicate, confuse and very often destroy people's lives?"

"I can understand the major's motives," she replied, quietly, "but what were yours? Why did you agree to our marriage? You knew you were only playing a game with her."

He lit another cigar. "An honest question deserves an honest answer, although I'm not very proud of it." He blew a large cloud of smoke toward the ceiling. "About the time you arrived, the situation between Camilla and me was becoming rather sticky. You see, I was running out of excuses why we couldn't get married. One of them was that silly business of being denied control of our finances. Lord, by then I was desperate. When you arrived, I looked at you. You were pretty, intelligent and very, very desirable. When my father explained the problem you had with your inheritance, I told myself, why not? Hell, it would solve both our problems. And so, I agreed. You would get your inheritance, and I would have the perfect excuse for not marrying Camilla. When I made that ludicrous bargain with you, I had every intention of abiding by the rules. Unfortunately, I hadn't counted on falling in love with you. Remember me telling you once that you were an unexpected complication?"

She nodded.

"Well, apparently I'm a master of understatement. Believe me, things were complicated enough without me becoming dotty over some little slip of a girl with a fiery temper and a perceptive mind. By the time I realized how much I wanted you—and I mean permanently

—you had seen Camilla and me in the library and believed we were having an affair. Lord," he muttered, "it was like walking the plank. I couldn't stop my seduction of Camilla without losing control of that damn confession. If she had suspected my ardor for her had diminished, she would have released those papers to the press just out of vindictiveness, and we would have been in for it. On the other hand, as long as I played the game with her, you pulled further and further away from me. So all in all, it's been a bloody little game of wits."

"It's been more than that, Christopher," Raven whispered. "It's been a murderous game."

He threw the cigar down and stomped it out as he sprang from the bed. "Don't you think I know that?" he snarled. "Oh Lord, there's not an hour that goes by that I don't blame myself for Aunt Jessica's death, but I honestly didn't think she would go that far."

"You didn't?" Raven asked sarcastically. "Did you perhaps think my being shot and having a stone thrown down on me just some nasty little temper tantrum? Oh, nothing serious, just a few trivial pranks brought on by minor fits of jealousy, but nothing really to be concerned about."

"That's not fair, Raven," he muttered.

"No," she screamed, "it's *not* fair! You knew very well what was happening. I tried to tell you, but you refused to listen. You intentionally set me up as a target. You admitted as much."

"I know that," he thundered, "but I never thought she would resort to murder. Then, when Aunt Jessica died, I realized just how dangerous she was, and all I could think about was how I could protect you. Why do you suppose I arranged for our hasty marriage? I thought once we were married I would be in a better position to watch out for you. I could be close to you, and at night you would be with me." He laughed harshly. "Foolish of me, wasn't it?"

"What is foolish," she cried, "is you not going to the authorities. Why hasn't she been arrested and put away? She's committed murder, Christopher, and very probably will again before you do something."

"Knowing something and proving it are two different things, Raven. Can you actually prove that Camilla shot you or threw that stone down on you or poisoned that brandy bottle?"

"Well, no, but—"

"Well, neither can Constable Wicks. I've told him everything I know and everything I suspect, but there's nothing he can do about it without proof."

Raven was becoming numb from the cold, and her fingers no longer had any feeling in them. She grasped her upper arms and rubbed them briskly. "So," she muttered angrily, standing up, "it seems that nothing has changed, has it? Camilla is still free to walk around and arrange for my death anytime she pleases." She headed for the door. "I just hope, if she succeeds," she flung over her shoulder, "she will leave some proof behind this time, otherwise your little contest of wits won't be any more successful than Marigold's."

She stormed from the room, leaving only Christopher to observe Marigold patiently clawing out a pile of dirt between the flagstones making up the floor.

By the time she reached her room, Raven was crying. She slammed the door and fell down on her bed to smother the sound in the abundant feather mattress.

After several minutes, she regained her composure and reached into her pocket for her handkerchief. Her fingers felt something cold and hard. She sat up and pulled out the mysterious object. It was a pendant, inexpensive but pretty, threaded on a broken chain. She stared at it for a moment and then remembered. She had found it wrapped around the bed in the cellar room the day Aunt Jessica had died. The pendant was about an inch in diameter with scalloped etching around its edge. On one side a "C" was engraved and on the other side was "M."

Michael, thought Raven. It must have belonged to Michael, the young man who had disappeared several years ago. She shivered. Why did that possibility frighten her? She knew why, of course. It was because she was certain he had never left. She quickly wrapped the pendant in her handkerchief and stuffed it inside the pillowcase on her bed. For some reason, she wanted to keep her discovery a secret. There was something very strange about Michael's abrupt departure, and somehow she knew this pendant would help solve the mystery of his disappearance.

That night, Raven turned in early. She felt more fatigued than usual, almost as if she had been drugged. The thought occurred to her, and she fought the inclination to shut her eyes with a good book from the library. But after two hours of struggle, she convinced herself that if she had been drugged, it would have taken affect before then, so she set the book down and went to open the drapes before putting out her candle.

It was another clear night with the moon's reflection glistening on the snow. The phenomenon was lovely and produced a faint cast of light into her room. That illumination together with the glow from the fire gave her a sense of security, and she crawled into bed and fell asleep almost immediately.

Several hours later, something woke her. She lay there quietly for several minutes, listening for any sound, but heard nothing. Then she became aware of a slight pressure on her stomach. She reached down and touched Marigold's fluffy tail.

"Well, it's about time you put in an appearance," she mumbled with affection. "But you're not about to sleep there." She extended her hand and tried to brush him aside.

Raven's heart began to pound. Marigold felt unnatural. With shaking fingers, she clumsily lit her candle and stared down at the hapless object in her lap. Marigold lay there, his mouth twisted into a snarl. There was a fuchsia sash knotted around his neck. Someone had strangled the poor thing to death and then had delivered it into her bedroom for her to find. Someone had sent her a death message. Camilla!

Chapter 16

Raven sat paralyzed with fear. She couldn't scream, she couldn't move, she couldn't breathe. She simply sat staring at Marigold's lifeless body and at what she perceived to be her own destiny.

It could have been moments or years, but at some point a log collapsed in the fireplace and movement returned to her limbs. The sound jarred her into action and she moved her adopted friend off her lap and with palsied limbs climbed from her bed.

Before she realized what she was doing, Raven found herself at the adjoining door to Christopher's room. With fingers almost useless because of their trembling, she turned the lock and opened the door.

Christopher sat in a chair before the fireplace,

fully dressed and staring morosely into the flames. In one hand he held a glass of brandy, in the other a decanter. So engrossed was he in his thoughts that he failed to hear Raven until she spoke.

"Christopher?" she called, her voice nothing more than a hoarse whisper.

Startled, he looked up. Raven stood in the doorway, barefoot and without her robe, clutching either side of the doorframe. The muted light in the room reflected on her chalk-white face and revealed the pinched look of sheer terror.

He dropped the glass and decanter and stood up. "Raven?" he asked, alertness in his voice. "What's the matter? What's happened?"

She took two drunken steps toward him. "Please, Christopher," she whimpered pitifully, "I'm so afraid. I . . . I . . . just need . . ."

He was across the room and had her in his arms before she finished the sentence.

Trembling violently, Raven clung to him in desperation. "Oh, please," she begged, "just let me stay with you. Please!"

"Raven, sweetheart, what's happened?" he murmured. "You're shaking as if you've seen a ghost. Tell me, what's frightened you so?"

"In . . . in there," she said, trying to point to her room. "He's dead, Christopher. She killed him and . . . and then put him on top of me." She began to cry hysterically. "It's a message, you see. She's telling me I'm going to die."

He began to pry her arms loose. "Who's dead,

Raven?" he barked. "My father? Who are you talking about?"

"No, no."

He moved her aside and started for the door.

"No!" Raven screamed and grabbed for him. "Please! Please don't leave me."

He hugged her. "It's all right, sweetheart. I've got to go see what's happened. I'm just going to see what's frightening you so. I'll be right back. I promise."

A few minutes later, Christopher returned, his face blanched and set in a grim expression. He closed and locked the adjoining door, then locked and braced the door leading out to the hall with a chair.

Raven stood rooted to the floor where he had left her, watching his movements until he came back to her and scooped her up in his arms. She grasped his neck as if he were saving her from drowning.

He placed her in the turned-down bed and just held her. "It's all right, sweetheart. You're safe now. You don't have to be afraid any more."

She couldn't stop shaking. "No, no," she whispered. "She'll come for me. I know it."

"No, she won't. She can't get in. Besides, I'm here and I won't let her."

Raven began to squirm. "The passage," she whimpered hysterically. "She can come through the passage."

"No, Raven, I nailed it shut after you found her robe in my room."

"You did what?" she asked, in vague surprise.

"I didn't want her creeping into my room again. I nailed yours shut, too. Haven't you noticed?"

"No," she moaned. And then she stiffened. "Christopher, how did she get in my room then?" she asked, her voice rising back to hysteria.

"She used the hall door."

"But she couldn't! I locked it. I distinctly remember doing so because I was afraid."

"Listen to me, Raven. She most probably used Mrs. Bagley's master keys. She leaves them hanging on a peg in the kitchen. Everybody knows that. Besides, I found your key on the floor where she had pushed it out from the other side. But she can't do that here, Raven. I propped the chair against the door so you would feel safe. But she wouldn't dare come in here, Raven. She knows I would kill her without the slightest compunction."

"Oh, Christopher, poor little Marigold," she sobbed. "How could she do such a terrible thing? And why? He was just an innocent animal. He never hurt anyone."

Christopher sat up, frowning. "I know," he murmured. "But she was afraid of him just the same, and now that I think of it, I should have expected it."

"Why?"

He got up from the bed and went to retrieve the spilled bottle of brandy. "Damn," he muttered, holding the decanter up to the firelight.

"Well, most of it spilled, but there's enough left, I think."

He reclaimed the glass, returned to the bed and poured the last dregs of brandy into the goblet. "Here, drink this," he ordered, pulling her into a sitting position. "You need it."

She took the glass and began downing the dark liquid in small sips. "Why do you men always believe spirits can cure any and every calamity that comes along?" she muttered, making a face because of the taste.

He took the empty glass from her and placed it on the bedside table. "Oh, we don't believe it cures them. It just helps in facing them. It deadens the senses, so to speak." He sat back down on the bed beside her.

Apparently he was correct because Raven began to relax. "Christopher, what did you mean when you said you should have expected Camilla to harm Marigold?"

He leaned over her and propped himself up on his elbow. With his free hand, he began to play with the ribbons of her nightdress. "A few minutes after you left the cellar this morning, Camilla appeared out of nowhere. When she saw Marigold scratching about around that trunk, she turned white as a ghost, and I thought she would faint dead away. She literally went into a frenzy and attacked the poor beast."

"Christopher, what is it about that trunk? I've tried and tried to discover what is so important about it, because both Marigold and Camilla and, yes, even poor Aunt Jessica were and are obsessed with it."

"I know, I know," he grumbled.

Raven's eyes began to dance with excitement.

"Christopher," she said, "what if it isn't what's in the trunk so much as it is the trunk itself? Maybe it's the confession. Maybe she's hidden the confession in the lining of the trunk!"

He left the bed and began to pace. "No, that's what I was doing when she walked in on me this morning. I had already ripped the lining out of the trunk, and there was nothing there. No. She was more interested in Marigold's activities than mine." He stopped suddenly, walked over to the bed and took her hand. "Come here," he muttered and dragged her from the bed.

When they reached the door, he removed the chair bracing the door before turning back to her. "I'm going to pay a little visit to Camilla, Raven. When I leave, I want you to replace the chair under the knob and don't let anyone in until I get back. Do you understand?"

"No," she wailed and clutched his arm. "Please, Christopher, please don't leave me."

He kissed her softly. "This business has got to end, Raven. She's got to be stopped. Look at the damage she's done. She killed Aunt Jessica, whether she meant to or not, and we both know it. She nearly caused my father's death, and she's terrorizing you, to say nothing of bleeding us dry financially. No, I can't let this insanity continue. Now, you'll be all right, if you do what I say."

A few moments later he was gone, and Raven

spent the next hour or so in terrified isolation before the soft rap on the door and Christopher's voice announced his return.

As he slipped through the door, he was panting from exertion. "She's gone, Raven," he announced. "I've searched the house from attic to cellar and she isn't here. She probably realized she had gone too far with that business of Marigold and decided to beat a hasty retreat before I had an opportunity to wring her despicable neck."

Raven reached for him, and he enveloped her in his arms. "Are you certain?" she asked, hopefully. "Maybe she's hiding somewhere in the passages."

He kissed the top of her head. "I don't think so. The back door was ajar, and she took some of her clothes. At least, I think she did. Her room is a bloody mess. There are clothes scattered everywhere. It looked as if she just grabbed some things at random and left the rest. No, she's gone. I'm certain of it."

Raven felt the tension in her body ease away, and she sighed deeply.

Christopher, caressing her back with gentle, soothing strokes, moved his hand up to the nape of her neck and pressed her head closer to his chest. "Are you ready to go back to your room now?" he murmured into her hair.

She tightened her grip around his waist. "I don't want to go back," she answered softly.

"If it's Marigold, I'll remove him for you," he offered gently.

"No."

"Raven, I don't think you realize what the result would be if you stayed. Right now my inclinations toward you are anything but chaste."

Raven's grasp around him tightened. "I wouldn't know about that," she sighed. "All I do know is that I want to be near you."

"If you stay with me, Raven, don't expect me to treat you like a sister," he warned. "Do you understand what I'm trying to tell you?"

She nodded.

"Are you certain? Think about it, Raven. Because if I make love to you, I want it to be with no reservations." He squeezed her lovingly. "Lord, I've nearly died from wanting you, but I don't want to take advantage of you. That's why I haven't pressed you any more than I have. Now, look at me."

She raised her head and looked into his handsome face. The brown eyes staring back at her with such intensity had the glow of candlelight in them, and they glittered with desire.

"This is not the time to test my noble instincts, Raven," he continued, "especially where you are concerned, because you'd lose. When you come to me, I want it to be because you are ready to spend a lifetime with me, and I don't want you to have any doubts about my love or my fidelity to you. I want you to trust me and believe in me."

"All those words are just confusing me," she sighed. "I only know that I love you and I want to be here in your arms always. Isn't that enough?"

He kissed her sensuously. "That's enough," he whispered. He picked her up, carried her back to the bed and deposited her in the same place as before.

Raven watched as he moved about, putting two more logs on the fire and extinguishing the candles burning inside the room, before returning to her. She felt the bed sag, and by the muted glow of firelight, she could see his faint outline undressing and then deftly sliding under the covers.

Immediately his arms reached out to her, and she was drawn into the firm warmth of his body.

Her first awareness of morning came when she moved slightly and Christopher's grip on her lessened. She stretched languidly, opened her eyes and quickly shut them again. It was morning, but she didn't want to move. She felt safe and warm and completely contented.

As soon as she had settled, Christopher's possessive hold on her tightened once again. It had been that way all night. Every time she had moved he had released her just enough to change positions and then his custody of her had resumed.

She sighed peacefully and slipped her arm around his bare torso to snuggle closer to him until her face was buried in the glossy dark hair on his chest. The sensation of his warm flesh against hers felt exquisite and brought back the memories of deep longings and flaming desires, deliciously quenched. She kissed the man responsible for her contentment.

He stirred. "Morning, little moppet," he breathed huskily, squeezing her tightly. "No, that's not very appropriate, is it? I'll have to think of something more suitable."

"Why?" she asked sleepily.

He bent down and kissed her deeply. "Because," he uttered against her lips, "you don't make love like a little moppet. You, madam, make love with all the fire and passion of a brazen hussy."

A delicious shock ran through her as she remembered her conduct during the night. She supposed it was true, but she couldn't help herself. Christopher had been kind and gentle though vehemently passionate. He had taken her through every level of emotion a man and woman could experience during intimacy, and she had reveled in and reacted shamelessly to every glorious awakening within her.

She kissed him back. "Do you mind?" she teased.

Christopher chuckled. "Not in the least, although I'm going to need more food and rest if last night is any indication of our future nights together."

She giggled. "You beast. No one forced you to ravish me with such enthusiasm—and so often, I might add. After all, I'm new at this. You're the one with all the experience."

"I know," he sighed, stretching languidly

himself. "But you, my little wench, are so tempting. Do you mind?" he teased back.

"No," she cooed happily. "I love you. Isn't that what it's all about?"

He sat up and stretched his arms over his head. "That's what the experts claim." He stifled a yawn. "Although in the past I've seen very little correlation between the two—up until last night, that is." He threw the covers back and grabbed his clothing.

"Where are you going?"

"Well, if I stay here any longer, I shall just make love to you again and that would never do. Right now, I need to ride into Dunsford and find Constable Wicks."

Raven searched around for her nightdress and found it on the floor beside the bed. She retrieved the flimsy garment and surveyed the damage as he continued.

"He needs to know Camilla has bolted. We hadn't counted on that. Maybe, just maybe, he can find her." He turned back to Raven. "Good Lord," he exclaimed as he caught sight of her gown.

Raven sat there, holding up what was left of a delicate lawn nightdress. The front was ripped down the middle and one shoulder had been torn in two.

Christopher snickered. "I hope you remember that the next time you decide to wear one of those blasted things to bed." He reached over and snatched the destroyed garment from her before throwing it aside. "Anyway, as I was saying, I want her prosecuted for killing Aunt Jessica. I don't know how we're going to prove it though, but I want to try just the same. As long as she was here, we thought we had time to obtain the evidence we needed against her, but now . . . Well, her disappearing has put us in a rather ticklish spot. She's forcing us to move before we're ready, and that may be our downfall."

"Well, you should have thought of that before you ordered her out of the house," Raven replied smugly.

He leaned over and kissed her. "Don't be impudent. Besides, I enjoyed that pleasure immensely. Now, come along. Get dressed and come have breakfast with your husband."

An hour or so later, Christopher left as did Jeremy and Julia.

As soon as everyone departed, Raven headed for the cellar. Curiosity ate at her. She had to find out for herself what mystery that room concealed.

When she arrived, she found everything as Christopher had said. The clothes had been thrown out of the trunk, and the lining had been ripped out and lay strewn about in pieces. She walked around the trunk, scrutinizing the disreputable shell.

When her foot caught on something, she almost tripped. Glancing down irritably, Raven noticed one of the flagstones had almost been dug out from its place in the floor. As if a thunderbolt had struck her, everything registered. She swore at herself for being such a fool.

Galvanized into action, she tore through the debris of clothing until she found an old metal tray she remembered seeing. She set to work.

The interest Marigold had had wasn't in the trunk or around the trunk, but under the trunk, she thought wildly. That's what he had been trying to tell everyone, and that's why Camilla had been so upset when Aunt Jessica had discovered her treasure. She had been terrified whatever was buried there would be discovered.

It didn't take Raven long to find the package. About six to eight inches below the surface, she hit something soft and pliable, and soon she held Robert's confession in her shaking fingers. It had been wrapped in oilcloth.

She stuffed the papers in her pocket and started to refill the hole when she spotted something shiny. She clawed the object out and discovered a rusted pocketknife. Something was etched in the handle. She grabbed her skirt and rubbed. There, in delicate script, was the name "Michael."

Raven dropped the knife and began digging hysterically. Now she knew where Michael was.

Almost immediately, her makeshift spade uncovered another shiny object. It slid off the tray, back down into the excavation. Raven picked it up. A pendant engraved with "M" and "C," identical to the one in her room, rested in her palm. The pendant was attached to a chain, but it was caught on something. She tugged on it.

"I wouldn't do that if I were you." Camilla's voice reverberated across the room. "Unless you want to pull Michael out of his grave with it."

Raven uttered a startled scream and dropped the pendant. She slowly turned. Camilla stood in the doorway with a gun pointed directly at her. Indescribable terror seized Raven. She sank back against the wall. "Cam . . . Camilla," she whispered, "how long have you been there?"

Camilla chuckled evilly. "Actually I've been here quite a while." She walked over and peered into the gaping cavity in the floor. "My, my, but you've been busy. Not only did you find Robert's confession but you found Michael along with our little love token."

"Love token?"

"The pendant. I had one, exactly the same as his, but I lost mine long ago. Michael had them made. Clumsy but sweet in a sort of homespun way, I suppose."

Raven blanched. "You and Michael were . . ."

"Lovers? Certainly. You know, I really am surprised at you, my dear, for not figuring that out. You're rather clever, you know."

Raven's head began to ring. "Camilla, why is Michael buried down here? What happened to him? How did he die?"

Camilla smiled. "And curious, too." She shrugged. "Well, why not? You'll be joining him soon, so what does it matter?" She walked over to the bed and sat down. "It's all very simple, really. Michael died because he forgot his place. He became too possessive. You see, this was

340

where we used to meet. One night, before I left, he announced he was going away. He wanted me to go with him." She giggled. "Can you imagine? Me, Camilla Mallory, leaving all of this for a common laborer?"

Raven's mind began to whirl. Of course, of course! Why hadn't she been able to put the pieces together? Flora had—at least, partially. She had recognized the obvious immediately and had even verbalized her suspicion that it had been a woman behind Michael's disappearance. That's why Camilla lost control that day during tea. The knowledge of Aunt Jessica prowling around in the trunk just above Michael's grave must have sent her into an emotional frenzy. When Flora actually made the suggestion that a woman had been involved, it must have been too much for Camilla. Her facade had crumbled.

Raven began to think frantically. She had to keep Camilla talking. She knew Camilla had no intention of allowing her to live, not after she had spoiled all her cunning plans to win Christopher and the Mallory empire. And now that she had found Michael? Never!

There was one hope, though. If she could keep Camilla busy, maybe Christopher would return and come looking for her. Maybe Mr. Purdy would come for some wine. Maybe anything.

"What did you do?" Raven asked, her voice barely above a whisper.

"I killed him." Camilla shrugged. "Well, I had to! He threatened to tell Robert about our affair, and I certainly couldn't let that happen, could I?"

Raven fought back her revulsion. She didn't want to hear anymore, and yet she did. There were so many unanswered questions. If she were about to die, then Raven wanted to know the cause behind her sacrifice.

"What happened, Camilla? How did it happen?"

"We had an argument. I tried to reason with him, but he wouldn't listen. His pocketknife was lying on the table. I grabbed it. When he lunged for me, I stabbed him."

"What happened next?"

Again Camilla shrugged. "Nothing. As it turned out, it didn't matter. Robert woke up and discovered me missing. He came looking for me and walked in right after I had killed Michael. I was hysterical, but Robert was quite cool and collected. He calmed me down, tore up the flooring and buried Michael."

Raven couldn't believe what she was hearing. She simply couldn't believe a brother of Christopher's could willingly become an accessory to murder, unless . . .

"He must have loved you very much, Camilla."

"Yes, but he did me no favor."

Startled by her lack of insight, Raven glanced up at her captor. "How can you say that, Camilla? He risked covering up a murder for—"

Camilla stood. "We've wasted enough time

down here, Mrs. Mallory. If we tarry much longer, your loving husband might return and try to prevent our departure. I can't let that happen. Get up, please."

Raven had thought her life would end there in the cellar, but apparently not. "I . . . I don't understand. Where are we going?"

"We're going for a little ride, but first I want those papers. Hand them over, please. Now!"

Raven knew she had to obey. She rose and handed Camilla Robert's confession. "There's something I must know, Camilla. What made you come back? Surely you must realize that it's over. You've lost. Christopher will never be yours now. You've done too much. So why did you risk coming back when you could have been safely away by this time?"

Camilla smiled wickedly. "I had to." She casually waved Robert's confession about. "I couldn't leave this behind, could I? Otherwise how could I bring down the great Mallory empire?"

Raven felt the blood drain from her face. "Camilla, please," she begged, "you don't really intend to make those papers public, do you? You can't! Think of Christopher. He's worked so hard. It would—"

"Precisely. It would break him. That is exactly what I want. If I can't have him and everything that goes with him, then I want him ruined. Now, take that lantern and lead the way." She waved the gun toward the door. "Move, Mrs.

Mallory, before I decide to alter my plan and succeed, here and now, in what I have failed to do thrice before."

Raven did as she was told and led the way out of the dark and dingy room that had been the grisly scene of ruination to so many lives.

"Camilla, please. Where . . . where are we going?"

Camilla laughed pleasantly behind her. "A picnic, my dear," she answered gaily. "We're going on a picnic!"

Chapter 17

They had no trouble getting out of the house unseen. With the various members of the household either absent or otherwise occupied in their rooms, the servants were busy attending to their chores and never noticed the two shadows drifting down the hall and out the door.

The weather had begun to improve. The soft breeze felt much warmer than in previous days, and the sun, shining with unfamiliar brightness, had begun the slow process of thawing the blanket of ice and snow coating the landscape. Because of the melting conditions, the snowy mantle had become wet and sticky, and soon both Camilla's and Raven's skirts were covered by a heavy layer of white paste as they trudged toward a low rise beyond the house.

Camilla had dressed for the elements, but Raven was ill-equipped. Her slippers, meant for indoor wear, soon filled with slush, and by the time they reached the crest of the small hill, her feet were numb and almost useless. Even her cloak, because she had fallen several times, had become more of a hindrance than a help due to its accumulation of liquefying ice.

On the back side of the slope, a horse stood, waiting patiently, and Raven sighed in relief. At least she would be able to get her feet out of the freezing mire. She plunged down the grade in hopeful anticipation of the luxury.

Camilla untethered the horse, climbed on the bay's back and pulled Raven up in front of her.

"Camilla, please," Raven cried miserably, "where are we going? I'm so cold."

"Don't worry, my dear," Camilla cooed silkily. "In no time at all, your discomfort will be a thing of the past." She turned the horse in the direction of the open moors and dug her heels into the stallion's flanks.

Minutes dragged by in deadly silence as the horse lumbered its way through the heavy and deceptive drifts of snow. When Raven couldn't stand the suspense any longer, she broke the stillness with a voice as numb as her body. "Camilla, why are you doing this? I mean, I know you plan to kill me, but why didn't you do it in the wine cellar? Why are you going to all this trouble?"

"Call it poetic justice, if you like," Camilla

replied pleasantly. "I feel it is important for us to end our association where it began."

"But our first meeting occurred in my bedroom at Heathglade, not out here," Raven reasoned.

"Oh, that was our formal introduction. Actually we met some hours earlier, and and it would have been our last if you hadn't decided to pick up your bonnet when you did."

Raven's stomach lurched. "So it was you who shot me," she exclaimed. "I always suspected as much, but I couldn't understand how. You were still away when Christopher and I left. How did you even know about me or where to find us?"

"Oh, but I did know about you. You see, Julia and I arrived back home shortly after you and Christopher left on your little outing. Well, we weren't out of the carriage before dear Jessica came running out to tell us of your arrival and the happy announcement of your betrothal to Chris. The only trouble was, she kept calling you Ivy. Because of that, Julia, quite naturally, dismissed her prattling as just another episode in her confusion with reality."

"But you didn't?"

"No. By then, I knew Jessica wasn't as rattle-brained as everyone else thought. Quite the contrary. I had learned long ago that she was more often right than not, and besides, I knew Roger was up to something. I just didn't know what, so I began to put the pieces together. First, I knew someone had arrived, obviously a woman, but certainly not Ivy. Ivy is dead, you see. She and Albert were lost at sea going to America some twenty years ago."

Raven was astonished. "Camilla, did Aunt Jessica know that?"

"No, of course not. Roger felt it was better to let her continue to believe that possibly one day Albert would come for her. He felt that some hope, however remote, was better than no hope at all. And, after all, I certainly wasn't going to tell her."

"But why not? If she had known, perhaps she could have put her grief away and begun a new life."

Camilla snickered. "That is precisely why I didn't tell her. I needed her fear of Ivy in order to control her."

"But why? Aunt Jessica was completely harmless. She wasn't any sort of a threat to you."

"Oh, but she was. She very nearly caught Michael and me on several occasions with her always popping up at unexpected moments. She was like that, you know, always appearing where she had no business being. So it became necessary to contain her movements. Once I had planted the seed of fear in her, that Ivy was coming for her, it worked beautifully. She became terrified of Ivy and began to hide in her room."

"But she didn't, Camilla. She prowled about in those passages constantly. It seems to me that would have been more of a danger to you than her known presence."

"Ordinarily, yes. But by the time she had gained enough nerve to begin her sneaking expeditions, Michael was dead and so it no longer mattered where she went or by what means."

Raven shook her head. "I don't understand, Camilla. If you loved Christopher as much as you claim, how could you marry someone else —never mind the fact that it was his brother— and then carry on an affair with still another man?"

"I was angry and I was bored," she replied defensively. "Chris flatly refused to leave that wretched island and come back to England so I simply married Robert to punish him. An added incentive, of course, was the fact that Robert was the heir. He would eventually inherit everything, not Chris. Unfortunately I soon discovered what a poor bargain I had made. Robert was dull and lifeless, nothing like Chris at all, and then when Michael came along, I saw a chance to recapture that excitement I had felt with Chris but would never have with my husband."

"But didn't it occur to you that if you married Robert, Christopher would be lost to you forever?"

"Not at the time. That came later."

Something gnawed at Raven. There were still some pieces missing. "You said earlier that Robert had not done you a favor by helping you dispose of Michael's body. What did you mean?"

"Only that Robert wasn't as saintly as everyone thought. You see, he wasn't above a bit of blackmail himself, and he wasted no time in disclosing his terms for silence."

"Terms?"

"Yes." Camilla's voice became as icy as their surroundings. "You see, he knew I still loved Christopher and that I wanted to go back to Barbados to be with him, but with his knowledge of Michael's murder as a threat, Robert was quick to realize he had a way of stopping me. He told me that as long as I lived I would be bound to him. If I ever looked at another man or tried to leave him, he would turn me over to the authorities. But that wasn't all. He said I had done enough damage to his family, and because of it, we were going away. He told me about embezzling all that money in an effort to keep me happy. To put things right, he intended to write out a confession and relinquish his inheritance in favor of Christopher."

Raven could well imagine how that piece of news must have set with Camilla.

"Robert's sudden death must have seemed an extraordinary piece of luck." Raven hadn't realized she had verbalized her thoughts until Camilla answered her.

"Luck had nothing to do with it, my dear. I wasn't about to spend the rest of my life living meagerly with a dolt who had suddenly decided to be noble."

Camilla's words jolted Raven. What was she implying? "Camilla, what . . . what did you do?"

"I waited and watched. Two nights later I saw

Robert slip the confession under Roger's bedroom door. After he left, I retrieved it, and early the next morning I encouraged him to take a morning ride to clear his head. Robert was a poor rider—he didn't like horses—but that morning he agreed. I walked out to the stable with him, and while he was talking to Mr. Bridges, I slipped a thorn under his saddle. Sure enough, the horse bolted. Robert was thrown and died in the fall."

"No!" Raven cried. "Oh, Camilla, not Robert, too?"

"Of course, I did! After all, I had nothing to lose. I had already killed one person. Besides, with Robert dead, that left me in complete control. I had Robert's confession, and I knew Christopher would be coming home. I buried the confession along with my other little secret. After that, all I had to do was sit back and wait for everything I ever wanted to become mine. But then," her voice turned venomous, "Roger became difficult and started throwing up barriers. The ultimate stumbling block came when he brought you here. If it hadn't been for his interference, Chris and I would have been married by now and everything would be perfect." Camilla sighed. "But he did, so I have still another obstacle to eliminate."

Raven had become so fascinated with Camilla's treachery that her fear had left and a sort of macabre interest had taken its place. "Camilla," she asked, curiously, "the day of the picnic, how did you know where to find us? I mean, the moors are so vast, you could have looked for days and never found us."

Camilla laughed. "On the contrary. Chris took you to Miller's Marsh. It's a favorite picnic spot out here where Chris and I have been many times. When Jessica said the two of you had gone on a picnic, I knew exactly where to find you. So I simply told Julia and Jessica I was riding over to the Carltons to make my apologies for missing their dinner party the night before. Instead, I went directly to Miller's Marsh."

"But why did you run the risk of killing someone before you were certain what you suspected was true? For all you knew, I may have been a distant relative just visiting or a friend of the family just passing through. Surely you didn't take everything Aunt Jessica said as the complete truth?"

"No," Camilla muttered. "That's why I went to see for myself. As I said, I knew Roger was up to something, and I began to think about it. What better way to accomplish his goal of keeping me and Chris apart than to marry him off to someone else? It sounded like something he would do. And remember, I was there, hiding in the foliage, and witnessed the way Christopher kissed you. I knew then that you had to be disposed of. You were much too pretty, and Christopher's reaction to you was too intense. No, you had to be eliminated—and quickly, before his affections were completely diverted."

"And so you simply shot me," Raven finished lamely.

"Yes. And the shot would have been fatal if Chris hadn't been in the way. I had to wait for him to bend down before I could fire, but by then you had begun to reach for your bonnet."

A flicker of hope welled up in Raven. How accurate was she with a gun? Women weren't normally known to handle firearms, let alone shoot them. Perhaps she had a chance, after all. "Camilla, how do you know about guns? Surely you aren't a hunter."

A peal of laughter drifted across Raven's shoulder. "Certainly not, although I do boast of several ribbons won in various shooting competitions, but always in the ladies division, of course. Actually, my father taught me. It was necessary to know how to protect yourself, given the wretched place where we lived."

"Wretched place?"

"Barbados." She shivered. "Those miserable savages were always sneaking about, working some sort of mischief. That's why I chose to leave. I wanted to live in a civilized country, where civilized behavior is practiced."

The irony of Camilla's words coming so soon after her bloodthirsty confessions nearly caused Raven to erupt in hysterical laughter.

They now were well out on the moors where the going became easier. Everywhere Raven looked, miles of rolling slopes stretched out in spotted splendor before them—desolate, silent and deserted. With each step the horse made, Raven knew she came closer to the fate awaiting her at Miller's Marsh, and the hope of being rescued began to melt away as fast as the snow around them. As long as they had been within the realm of human contact, there had been a chance of help arriving, but out here there was no one.

At least Raven now knew their destination. It was indeed poetic that her life should end where she felt it had begun. For there, at Miller's Marsh, her feelings for Christopher had changed and blossomed in one short afternoon with the mere brush of his lips.

The horse stopped suddenly, and Raven looked up. Miller's Marsh stood before them, bleak and barely recognizable. Gone were the lush leaves of spring. Now, only bare twigs stood rooted in the frozen ground.

Camilla pushed her off the horse, and Raven landed with a hard thud, jarring her senses.

"Get up, Mrs. Mallory," Camilla hissed, sliding off the horse gracefully. She pulled the gun from her pocket where she had placed it for safekeeping. "We've only a few more steps to go and then all your worldly worries will be over."

Raven staggered to her feet, brushing off the clinging ice crystals attached to her soggy cloak. "Camilla, please," Raven begged. "How will killing me correct what has happened? It's too late. Don't you see? Killing me will serve no purpose."

Camilla motioned Raven into the cluster of skeletal trees and shrubbery. She laughed, and for the first time Raven noticed a wild resonance in her voice. "Oh, but it will, my dear. It will serve a very great purpose. You see, your annihilation is to be Chris's final punishment for his foolish defection from me. He is in love with you, and your absence undoubtedly will give him many long, lonely years in which to ponder your whereabouts. He will pine for you and perhaps wonder if you didn't run away only to find happiness in the arms of another." She laughed again, a crazy, out-of-control cackle. "Oh, I know how our darling Chris thinks. It will break him. And then, of course, he will come here to recall the memory of that idyllic afternoon the two of you spent together. He will ache for you and all the while never know just how close to him you truly are."

Raven knew Camilla had crossed the border into insanity. The tone in her voice, her obsession for revenge, the very process of her reasoning, were all classic indications of a sick mind. "I . . . I don't understand," Raven babbled, fighting back the realization that her fate rested in the hands of a raving lunatic.

Camilla's eyes shone with fiendish glee. "But of course you do. Why, this is the perfect place. Your shrine for all eternity. He will come here, distraught with loneliness, trying to recapture the closeness the two of you shared. And you shall be here, waiting patiently for his visits, resting comfortably at the bottom of Miller's Marsh."

The sudden realization of Camilla's intentions, the thought of sinking slowly into the murky depths of a bog until the breath of life had been denied her, spurred Raven into action. She took a deep breath and hurled herself forward. She didn't have time to think about what she was doing. She simply lunged at Camilla, and they both toppled to the ground.

Camilla hadn't expected the sudden attack and was stunned, but Raven had the potency of fear stimulating her. She scrambled up off the ground and fled into the dead shrubbery surrounding them.

Raven heard Camilla utter an oath and then scream in rage. "You can't get away, Mrs. Mallory. There is no place for you to run." She laughed again, and the sound of madness reverberated through the stillness, echoing off the dead trees standing in mute observance.

Raven huddled on the ground behind the bare twigs of a forlorn bush, trying to catch her breath.

She heard branches snapping and then a demented giggle. "It will do no good to hide, Mrs. Mallory," Camilla cooed with deadly calm in her voice. "You know I'll find you in the end, so why prolong the inevitable? It would be much better for you to just accept what must be."

Camilla seemed to sense where her quarry lay hidden. She started forward. Raven tried to move, but her cloak had caught on some spiny branches. With shaking fingers, she frantically untied the strings binding the cape to her and slid out of its grasp.

"Come, come, Mrs. Mallory," continued

Camilla with deceptive pleasantness, "we're wasting time. You must follow the plan, my dear. You really must."

Raven began to crawl on all fours. If she could circle around Camilla, maybe she could reach the horse standing patiently just outside the ring of brush that had become their playground of death.

A twig snapped, and Raven glanced down to find her skirt had caught on a straying branch. The tension had broken the limb off at its joint.

Camilla heard the noise and whirled around. "So," she chuckled, "there you are." She started toward Raven.

The growing rumble of a horse galloping at full speed made Camilla stop. The sound grew louder and louder until the clamor of hooves abruptly stopped. Then the unmistakable echo of wood splintering broke the deadly silence.

Christopher suddenly appeared out of the lifeless undergrowth. He stopped when he saw Camilla facing him with the gun pointed directly at his chest. "Where is she, Camilla?" he hissed between clenched teeth. "So help me God, if you've hurt her . . ."

The frenzied peal of madness cut through the air. "Such an eager postulant," Camilla babbled excitedly. "But you are too soon, my darling. Your revered wife is not yet in her tomb. You must come back tomorrow." She smiled at him pleasantly. "Yes, that will be much better. She will be able to receive your homage then."

Christopher stared at her. "You're insane," he whispered incredulously. "You're completely mad."

A low, deranged giggle emerged from Camilla's throat. "I know you're disappointed, my love, but you must learn to be patient. After all, you will have the rest of your life to visit her."

"Where is she, Camilla?" Christopher snarled. "What have you done with her?"

Raven slowly emerged from her hiding place. "I'm here, Christopher," she whimpered softly.

Camilla giggled again. "There, I told you," she announced childishly. "She isn't ready yet. She's still alive, you see, and that will never do. After all, how can you mourn for someone who is still alive?"

Raven stood roughly between them, perhaps 15 feet away.

Christopher's gaze raked over her. "Are you all right? She hasn't hurt you, has she?"

Raven shook her head. "No, no, I'm all right, but she's completely insane. She . . . she killed Michael. He's buried in the wine cellar. And . . . oh, Christopher," she finished in anguish, "she killed Robert, too."

Christopher stiffened and his mouth hardened. "It's all right, Raven," he muttered with calm detachment. "Right now, we must concentrate on getting you and Camilla back to Heathglade. It's unpleasant out here, and back home there are dry clothes and warm fires waiting for us." He took several steps toward Camilla. "Come along, Camilla, it's time to go home."

The ploy didn't work. Camilla jerked to attention and held the gun out. "Stop," she warned, and then she smiled vacantly at Christopher. "You, my darling, must go, of course. But Raven and I must stay. She has to die, you see. She can't be allowed to live after all the trouble she has caused."

Christopher began to inch his way between Camilla and Raven. "No, Camilla, Raven isn't important any longer. Let's just leave her and be on our way. We can be on our way back to Barbados or anywhere you like before anyone is the wiser."

"Please stop, Christopher," Camilla barked. "I would truly hate to kill you, but I will if I have to."

Christopher stopped and smiled at her. "Camilla, dearest, you know that I love you. Now, why on earth would you want to kill the man who worships you?"

"I no longer believe you, darling," she replied, smiling back. "It's all your fault, you know. If you had only come back to England with me, then none of the others would have had to die. But no, you had to make things difficult, and then our darling little Raven came along and you transferred your affections to her. You shouldn't have done that, Christopher."

Christopher's facade vanished and his face

expressed revulsion. "I stopped loving you long ago, Camilla," he muttered cruelly, "as soon as I realized how completely selfish and greedy you were. That was long before I ever knew of Raven's existence, but you don't want to kill her because of that, do you? Oh, no, it's because you want to hurt me. Well, here I stand, Camilla. You have the gun. Why don't you exercise your revenge on the proper person responsible for your unhappiness."

"But I don't want you to die," Camilla exclaimed. "Don't you see, darling, you're spoiling everything? If you die, then how are you going to regret your mistakes?"

"Then give it up, Camilla. Accept the fact that your plans have failed, and, rest assured, I will have plenty of regrets to plague me in the years to come."

"No," Camilla grumbled obstinately. "That isn't enough. You will still have your loving wife to comfort you, and I can't allow that."

Camilla turned and pointed the gun at Raven. "She has to die, Christopher. It's the way I've planned it, you see."

Before Raven realized what was happening, she heard the gun go off and saw Christopher dive in front of her. He landed two feet in front of her and lay motionless.

For a moment, Raven couldn't comprehend what had happened. It seemed like a dream, a nightmare from which she would wake at any moment—except, of course, it wasn't. Christopher lay in front of her, blood slowly covering the handsome tanned face, strangely still and silent.

At last, she screamed and rushed toward him, but Camilla grabbed her by the arm and dragged her to her feet before she could determine his condition.

Camilla, completely out of control, shook Raven violently, her eyes wild with madness. "Now, see what you've done?" she screeched. "You've spoiled everything. You've always spoiled everything."

This time it was Raven's turn to go mad. She clawed at Camilla's fingers until her arm broke free of the talons grasping her. Then, in one deft movement, Raven attacked. She flew at Camilla, hitting her full force in the middle, and both women went down in the brittle shrubbery. Arms, legs and petticoats became intertwined. Black hair and blond caught and tangled among the spiny twigs clawing at them. The desperate struggle continued until Camilla's arms suddenly went lax and Raven found herself clutching a limp rag doll.

She struggled to her feet and noticed her hands covered with blood. Turning Camilla over, Raven found a sharp splinter of wood wedged in her back. With numb fingers, she pulled the makeshift dagger from Camilla's body before turning toward Christopher.

Christopher lay on the ground, blood leaking from a wound surprisingly similar to her own, only his was to his forehead near the left eye.

Crying softly, she picked up his head and

nestled it in her lap. "Christopher?" she whispered in anguish. "Please wake up. Please!" There was no response.

When a twig snapped behind her, Raven's heart began to hammer in renewed dread. She gently placed Christopher's head back down on the ground and rose slowly before turning around.

Camilla staggered toward her, the bloody splinter of wood clutched in her hand. "Your tomb is waiting, Mrs. Mallory."

Raven inched backward, keeping a steady distance between them. "You're hurt, Camilla," Raven began. "We must get you to a doctor." She raised her bloody hands for Camilla to see. "Look. You're bleeding. Your wound needs attention."

"There will be time enough for doctors when you are safely in your grave."

They continued their bizarre dance, slowly snaking their way through the foliage until the unexpected shock of icy water forced Raven to gasp. She looked down and found herself standing ankle deep in a large bog. Frantically grabbing a limb from a nearby bush, she pulled herself up on solid ground.

Camilla stopped and smiled in demented delight. "How very convenient that you should find your watery crypt on your own. You have saved us both a lot of time by doing so." Then she frowned. "But look what you've done. You've pulled yourself out. Now, that was foolish, my dear, since you will just have to step right back in."

Grim determination sparked Raven. "No," she said defiantly, "I won't."

Camilla's mouth twisted in hate. "Then it appears as if I shall have to persuade you." She leapt at Raven.

Raven anticipated the attack and twisted sideways just as the sound of a shot ricocheted through the dead trees. Camilla's body slid past her and fell into the soggy marsh.

Dazed and shaking, Raven slowly rose from her crouched position and watched as Camilla's body sank beneath the surface. Next, she turned her attention in the direction from which the shot came. Christopher stood a short distance away, his arm outstretched, holding a gun. The smoke caused from the firing of the gun floated lazily skyward, framing his bloodied face in a silver-blue haze.

"Christopher," she screamed and rushed toward him, only to be smothered in his arms.

"Oh Christopher," Raven sighed, "I thought you were dead. But you're not! You're alive! You really and truly are alive!"

Christopher chuckled and held her away. "Yes, I'm still in one piece, as you can see." He reached up and wiped an accumulation of blood from his eye. "Perhaps a bit dented, but nevertheless still intact."

"Oh, your forehead," Raven cried belatedly. She reached up to examine his damaged brow.

"Stop fussing. It's only a scratch."

"Yes, but you're bleeding. It needs attention."

"Well, I admit it's a bit of a nuisance." He reached up and wiped the blood dripping off his chin. "But first we must see to Camilla."

"It's too late for that," Raven informed him. "She fell into the bog and was sucked under."

He dropped the gun. "I wish I could say I'm sorry, but I can't. Lord, what a shamble she made of our lives."

Raven slipped comfortably into his arms. "Yes, but it's over now," she whispered. "We can begin to build a new life, free of hate and deception. Heathglade will be a happy place again. You'll see."

Raven's words seemed to revive him, and he squeezed her gently. "Well, why don't we go and find out? Let's go home, and if you still insist on nursing me, then you can do it there while you explain how on earth you came to be out here with Camilla."

Several hours later, Raven and Christopher sat before the fire in the salon, sipping brandy and soaking up the warmth emanating from the flames. She had told her story from beginning to end while she had cleaned and bandaged his wound. Now there was nothing left to do but wait for Constable Wicks to arrive when she would have to repeat the whole tale once again.

Camilla's bullet had grazed Christopher's forehead, just above his left eye. It would leave a scar, similar to the one on Raven's cheek, and they had laughed about their common blemish being further evidence of them belonging together.

Raven finished her drink, slid out of her chair and knelt down in front of him. "Christopher," she murmured contentedly, slipping her arms around his waist, "how did you know Camilla had come back and how did you know where to find us?"

He caressed the black silky mane in his lap. "I didn't—at least not until I arrived back home and found that hole in the cellar. You see, when I couldn't locate Constable Wicks, I left word for him to contact me as soon as possible and hurried back home." There was a slight pause. "I don't know," he uttered almost to himself. "It's strange, but something in the back of my mind kept telling me to get back home. When I did and couldn't find you and then found the cellar floor torn up, I knew something was terribly wrong. That's when I found your tracks in the snow leading away from the house. They were fast disappearing. Still, there was enough of them left to follow for a while. Later, of course, I knew where they were leading."

Raven raised her head. "How?"

Christopher shrugged. "There was nowhere else to go. The tracks I had been following were headed directly for Miller's Marsh. Lord, I ought to know. I've gone that beaten path a hundred times and know there is nothing else out there."

"Christopher," she murmured, "do you suppose we will ever be able to forget Camilla and the terrible damage she inflicted?"

Christopher reached down and pulled her into his lap. "I don't want to forget, Raven," he whispered. "To do so would be to forget Robert and Aunt Jessica, but most of all it would be forgetting the reason you came into my life. That alone is enough to make me want to remember every moment of the past."

"What do you suppose the future holds for us?" she asked quietly.

"Whatever we choose," he whispered against her ear. "That is for us to decide." Then he forged a trail of soft caresses across her cheek to her mouth. "Tell me," he murmured huskily before kissing her, "do you have any thoughts on the matter?"

That sweet longing he always evoked within her suddenly begged to be quenched. Yes, she thought drunkenly, she had quite a few ideas on the subject.

Leona Karr

Colorado's Romance Writer of the Year!

FORBIDDEN TREASURE. Beautiful and unconsciously alluring, young Alysha had resigned herself to the dreary life of a seamstress. Then a carriage accident left her stranded at a lavish French castle, and Alysha was lured into a world of seduction and danger by darkly handsome Raoul de Lamareau, master of the chateau.

_____2707-0 $3.95US/$4.95CAN